PRIVATE WAY

Flyover Fiction

SERIES EDITOR: RON HANSEN

Private Way

A Novel

LADETTE RANDOLPH

University of Nebraska Press
LINCOLN

Library of Congress Cataloging-in-Publication Data
Names: Randolph, Ladette, author.
Title: Private way: a novel / Ladette Randolph.
Description: Lincoln, Nebraska: University of
Nebraska Press, [2022] | Series: Flyover fiction
Identifiers: LCCN 2021040741
ISBN 9781496230492 (paperback)
ISBN 9781496231185 (epub)
ISBN 9781496231192 (pdf)
Subjects: BISAC: FICTION / Literary
Classification: LCC PS3618.A644 P75
2022 | DDC 813/.6—dc23
LC record available at
https://lccn.loc.gov/2021040741

Set in Janson Text by Mikala R. Kolander.
Designed by N. Putens.

For
Lulu and Jack
Bird, Charlie, and Atlas

Author's Note

This is a work of fiction and any similarities to actual people, places, or events are purely coincidence, with the exception of a few imagined scenes involving the following actual people:

The scenes in which legendary Nebraska state senator Ernie Chambers appears are not based on or inspired by actual events and in no way reflect actual words, actions, or beliefs by the senator (though it's true that he has a long-standing policy of not accepting gifts of any kind). Senator Chambers is known for his on-the-spot, witty limericks. The limerick ascribed to him in these pages is my creation and does not fairly represent his wit and humor.

Although the Attic Theater is a fiction, it was inspired in part and shares similarities with the talented young people who founded the remarkable Colonel Mustard Amateur Attic Theater in Lincoln, Nebraska.

It's well-established among Cather scholars that Willa Cather based her beloved character Ántonia on an actual Czech woman named Annie Pavelka. The Sedlacek-Pavelka family portrayed in this novel is purely my own creation and is in no way meant to be confused with actual heirs of Annie Pavelka. Nor did Willa Cather have any known ties with the town of Wilbur, Nebraska. Any opinions, ideas, or judgments expressed by these characters are imagined and should not be interpreted as those of anyone in the Pavelka family.

My former colleague, Jana Faust, some years ago had a cat named The Lord. Her delightful stories about The Lord's antics inspired the name for my fictional cat.

Frederick Fields is a fictional character and is not based on any actual historical man. Fieldcrest Manor and Fieldcrest Manor Drive are also fictional constructs. Any similarity to actual places is a coincidence.

The extreme weather events described in this novel are not intended to be historically accurate. They are meant only to enhance the narrative and do not reflect actual meteorological events in Lincoln, Nebraska, in 2015–2016.

This novel was started in 2012, long before cyberbullying came to mainstream attention. The cyberbullying event described in this novel is fictional, though it was informed by the details reported around actual trolling events.

Similarly, the conceit of pie activism in this novel also predates the phenomenon of pie activism that arose after the 2016 election. PIE was not inspired by nor is it based on any actual social media platform and is a product of my imagination.

PRIVATE WAY

CHAPTER I

Empty Houses

I have a long history of secrecy and solitude. Whenever I don't catch some pop culture reference and people tease me about living under a rock, I laugh along, but the truth is, I did grow up under a rock of sorts. My mother always said we had to avoid attachments. We couldn't afford entanglements. She was a vagabond before I was born in Oakland in 1987, and for the first five years of my life she continued her vagabond life, mostly housesitting.

Between housesitting gigs, we crashed with her friends and she worked short-term jobs walking dogs, or waiting tables, but mostly doing odd jobs as a carpenter. She'd learned her carpentry skills from her dad when she was growing up in Nebraska. According to her, he was the only good thing about that state, and after he died (before I was born) she never went back, which is why I didn't meet my grandma until I was six.

Everything changed when I was five and she met Rex while we were housesitting in Palm Springs. He was a retired stunt man, almost twice her age. Like a lot of guys, he fell hard for her, with one big difference. He wanted to marry her and to adopt me. We moved in with him. He taught me how to swim in his backyard pool, and that first Christmas he built me a kid-sized play kitchen. I started kindergarten in Palm Springs and even made it halfway through my first-grade year (the longest I'd ever attend one school) before Rex died of a heart attack.

He and my mother weren't married yet, but after he died she found out he'd already changed his will and had left his house to her.

She had zero interest in living in Palm Springs without Rex, so she sent me to Nebraska to stay with her mother—a complete stranger to me at the time—while she rehabbed Rex's house. In the process of selling that house she taught herself about California real estate laws and found her calling.

For the next eleven years, as she bought and sold houses throughout the Inland Empire, she insisted we travel light. We fit everything we owned into the back seat of our car, reserving the trunk for her tools. We didn't own a television, and the only radio I heard was the car radio. We didn't subscribe to newspapers or join local organizations in the towns where we stayed for only a few months. My mother was all business, focused on finishing the job, selling the property, and moving on to the next project.

We slept on tatami mats in construction zones, some houses more disrupted than others. Most of them she brought back to life by stripping wallpaper, sanding wood floors, refinishing woodwork, rewiring, putting in new plumbing, and painting interior and exterior walls. A few of them needed major renovations so she subcontracted with roofers or foundation experts. For periods, we lived in houses without electricity, sometimes without plumbing, using buckets to do our business. In one house, the floors were so damaged, she had to pull up all the floorboards. For weeks before she finished laying the new floors, we walked around on plywood paths over open floor joists and slept on a plywood platform.

Instead of watching TV or playing sports or music, I spent my childhood in lumberyards and hardware stores, paint stores and cabinetry warehouses. As I got older, I took notes for my mother as she estimated costs. She wasn't patient enough to teach me her carpentry skills, but she used me for unskilled labor. I lugged muck buckets, swept up after demolition, stripped wallpaper, and painted. Once I got my driver's license I was her gofer. Through it all, she relied on me to listen as she talked herself through one construction problem or another. By sheer repetition I learned to see houses in their component parts and for their potential.

We lived like this until nineteen houses and fourteen schools later we landed in the house on Henrietta Street in Redlands, where my mother, semiretired, bought into a real estate company, and where I finished my senior year.

She was a hard worker, I'll give her that, but she was a careless mother. She left me alone a lot of nights in those half-finished houses. For all her talk about avoiding entanglements, she always found a way to connect with men wherever we had landed.

The only break I got from this life were the seven summers my mother sent me back to Lincoln, Nebraska, to stay with Grandma. Those summers—from the age of six to twelve, the year Grandma died—are the only consistent thing in my childhood. Grandma took me fishing on the lakes around Lincoln. She took me wading in creeks and rivers. She fixed up my mother's old bike, and we rode on Lincoln's flat streets. We went to the Children's Zoo and the Children's Museum, and each summer we made one big trip to Omaha's Henry Doorly Zoo before I went back to California—always on the hottest day of the summer, we liked to joke.

And, she taught me how to bake a pie. Something neither of us imagined would become one of the most important things in my life.

My mother often says she "shook the dirt" from her feet when she left Nebraska at sixteen. She has a fierce temper, and I was a watchful kid, careful not to set her off, but if I ever wanted to get under her skin all I had to do was tell someone she was from Nebraska. Even knowing this about her, I was still shocked when after Grandma died she didn't seem to have any feelings at all for her. It mystified me then and mystifies me still. I watched my mother dismantle the house where she'd grown up with as much dispassion as she would have one of the houses she was flipping, sorting things into two categories: garbage and donations. The only tiny bit of sentimentality I witnessed was one time when she sat down and looked through an old photo album before she tossed it into a trash bag.

When she caught me salvaging Grandma's pie tins and rolling pin from one of those garbage bags, she accused me of "crap dragging," but in a rare show of resistance I stood my ground. Otherwise, I'd have no memento of Grandma. I've carried that rolling pin and those pie tins with me ever since.

So, yeah. I grew up under a rock. I've never fit in with my cohort, the so-called millennials, or any other cohort for that matter. Here's one way that I'm apparently like everyone else in the world, though: I blame my mother.

CHAPTER 2

Pie Girl

I tell myself I've forgiven Kylie for how things ended, but I'm surprised now and then at how the memory of it will still feel like a gut punch. When I left California in July of 2015, Kylie was my oldest—in truth, my *only*—friend. We were roommates at Redlands University our entire four years there. She was so open, so nonjudgmental, I broke my own rule about avoiding attachments and let her into my life. For many years, she was the only person I'd ever told about my past.

She grew up in San Francisco and came to Redlands U on a music scholarship. I forget sometimes that for about five minutes she was a voice major before she switched to business. We lived together and then we went on to work together for several years, and in all that time I never once heard her sing, not even in the shower.

After our graduation in 2008, I started a strong contender for the least-likely-ever-to-succeed social media platform, a platform dedicated to all things pie: recipes, stories, techniques, obsessions. PIE—Pastry Innovations and Expertise—was the result of a series of coincidences: a free-for-all social media landscape and just plain dumb luck. No one was more surprised by its success than me. I was twenty-three at the time, and it was only natural to bring Kylie onboard as soon as I saw the thing had grown legs and was starting to run away from me. She was there at every stage—from its ridiculous genesis, to overseeing its off-the-charts financial growth, to the crisis that ended our friendship.

To her credit, she's still there, the one who kept things going after I went AWOL.

By July of 2015, I couldn't have begun to untangle the wheels within wheels of financial complexity Kylie and her dad—the president of our board—had put into place. We had millions of users, and we were responsible for an army of employees. It had always suited me to be in the background: strategic planning, setting priorities, trouble-shooting, and creating ways to attract new users. As founder and owner, my vision for the company carried weight, but I see now how I was sidelined early on.

In the second wave of the company's success, the numbers were so large I started to get suspicious. In hindsight, I see the ways Kylie framed our quarterly reports to avoid my questions. It's obvious now, in ways it wasn't then, that we'd been harvesting and selling user data for a long time. I can't blame all that on Kylie, though. I'm guilty too. I wanted to avoid confrontation, and that's on me. Those days, I operated on a split screen: seeing yet willing myself not to see—the very definition of denial—and that's on me too.

If that had been our only disagreement, our friendship might have survived.

CHAPTER 3

No Empty Threats

My mother is still a vagabond at heart. When I went to stay at her house on Henrietta Street in early July of 2015, the house had been closed up for seven months while she was in St. Thomas with a guy she's only ever referred to as Mr. Gaston, making me think he's some kind of criminal.

People who haven't been trolled must wonder what the big deal is. It's just words after all. Hard to explain how intimidating it is to read hundreds, thousands (I'm not exaggerating) of tweets and emails from strangers calling you horrible names, threatening to rape you, kill you, kill people you love, posting messages so fast you can't block them. And later, when they put up YouTube videos describing in detail how they're going to make you suffer before they murder you, it starts to feel like more of a real threat. The team that managed my social media accounts at PIE did their best, but even they were overwhelmed. And still Kylie insisted, "These people never actually do the things they threaten to."

Both of us thought it would blow over eventually, but once the customer service lines at PIE started jamming up with calls from trolls, Kylie decided the platform had to go on the offensive and distance itself. From *me*. She was adamant about it. Despite my argument that we should create a companywide response protecting both me and the platform, she remained firm. She played an old hand against me, a long simmering resentment. She hadn't needed to say I told you so. She'd been warning me for years that a small group of our earliest users—the pie-action stringers as I called them, or the crazy activists according to her—were courting trouble. I'd always defended these users, finding new ways to manage their posts without shutting them down completely the way Kylie thought we should. She wanted me to own that decision now, and I felt chastened for not having listened to her earlier warnings.

By the time the trolls doxed me, hacking into my personal email and my medical records, attempting to hack into my bank accounts, Kylie had moved on. As long as it wasn't hurting PIE it didn't interest her, so when I discovered the trolls had been staking out my condo, I had nowhere to turn except to my mother. She listened but couldn't seem to grasp what I was telling her. How could she? She didn't know anything about social media, let alone cyberbullies. Her focus was my state of mind.

She sounded almost cheerful as she said, "Well, little bug, it sounds like you're having a good old-fashioned nervous breakdown." I pictured her sitting poolside at Mr. Gaston's villa, drinking mojitos while recommending I commit myself to the psych ward. "Take a few weeks off, rest up, and get your feet back under you." She made it sound like a visit to the spa. After I made it clear I wasn't going to do that, she suggested I at least go stay at her house in Redlands for a while. "And Vivi," she said with a little more urgency before I hung up, "Please go see Dr. Smith. She'll give you something to calm your nerves anyway."

I liked the idea of something to calm my nerves.

A few days later Dr. Smith was smiling as she came into the exam room. "It's good to see you, Vivi." She looked down at my chart. "It's been four years." She'd changed her hair since I'd last seen her, and the asymmetrical cut didn't flatter her round face. "So, what brings you in today?"

I tried to make light of it, telling her I'd been under some stress at work. She nodded and held up her stethoscope to listen to my heart and lungs just as my phone began to vibrate. I reacted like it was a charging rhino and scrambled to mute it. When I looked at her again, Dr. Smith was staring at me, open-mouthed, still holding the stethoscope to my chest. "What on earth was that about?"

I shrugged my shoulders. No big deal. But she wasn't buying it. She finally dropped her stethoscope. "Vivi, I've known you since you were seventeen years old, and I've never known you to be someone prone to anxiety." She made a vague, dismissive gesture toward my phone, "Whatever that's about, it's not worth risking your health over." She moved away from the exam table and sat down. "Something's really wrong with you. Tell me what's going on."

Once I started talking I couldn't seem to stop myself. Dr. Smith listened without emotion until I'd finished. She pursed her lips a little. "I'm so sorry this is happening to you," she said, and when she reached across the space between us to take my hand, I fell apart. I sobbed.

Once I'd calmed down, Dr. Smith took a deep breath. "Vivi, you're having serious anxiety attacks." She raised her hand and pinched the tiny space between her thumb and first finger. "You're this close to my insisting you be hospitalized. Nothing is so important that you can't take a little time away from your work." My face must have reflected my impatience with this advice, because she said, "I'm *very* concerned about you. I need you to take this seriously."

My mother's house is still bare-bones. There are no beds, only mats; no furniture in the living room except pillows and a low table. No place to eat except at the kitchen island. It had never occurred to me how awkward it all was until Kylie called to say she was driving out to Redlands to bring me some things I needed to sign, and I imagined inviting her inside.

On the morning she was to arrive—what would end up being my last day in the house on Henrietta—I woke up in my old bedroom to a sky so clear I could see across the valley to the San Bernardinos. I'd been taking early morning walks to avoid the heat, and that morning I walked my usual route up Ridge to Caroline Park, across to Sunset and down to Pacific before heading back. There'd been heavy winds in the night, and I'd had to navigate around a few big widow-makers they hadn't yet cleared from the streets. Everywhere I walked, yards and streets were littered with downed branches from palms and pepper trees. By the time I got back to the house, the sky was hazy, and I couldn't see the mountains or the valley below.

I'd been working remotely for months, wearing only shorts, flip-flops, and T-shirts, but this morning after showering, I combed my hair and put on a cotton dress I found in the back of my mother's closet.

Given the windstorm the night before I wasn't surprised when I opened the patio blinds to see the pool was covered with debris. I wanted things to look good for Kylie and went out with the pool net to remove the worst of it. Expecting to find only downed branches from the orange trees in my mother's backyard, what I found instead horrified me. Dead rats. Over a dozen of them floating in the water.

A guy from my mother's pool service came right away, telling me as he got out of his truck that he'd been on another job just down the street. He was laughing and joking as we walked to the backyard, but the dispatcher must not have told him what kind of mess it was, because he took one look at the pool and jumped back. "Jesus Christ," he said, not laughing at himself like I expected.

"So, this isn't normal?"

"Christ, no." He wiped a hand across his mouth like he might be sick. And that's when I knew. The trolls had already found me here. I looked at the high stone fence surrounding the property. It would have taken some doing to climb over it. Just to threaten me? But why?

The pool guy went to his truck to get a bucket and a larger net. He'd put on heavy work gloves and did nothing to hide his disgust as he fished the rats out of the water. Even after he'd finished he seemed irritated with me as if I were the problem. He left the rats in a soggy pile by the garbage cans outside the fence and told me he didn't have any way of disposing of them, advising me to call the garbage service or animal control. I didn't entirely believe him, but I let it go since Kylie was pulling into the driveway.

She was smiling as she got out of the car, but I couldn't manage to smile back; instead, I wordlessly pointed toward the garbage cans. She frowned at my rudeness.

"Well, good morning to you too," she said, still frowning as she walked toward me until she saw what I was pointing at and, like the pool guy, stumbled back. "Holy shit." She looked up at me, her eyes wide. "Is that . . . ?"

I nodded, and she looked at me again like she hadn't seen me for a long time, which, truth be told, she hadn't. "Do you think it's . . ."

"No doubt."

"Holy fuck." Her eyes widened further. "This shit just got real."

I felt my face flush. My heart kicked. If she'd said, "I'm so sorry, Vivi" or "I had no idea things were this serious," I might have been fine, but as it was, something snapped in me. "*Just* got real, Kylie? Are you seriously saying this?"

Her eyes narrowed then, and her expression shifted from one of horror and sympathy to one of judgment. I knew what she was thinking, the same thing she'd been thinking for months: You brought this on yourself. I remembered how irritated she was by my surprise after one of the pie-actions blew up in exactly the way she'd always predicted. A dozen attractive young women bearing pies, accompanied by the media, disrupted a secretive vote by the Stillwater, Oklahoma, City Council to change the laws protecting historic buildings so developers could move in. This pie-action, like all the others before it, was a peaceful demonstration—meant to expose political self-dealing and abuse of power. It was documented with videos and irreverent testimonials. Previous pie-actions had gone viral, but nothing like this one did. Who could have guessed it would attract the attention of a prominent right-wing radio commentator. He went nuts, calling PIE a front for dangerous feminists, a cover for a radical left lunatic fringe, accused us of planning to overthrow the government and make men obsolete. I'd thought it was hilarious. Where do people come up with this stuff? Who listens to them anyway?

Long before this happened, Kylie had shown me data analytics indicating the majority of our dedicated users weren't interested in the pie-action testimonials and were in fact more often than not offended by them. She'd given me an ultimatum: I'd have to come up with a way to mediate the comments or we'd have to shut them down. I don't think she expected me to solve the problem, but I did, coming up with the pie icon as a way to allow users to express opinions—a full pie meaning they didn't agree at all, an empty pie meaning total agreement and everything in between signifying what you'd expect—without devolving into the nastiness so quick to take shape on social media.

The pie icons had worked to a point, but it turned out a lot more people than I expected listen to kooks on the radio, and they weren't the type of critics we usually encountered. Even then, I insisted the pie-action had been successful. It had achieved its purpose to get attention for a shitty backroom deal. Why should we back down from that?

In previous arguments about the pie-actions, Kylie hadn't once brought up her father, but that day she did. I knew she regretted it as soon as she said it, but instead of apologizing like she would have in the past, she dug in. I should have fought back. I should have been more forceful. I should have reminded her we'd repaid her father's investment long ago and had paid generous dividends since. I should have acknowledged that as our board president, he had a serious conflict of interest. I should have insisted we put up guardrails around his involvement to protect myself. I made a critical mistake in ignoring it. The thing I'd always feared but had overlooked because I trusted her was that Kylie had a powerful ally who could side with her against me if push came to shove.

Here's the thing about Kylie. She's intimidating in her way. She's very pretty. Always dresses perfectly, and that day was no exception. I remember she was wearing a pink linen top and narrow black pants, strappy black sandals, her dark, curly hair cropped close. I'd planned to invite her inside for iced tea, and the day before I'd gone downtown to

Mozart's and bought a pretty pitcher and two glasses. I'd also bought a few nice teas from Augie's hoping we'd get caught up after weeks of not talking about anything but work. Clearly, none of that was going to happen. Within ten minutes she was gone.

Before her car had left the driveway, I was on the phone with the garbage service about the rats. I went inside the house where I saw the pitcher of iced tea waiting on the kitchen counter. A puddle of condensation had formed beneath it. Suddenly I hated everything about my life. In the time it took for me to pour the tea down the drain and to dry the counter, I'd decided to call my business manager. I had only a vague plan in mind when he answered.

"I'm thinking about doing something, Jeff, and I want your help."

"Okay. What's up?"

"Nothing radical." Giving myself away, I laughed a dry little laugh. "Well, not *too* radical."

"Okay." He hesitated a little. "What's up?"

In the short time we'd been on the phone, I'd begun to firm up my plan. "I've decided to de-grid. Just for a year."

"And why would you do that?"

"I shouldn't have to tell you why, Jeff? You know what's been going on."

"Yes, but . . ."

"No buts. This is something I need to do. I don't see any other way out of this." I was sure a year would be enough time for the trolls to lose interest. I'd come back next July and start over where I'd left off before all this nonsense began.

"All right then. And what do you need from me?" Jeff said.

I told him what I needed from him, promising I'd send a mailing address once I got to where I was going. I had no idea at that point where that might be.

He was dubious even as he confirmed each of my requests. "Obviously, I'll do whatever you need me to do. But, and I'm saying this as a friend, are you sure about this?"

"I am." The resolve in my voice sounded convincing, even though I had no idea what I'd do for a year. It was enough, though, to help when I called the heads of marketing and operations at PIE to give them directions for how I wanted them to carry on for the next year without me. I knew I could trust all of them to carry on. I couldn't see any major issues facing operations in the coming year that couldn't be solved in my absence. If something came up, I assured them, Kylie would handle it.

I'd sounded calm, but the entire time I was on the phone with them my mind was scrambling. By the time I hung up, I'd landed on a solution. I'd go back to the only place where I'd ever really felt safe. Lincoln, Nebraska. True, Grandma wasn't there anymore, but for lack of a better plan it sounded as good to me as anything else.

The last thing I did online was to search for a place to rent. Nothing stood out until I saw the ad for a "cottage on a meadow in the city." While it seemed a little pretentious to call the small house a cottage, it was also a little adorable. The blurry photos of the house's interior told me nothing about it, but several shots of the meadow and what the ad said was "a wooded creek" led me to fantasize about a place so out of the way the trolls could never find me. It was a bargain by LA prices, and I paid a year's rent in advance.

Later, I was relieved to reach my mother's voicemail instead of her. I left a message thanking her for the use her house and let her assume I was going back to my condo. I told her I was planning to take a little break from the internet, that I'd be out of touch for a while, but there was no need to worry. She'd freak out if she knew I was going to Nebraska.

Two hours later I locked the door of her house with my phone and laptop inside, and I left California.

CHAPTER 4

Like Madness

It took me five days, two more than I'd thought it would, to drive across the West. I kept the atlas I bought at a gas station outside Elko, Nevada, open on the passenger seat, my route highlighted in yellow. At night, I studied maps of each state I'd be going through the next day, making careful notes about where to turn. In spite of that, while driving, I regularly ignored the route I'd planned the night before. Caught up in daydreams, forgetting my GPS wasn't there to warn me, I overshot turnoffs or made wrong turns because they *felt* right. When there was a choice to be made, I almost always chose wrong.

Over and over those days, I repeated to myself, *I have lost the thread of my life.* I was beyond any world I knew. Day after day, only the wind, and the blank, blue summer sky, and the dirt. So much dirt: red dirt and brown dirt, yellow dirt and black dirt. And the endless roads through bleached to bone hills, through green valleys, over red mesas, and across gray flatlands: mountains, buttes, badlands, and grasslands—everything burned to parchment in the summer heat. Rivers, lakes, ponds, clouds, all of it mixed together into a gauzy haze, like memory, like madness.

Without my phone, I felt I was missing something big, like a limb or one of my vital organs. It felt like I'd lost one of my senses. I was a burrowing animal. Blind and deaf, cut off from the world outside and scrabbling underground. A hundred times a day I reached for my phone to check Twitter and Instagram, to know what was happening. Without it, I wasn't sure I existed at all. Life was happening out there, and I wasn't a part of it. I had no idea who I was or where I was, and no one else knew where I was either.

The heat was intense that July. Fires burned across the West, and everywhere I drove, local DJs interrupted programming to issue fire warnings. In spite of that, I never once saw a fire, only a wisp of smoke now and then on the horizon. A blessing maybe, but I'm hardly one to count my blessings. When I was a little girl, I kept a list of all the things I'd lost: the kid-sized kitchen Rex had built for me, all the houses we lived in, even the ones I hadn't liked, and the schools, same thing. I kept track of little things too: the blue sweater I'd loved and left on a bus when we almost missed our stop; a five-dollar bill my mother threw away with a birthday card; a one-eyed doll I'd had since I was a baby and kept in the bottom of my suitcase; a little clasp purse Grandma had given me when I was eight. And all the books I collected that my mother made me leave behind each time we moved on.

If I still had that list, I'd add this: *I have lost the thread of my life.*

I didn't talk to a single person those days except motel clerks and gas station attendants. My music was all on my phone, and I hadn't considered an alternative. Somehow, I couldn't get my head around buying CDs. And the voices on the radio were no kind of company: radio preachers, obnoxious DJs on classic rock or country stations, hysterical whack jobs talking about the end of the world, still more loons spouting conspiracy theories. I didn't trust any of them to give me advice or answer my questions. They couldn't give me instructions or directions or fill in the gaps of what I knew about the places I was driving through. I was on my own. Plus, the radio voices were enthusiastic, and I distrusted enthusiasm almost more than anything.

Blame that on my mother too. All of our moves started with the seed of her enthusiasm and sprouted in the warmth of her optimism as she imagined the perfect buyer, the house she'd sell this time and make a fortune, the new lover she was destined to meet. In all my years growing up, she never seemed to learn from the past, never seemed to question her judgment. Each time we left somewhere, the world was new again, and she was a blank slate, a perfect innocent, ready to jump into the next thing, the thing that would finally make everything right. I told myself I wasn't anything like her, but I worried now that I'd been kidding myself.

There were things I forgot to do before I left. I forgot to tell Kylie where I was going. I forgot to write down the numbers programmed into my phone, so that even now if I'd wanted to contact them I couldn't. By the time I reached the Great Plains, all that space, all that sky, all those miles between tiny towns, I knew I'd made a huge mistake leaving California. The only thing that kept me going forward was a new kind of inertia.

I'd gotten myself good and turned around by the time I got on I-80 toward Nebraska. As I crossed the Missouri River I wondered how deep it was. I thought about Mark Twain and how he'd made this river famous. At least I thought it was the Missouri he'd made famous. Or was it the Mississippi? Maybe it was the Mississippi.

These were the kinds of things I would have asked my phone. Quick question. Quick answer. If I forgot, I'd ask again. I could ask the same question all day every day for a month and each time Siri would answer in the same reasonable way. There'd be no attitude, no eye rolling, no frustration, no judgment. It was only one of the many things I loved about it. I wanted to hear Siri's voice say, "The Missouri is x feet at its deepest. The writer and humorist Mark Twain made it famous. Twain's characters Huck Finn and Jim made their escape on a raft down the Missouri River."

Now if I wanted to know the depth of the Missouri River, or if in fact it was Twain's river, I'd need to find a reference book, or ask a reference librarian, or ask a local smart person. I couldn't think of any alternatives beyond those three, and since I needed to stop for gas, I opted for the latter.

The guy behind the counter looked nice enough, even if he didn't strike me as maybe the smartest local person, but then I didn't know anything about the locals. His mouth dropped open a little when I asked how deep the Missouri was. He looked stupefied by the question, but it turned out he was just thinking. After a few seconds, he turned around and took a book out of a kiosk behind him, a book for tourists to Nebraska. I hadn't known there was such a thing. He went straight to the back of the book like he knew what he was doing, found the page he wanted, and said, "The Missouri River is the longest river of the United States and the principal tributary of the Mississippi River. The length of the combined Missouri-Mississippi system is 3,740 miles."

He glanced up at me, maybe to see if I was properly impressed, which I was, but I also thought it was a little slick of him finding the information so quickly. I wondered if maybe he was making it up; I wanted to test him a little, to say something like "show me where it says that," but I thought it might hurt his feelings, me insinuating he was a liar. He looked at the book again and then back to me, "I'm afraid that's all it says, miss. It doesn't say anything about how deep it is. Anything else you want to know about Nebraska pretty much'll be in this book." He held the book up. It was for sale. He wasn't only selling gas and snacks and sodas; he was selling books as well. It hadn't once occurred to me to buy a travel guide to Nebraska.

"I'll take it." I laid down my credit card. "I'm on pump 5. Just add it to the gas."

"Will do." He didn't smile when he said this, but I sensed—along with his surprise that someone had finally come along and bought that Nebraska tourist guidebook, the only copy in the kiosk—a sort of pride in his sales skills. If, right then, I'd been in a position to hire for our marketing team, I'd have suggested he apply. He'd surprised me, and as I drove on I-80 toward Lincoln with my new tourist guide, I made a resolution to try not to let looks deceive me. At the time, I meant it.

I'd wanted to be alone, but until I was on the road I hadn't known what an oppressive thing real solitude can be, an ordeal all its own.

Still, other people scared me more than being alone. I'd learned how unpredictable, how dangerous people are. I'd learned how people, even the one person you think you can trust, will turn on you. How one minute you feel safe and the next your life falls apart, and things you counted on, the person you thought had your back, becomes your worst nightmare. Fear and betrayal. Those things will rewire your brain.

I wanted to shut my eyes, to pretend the things that were happening weren't really happening, to escape any way I could. But I couldn't seem to outrun the things I'd left behind. Every time I closed my eyes, I saw it playing over and over again like a little movie in my head. Plus, where could I hide in a world where it seems like everyone can be found?

CHAPTER 5

A Spy in the Hinterland

The afternoon I arrived in Lincoln was so hot the edges of things seemed to quiver and blur; the straight streets wavered like water. A bank marquee downtown said it was 106 degrees, nothing for summer in LA, but add the humidity, and it was an ordeal.

I knew the cottage was south of O Street between Fortieth and Forty-Eighth but that's all I knew without a map of Lincoln. For half an hour I drove slowly up and down streets, squinting at street signs before I finally asked for directions from a woman out walking her dog. She pointed with a sympathetic smile before explaining Fieldcrest Drive was hard to spot because it was a private way.

She didn't mention how the entrance was also hidden by overgrown yews and a giant elm whose branches leaned across the drive. In lieu of a street sign, I finally found, partially hidden in the undergrowth, an old bronze marker: FIELDCREST MANOR. Once I'd turned onto the narrow street, though, I felt a childish thrill at discovering what felt like the perfect hiding place. Once past the entrance, the lane widened and wound up then down again before curving to the left.

All those days on the road, I'd been comforted by the idea of a cottage alone in the woods, and I wasn't happy now, as I rounded the last corner, to see the cottage wasn't alone. It was surrounded by three other houses.

I parked in front of the cottage, a small saltbox surrounded in front and back by a graying cedar fence. Inside the fence, leggy flowering plants wilted in the heat, but a large maple tree outside the back fence shaded the house from the late afternoon sun. Behind it I recognized the meadow and the row of trees I'd seen in the ad.

In my brief email exchange with the landlord, I'd been told to pick up the keys at the back door of the "big house," which I guessed was the sprawling house at the end of the lane: what had to be the original Fieldcrest Manor. I estimated it had been built in the 1880s out of the same rough-cut red stone I'd seen on historic houses in Lincoln when I was a kid. It was run-down: the gutters sagged, doors and window frames needed paint, the roof buckled in places. This was the kind of house my mother would have snapped up when I was a kid. All it needed, I could hear her say, was a little paint and some elbow grease.

My T-shirt was already soaked with sweat by the time I'd walked a few steps. I heard the sound of a loud electric guitar coming from one of the upstairs windows, and as I got closer, from the back of the house, I heard someone playing the cello. Closer still, I could hear kids playing outside and someone trying, without success, to start a motorcycle.

I met the motorcyclist first. On the driveway beside the house a short, squarely built woman, her face contorted with frustration, was jumping the clutch. She didn't see me until she got off the bike and was walking toward a row of tools lying on the edge of the driveway.

"Oh, you scared me," she said, before recovering herself. "You must be Ms. Marx."

"Yes, I'm Vivi."

"We expected you a lot earlier than this," she said and craned her neck to look down the street toward the cottage. "That all you brought with you, what you have in that little Fit? I'll bet your ass is sore from riding in that little golf cart all this way."

"Are you Matilda?"

"Naw, I'm Mary Garlic, Tillie's partner." She swiped at her greasy fingers with a green rag before she reached out to shake my hand. "Come on in. I'll introduce you to the tribe."

As I followed her, children, like iron filings to a magnet, attached themselves to her legs. She made grumbling noises but didn't shake them off. "These are our three youngest," she said, panting a little with the exertion of dragging the kids along with her.

Inside, in spite of its shabbiness and clutter, the house was still elegant. Large rooms with high ceilings, wood floors covered by beautiful old rugs, dark wood paneling, ceiling molding, and chandeliers. I sensed rather than saw on that first visit the alcoves and wings beyond those rooms.

As I followed Mary Garlic through the large entry hall, I felt a vague happiness, some memory I couldn't quite place. Mary Garlic stopped at the door of a dim conservatory ringed with dusty windows and covered on the outside by creeping ivy. A thin, dark-haired girl stopped playing the cello when she saw us.

"Harmony," Mary Garlic said with a gesture, "this is Vivi." Harmony smiled and set aside the cello. The three little ones had long since detached themselves from Mary Garlic, and I heard them again outside. When Tillie finally appeared, I mistook her for another kid. She ran down a wide stairway; her long, unruly dark hair and the strange billowy dress she was wearing flying behind her. "Til, this is our new renter, Vivi," Mary Garlic said.

Tillie pressed her hands together. "Oh, what a wonderful cottager you found for us MG," she said in an accent I didn't recognize. She looked me up and down twice before she smiled and said, "We're eating soon, Gigi. Outside on the patio."

"Vivi. Her name's Vivi, Til," Mary Garlic said.

Tillie looked momentarily confused by this before shaking her head and going on, "We don't have air-conditioning, as you've probably noticed, so we've been eating and sleeping outside this entire horrid summer. If you can't beat it, join it, right? Harmony's garden is bursting, and at night we throw things on the grill and see what happens. You'll stay and eat with us."

She pressed her hands together again and turned to Mary Garlic before I could answer. "Did you ever figure out the problem with your motorbike?" She made it seem like the most pressing problem of their day.

"I think so."

"Oh, what a relief." She took my hand then. "Come on, Gigi, come help us chop," and pulled me with her to the kitchen where Harmony was already at work washing vegetables at a deep soapstone sink. I quickly took in the pale green subway tiles, wide-plank pine floor, butcher-block counters, open shelves cluttered with stoneware, and an ancient iron stove standing alone against one wall, brooding over the room like an imperious head cook, all of which led me to conclude the kitchen hadn't been updated for at least a hundred years. A large basket on the long harvest table in the middle of the room held cucumbers, green peppers, green beans, kale, chard, hot peppers, eggplant, tomatoes, onions, garlic, leeks, and carrots.

"Harmony's been gardening since she was a toddler," Tillie was saying.

"Not quite that young. My mother tends to exaggerate."

"Whatever," Tillie said. "Pretty young. I don't know what we'll do if she leaves home next year when she and Moss graduate."

As Tillie was talking, I suddenly felt overcome with nausea and realized I had a fierce headache. Without knowing how, I'd let myself get lured into this situation when all I wanted to do was get to the cottage.

"I'm sorry," I said, interrupting Tillie, "it's so nice of you to invite me for dinner, but I'm afraid I have to take a rain check. I'm exhausted. From the trip. If possible, I'd just like to get the keys to the cottage."

Harmony nodded in understanding, but although she was looking right at me, Tillie seemed not to have heard me. Instead, she wordlessly handed me an eggplant and a knife.

It was only later as I silently peeled and chopped vegetables that I remembered why I'd felt so at home when I'd first walked in the door. Their house reminded me of a house I had loved as a girl where we'd stayed for a month with my mother's friend Ruth when I was ten and one of the places my mother was flipping had sold earlier than expected. That house, like this one, was old and large and well lived in. It wasn't a particularly orderly house, and I'd been able to disappear in all the clutter. Mostly I disappeared into the library (the first time I'd known there were rooms just for books).

It was summer then, too, and I'd read for hours every day in a big leather chair. Ruth had noticed me there, but instead of scolding me like my mother would have, she praised me for reading. When we left, Ruth gave me a box of books she'd picked out especially for me. I'd had to leave all of those books behind later that year when we sold the house my mother was flipping.

That night, after a dinner of grilled vegetables on the patio, dusk settled around us, and I listened to the sound of the cicada. There was another sound, too, that Moss, Harmony's twin brother, told me were bullfrogs in the creek that ran parallel to the private way. It was almost dark when Mary Garlic plugged in a string of multicolored Christmas lights strung randomly through the bushes surrounding the patio.

By then, I'd learned the names of the three little ones: Lake, Kettle, and Spur, and, no, they weren't nicknames, Mary Garlic said before grumbling about how Tillie had a habit of naming the kids the first word that came into her head. Lake chattered and fidgeted through dinner, sometimes getting up to run around the yard before settling back into her seat again; Kettle complained about not liking his food, and left most of it on his plate. Spur threw a couple tantrums and accused the other kids of picking on him.

Harmony was telling me about her garden when she was interrupted by a loud noise coming from nearby. At my look of confusion, Mary Garlic gestured with her head down the street. "That's just the neighbor Chuck getting his buddies wound up. He's quite the comedian."

Moss, who was slouched at the end of the table, one leg thrown across the arm of his chair, looked down the street and shook his head, the only indication he'd been listening to any of our conversations.

"So, Gigi, what brings you to Lincoln?" Tillie said. While I should have been prepared for this question, I really didn't know why I was here. Why was I here?

"I'm here . . . I'm just here taking a . . . taking a break. From my job."

In my long history of evasions and secrecy, this sort of half-truth usually worked, but not with Mary Garlic. She lifted her head quickly. "What do you mean taking a break from your job? For a whole year?"

"Well . . . yes. I've done all right, and . . ."

"I'll say you've done all right, if you can take off a whole year." I was concerned when I noticed suspicion, and maybe resentment, gather in her eyes.

"It's hard to explain. I'm just taking a break, that's all. I needed to take a break."

"You get fired or something?" she said.

Her hostility surprised me. "No, nothing like that. I just had to de-grid for a while, you know. I'll go back in a year. It's no big deal."

Mary Garlic's reaction told me I was saying exactly the wrong things. She looked across the table at Tillie before shifting in her chair, leaning on one haunch, and turning toward me. She gestured dismissively with her left hand. "So, this de . . . de-ridding thing you're doing . . . ?"

"De-*gridding*, MG, not de-ridding. It means taking a break from the internet," Moss said with an edge of impatience.

Mary Garlic frowned and shook her head. "I don't know anything about whatever the hell that is. Is that why we couldn't reach you when we tried to call? Because we thought you might have been dead on the side of the road or something when you didn't show up when you said you would."

"I'm really sorry about that. It was a longer trip than I'd expected. It's a long way out here from California."

Still frowning, she said, "You don't want to use your phone, that's fine, but we need to be able to reach you. We'll give you one of our old flip phones. You can use that, can't you, and still be de-whatever, and all?"

Lake, who had been shifting back and forth in her chair, sat up straight now and looked at me with her eerie, icy-blue eyes. "Are you a spy?"

At this, Kettle and Spur grew attentive, and when I didn't answer, Lake jumped up, followed by the boys. They ran around the table, shouting in mock fear, "A spy! A spy!" until Mary Garlic snapped her fingers and they all went back to their chairs, shivering dramatically, still thrilled by their game. Lake kept looking at me with suspicion until I wanted to reach over and pinch her little leg under the table.

Fortunately, Moss gave a low whistle and everyone's attention shifted from me to the gangly gray mutt that came crashing through the shrubs to join us on the patio. The little kids cried out, "Mr. Shipley!" and Moss jumped up from his chair and ran around the yard with the dog for a few minutes. The air was thick and humid, and I watched as they wove among the fireflies. I felt like I must be dreaming all of this: the laughter and the voices droned in the background, and I felt a sharp stir of desire for that beautiful boy, shirtless in shorts, as he effortlessly dodged Mr. Shipley.

It was this drifting desire that finally startled me awake. The son of my new landlord. A *boy*. Get a grip, I told myself. Moss finally returned to the table, and Mr. Shipley settled at his feet after a few sloppy kisses and a wagging tail had created havoc with our empty plates.

In silence, we were all watching as the sky filled with stars, hazy in the humid night air, when Tillie asked in alarm, "Has anyone seen The Lord today? When was the last time anyone saw The Lord?"

They all joined in. They'd seen The Lord in the meadow; in the middle of the street; on the roof of the garage, under the bushes in the front yard; he'd been spotted behind one of the couches upstairs and twice in the kitchen. For a few minutes I thought I was over-hearing the ritualistic practice of a bizarre religious cult, when Spur shouted, "There's The Lord," and a muscular, black cat sauntered into the dim light at the edge of the patio. He stopped just short of the bricks and began to lick himself, ignoring everyone as they fussed over him. "The Lord! The Lord!" the little kids said as they gathered on the grass to pet him.

By the time I got to the cottage late that night, the only light on the street was that coming from the small yard lights in front of each house, except mine. I was so tired I grabbed only my suitcase from the trunk of the car. The only other things I'd brought with me were a floor lamp and two boxes, one of them holding Grandma's pie pans and rolling pin. Until that night, it hadn't occurred to me how ridiculous it was to have brought that lamp. Weren't there things I needed more? Sheets? A pillow? Towels? A flashlight? I wondered as I tripped on the step leading to the front stoop of the cottage and then struggled blindly for a few seconds with the lock before tripping again on the high transition into the kitchen.

Inside, the windows were all open, but the air was still and oppressive. I smelled new paint, a faint whiff of herbicide, and the mustiness of an old house that has been shut up for a very long time. After a quick tour—easy to do with only three rooms and a bathroom—I was so tired I didn't unpack anything, not even my toothbrush. The bare mattress on the bed was sticky in the heat. Miserable, I lay awake thinking about how there was one more thing I'd forgotten before leaving California—I forgot to reconsider Nebraska, of all places. I'd headed here first thing when it felt like the world was falling apart because those summers I'd stayed with Grandma were the only times in my life when I'd felt completely safe, but Grandma had been dead for fifteen years, and I didn't know another soul here. That night, as I tossed on the sticky mattress, I could see her again standing at her kitchen counter, rolling out a pie crust, looking back at me, smiling as she said, *When in doubt, bake a pie.*

Outside, I heard an owl somewhere in the trees along the creek. Once, I thought I heard a coyote yipping in the distance, and under the open windows the sound of crickets. It was very late when I heard Tillie and Mary Garlic's strange little kids, still awake apparently, calling, their high voices echoing across the dark private way, "Here, The Lord. Come home. Come home, The Lord."

CHAPTER 6

How Mary Garlic Ruined
Mary Garth for Me

I woke up before dawn in the backyard on an old chaise longue, its vinyl cover torn and rust stained, confused about where I was and chilled by the humid predawn air. Then I remembered how I'd tossed for hours in the stuffy cottage until I'd finally gone outside.

A familiar fist of panic seized me that morning as I reached for my phone and didn't find it there beside me. I'd been repeating this action with the same futile result every few minutes since I'd left California. This morning, though, I decided it was time to end my little experiment. I'd been an idiot to think that de-gridding would be a cure for fighting the trolls. What had made me think disappearing could magically erase the past?

Long before the sun came up I decided to admit defeat. I'd stay long enough to rest up before going back to California. I'd eat the year's rent, it'd be worth it to get out of here. But as I started to make concrete plans for the return drive, I felt a surge of the same anxiety I'd experienced in Dr. Smith's office. While my mind yo-yoed from firm resolve to cringing despair, I watched as a line of red seeped along the eastern horizon and slowly became a smudge of pink, until all at once the sun popped above the Earth and sat on the edge of the world, fat and orange, like the stone Buddha in the garden of my condo building in Echo Park. With the sun's arrival, I shifted my thinking: I'd stay put for the time I'd prescribed for this inconvenient disruption to pass. Once the year was over, I'd go back to California, stand up to Kylie, and take control of PIE again.

Later that morning, I caught a glimpse of myself in the bathroom's grainy mirror. No surprise. I looked like crap. I hadn't been taking care of myself for months, and three big zits formed a lopsided triangle on my chin. Already at this early hour, the heat was intense, and any effort at grooming seemed pointless.

I inventoried the rooms in the cottage: kitchen, small living room, small bedroom, bathroom. The only furniture: two chairs with a little table between them and a bookcase in the living room; a narrow wood table and four mismatched chairs in the kitchen; in the bedroom, a black iron bedframe (Mary Garlic had assured me the mattress was new), a small bedside table, and a dresser.

The bathroom was crowded with a claw-foot tub and a wide pedestal sink, both with graying porcelain and heavy rust stains under the faucets. Several tiles were missing in the black-and-white mosaic flooring and in those places the old grout had crumbled to powder. In the kitchen, a single deep sink in a porcelain counter, an old Hotpoint stove, a newish refrigerator, faded green cabinets. Even my mother would have passed on this place.

I noticed again the faint smell of mildew and herbicides and remembered Tillie telling me the cottage had been used as a garden shed for fifty years. When Mary Garlic had handed me the key, she told me it had been built for the longtime gardener at the manor house in the 1930s. The only thing she knew was that he'd died sometime in the early '60s. I was their first renter. Most of the furniture, Tillie told me, had belonged to the gardener. He'd died in the cottage, and I remembered her saying, "I hope you won't mind using a dead guy's things." By the time she'd told me this the night before, I was so tired I couldn't have cared less, but now I couldn't stop thinking about how someone had died here.

While I brought in the rest of my things from the car, I replayed details from the night before. What had I been thinking to stay at their house so long? It wasn't only the maniacal teasing of the kids that bothered me, it was also Mary Garlic attacking me the way she had. Who was she to judge me? She didn't know anything about me. And why was I still feeling so defensive? She was an ignoramus, and she and Tillie were raising another generation of ignoramuses. Hayseeds, I thought, resurrecting the derogatory term my mother always used for people from her home state. I couldn't say I hadn't been warned. My mother had never glamorized Nebraska. One thing was sure, if I was going to make this year work, I needed to keep my distance from the neighbors.

It was a Saturday, and my going back and forth to the car that early morning was the only movement on the street. Each time out, I looked more closely at the two other houses on the street. I couldn't stop seeing them the way my mother would have. Across from the cottage and Tillie and Mary Garlic's house, a narrow asphalt driveway led up to a midcentury modern perched on a steep rise. Its wide front lawn fell like an apron to the street below. The ornamental grasses that grew along the bluestone steps leading up the hill had wilted in the heat. The house itself seemed to be looking down on the rest of the street. There was something slightly authoritarian about the bank of large windows across the front wall. It's hard to believe now, but that day, I decided I hated that smug house and disliked whoever lived there.

The other house was on the same side of the street, the kind of new house I'd seen scattered among the Victorians in Redlands, what my mother called a McMansion. It was a collage of past eras of architecture with no logic or coherence. The lawn was unnaturally green. Bushes and ornamental trees grew in beds and berms along the street. A white privacy fence stretched along one side. A portico covered the horseshoe-shaped drive where it met the house. Everything was supersized: huge double doors, a large arched window to the left of the doors, enormous wrought iron light fixtures hanging on either side of the entryway. The house wasn't proportional to its gigantic details, and strange little economies stood out against this excess, like the bare concrete foundation.

As I settled in that morning, something kept needling me, some core disappointment deeper than my frustrations about the night before, but it wasn't until I was washing the dishes from the cupboard that I finally located the problem. *Middlemarch*.

I'd fallen in love with *Middlemarch* the first time I read it when I was twelve, and I fell in love again after rereading it during a long summer trip to Maine with my mother when I was twenty. The second reading had been a revelation, the way it forced me to reconsider the strong impressions I'd formed in the first reading. The experience had made me question all of my memories and to second-guess my entire sense of reality.

When I was twelve I didn't notice the prologue where George Eliot lays out what the novel is supposed to be about—a study of the history of man under the pressure of Time, or something like that—or the little story about St. Theresa as a girl, her baby brother in tow, both of them leaving home to become martyrs. When I was twelve, I'd related to Dorothea Brooke, the most obvious martyr in a novel full of them, not because the novel starts with her but because she was pretty.

By the time I reread the novel, though, I felt sympathy for Dorothea Brooke, it wasn't because she was pretty but because she was tragic, her idealism blinding her to reality. Pretty Rosalind was no longer simply a silly woman but a very selfish, dangerous one. Instead, as I felt George Eliot had intended, I related entirely to Mary Garth, the eccentric, minor character, a plain girl, who was, nonetheless for me that summer in Maine, the most vivid character in the novel and the most subversive, testing the rigid rules of the marriage plot by insisting on her independence and resisting the charms of her rich suitor, Fred, because she believes he's unworthy of *her*. I loved, still *love*, this character. And ever since that summer, Mary Garth has been a kind of private test for me, a clear dividing line between the kind of women I want to know and those I'd rather not know.

Now, because of the freak coincidence of their similar names, I'd begun to conflate Mary Garth with Mary Garlic. Among my other complaints with her, I was furious with her that morning for how she'd co-opted something so private and precious to me, my affection for Mary Garth.

Already wringing with sweat at 8:00 a.m., I was at the kitchen table making a list of the things I needed to buy when I saw through the screen door an older woman walking down the bluestone steps across the street. She was carrying a tray, and I'm ashamed to say I didn't do anything to help her even as I watched her balance the tray on one hip to open the gate in front of the cottage, saying as she came up the little brick walkway, "Yoo hoo. Good morning. Anybody home?"

"Welcome to Fieldcrest," she said when I came to the door. "I'm Audra. I live across the street." She nodded for me to take the tray. "I brought you a little tea and some muffins for breakfast. I don't want to interrupt, but I know how it is the first morning after a move."

She told me I could return the tea things to her later, adding before she left, "If you need anything, just holler."

Once I saw she'd started back up the steps to her house, I opened the teapot and dumped that good smelling tea down the drain. What had she been thinking? Hot tea on a hot day? I'd begun to feel a little suffocated, and it wasn't only because of the heat.

As soon as I turned onto Forty-Eighth Street to go to the store that morning, I had a distinct memory of how as a little girl I'd been fascinated by the long, straight streets of Lincoln. It felt now a little like a toy town, the way the streets were laid out so carefully. Numbered streets running north and south, lettered streets east and west. One time, Grandma had driven me across town from West O Street all the way east across the city to where the highway began. She'd told me it was the longest main street in America, a fact that had impressed her more than it had me. I remembered how there had been a Vietnamese restaurant she'd liked on North Twenty-Seventh Street, and I detoured on Twenty-Seventh to drive north of O toward I-80. Things had changed in the fifteen years since I'd been on this street, especially beyond Cornhusker Highway, now crowded with big-box stores. I could have been anywhere. But before Cornhusker Highway, the streets were still lined with immigrant-owned businesses, a few of them the same ones Grandma had gone out of her way to point out to me.

After I finished shopping and had taken another shower, I finally climbed up the steps toward Audra's house to return her tray. As soon as she opened the door, I felt a rush of cool air so irresistible I couldn't say no when she invited me to come inside. My first impression of Audra was that she was a mouse woman: gray clothes, short gray hair, and rimless glasses that blended into her grayish skin. She looked like someone in the process of disappearing.

Like the woman, her house was spare. She told me most of the furniture was handmade. The rugs and wall hangings and the things on the shelves were, what she called, "specimens from their travels." As she showed me around, she seemed reverential in some way, more like a housekeeper or the caretaker of a house that belonged to someone else. The house felt sterile to me, hushed, like a museum, a place where no one lived. Just as her welcome-to-the-neighborhood tea tray had felt a little scripted, so did this tour of her house. I'm ashamed to remember it now, but that day I thought Audra was the most boring person I'd ever met in my life.

She mentioned at one point that her husband was "the brains in the family," adding that he'd been sick lately and was in the hospital. I was only half listening, prolonging my stay only so I could enjoy the luxurious air-conditioning. As we later stood in her sweltering backyard looking together at the arrangement of rocks and small succulents she referred to as "the garden," I couldn't figure out why she was showing it to me. It seemed like the admission of a failure. I mentioned then that I'd seen Harmony's garden the night before, and her smile at this took me by surprise. It changed everything about her face. For a few seconds before her smile dropped, she wasn't a mouse anymore.

"Yes," she said, pushing away the sweaty hair stuck to her forehead, "I know that garden well. I'm a regular beneficiary of their bounty." *A regular beneficiary of their bounty?* What a thoroughly odd woman.

"My folks . . ." the downhome word *folks* surprised me, "always had a big garden like that. I grew up on a farm just outside of Fayetteville, Arkansas. When I was a kid, we always put up all sorts of fruits and vegetables. By the end of summer, our root cellar was full of canned goods." Standing in the heat, listening to these stories about root cellars and home canning was not my idea of a good time, but she continued. "I still put up produce like that, but there's no need for all that food now, of course. Our basement shelves are full of food I'm afraid we'll never use. Still, I can't seem to stop myself." She followed this comment with another beautiful smile.

As if she thought I hadn't believed her about those basement shelves, she insisted on taking me to the basement to see them for myself. I followed her around her spotless basement, dying a little inside as she pointed out the various improvements she and her husband, Jim, had made to the house's infrastructure, saying once that "it's the stuff you can't see in a house that matters the most," which I was sure had to be a direct quote from her absent husband, and not something my mother the house flipper would necessarily have agreed with.

When we got to the room where she kept the canned goods, I had my first about-face. On floor-to-ceiling shelves were jars filled with everything imaginable, including preserved fruit—peaches, pears, spiced apples, cherries, pickled watermelon rinds—so gorgeous I kept reaching for my phone wishing to photograph them. If all things were normal, I'd be asking about canning techniques, sending photos to the marketing department at PIE, along with a few pie recipes I'd come up with to suit these ingredients: pear-lavender pie, a pear custard, sweet cherries in rum sauce, spiced apple crumble. I knew how the marketing group would post them with an invitation for our users to share their own recipes for baking pies with home-canned fruits.

For the first time in months, I was inspired in a way that felt completely natural. For those few minutes, I'd been able to think about PIE without feeling anxious. I'd been almost happy until Audra started in again about her folks in Arkansas. I started to worry she might keep me there all day listening to her stories and made up an excuse about needing to finish unpacking. She was so apologetic then she rushed me back upstairs and out the door like it was an emergency. It says a lot about me that I was almost grateful for the oppressive heat as I practically ran down her bluestone steps to the cottage.

Before I could get inside, though, I was waylaid by the last of the neighbors: Bridget and Chuck Clark, giving me the impression they'd been watching and had timed our meeting to seem like a coincidence. Why else would someone in their right mind be out walking on a day like this?

The first thing I noticed about Bridget was her height. She was even taller than me, and I'm a tall woman. That's where all comparisons between us stopped, though. She was vivacious—*ebullient*, a word I'd never used before, popped into my head. She was striking rather than beautiful; her green eyes bright against her deep tan, her thick blonde hair pulled up into a loose bun. Her personality seemed so transparent I felt like I knew her instantly. She was familiar to me, like her house, a type I knew from California. I remember resenting a little how she managed to look so cool in spite of the heat that morning, while I kept mopping my face and neck as we stood talking in the sun.

Chuck was a few inches shorter than Bridget, broad-shouldered and muscular with hairy arms and legs. He wore khaki shorts and a long-sleeved white shirt with the sleeves rolled back against his thick forearms. He was handsome in a traditional way, a strong jaw and large white teeth, deep-set dark eyes.

Behind the privacy fence they had a pool, and Bridget invited me to swim at their house. "Anytime," she emphasized. "Don't be shy about coming over even if we aren't home. Everyone on Fieldcrest has a standing invitation to swim. Please come by. Lord knows it's too hot to do anything else. Do come."

CHAPTER 7

Imaginary Family

In the gardener's cottage, I made two discoveries. The first was the old books in the small bookshelf. I guessed they must have belonged to the gardener. On the top shelf, a book of Keats's poetry, *The Odyssey*, *The Virginian*, a book of North American birds, and a handful of gardening books. On the bottom shelf, several novels by Willa Cather. I'd heard of her but had never read any of her books.

I took every book off the shelf and opened each front cover hoping I'd find the gardener's name inside. I thumbed through the pages looking for notes in the margins, a pressed flower, anything that might tell me who he'd been. I didn't find anything until I opened Cather's novel *Lucy Gayheart* and a yellowed newspaper clipping fell to the floor, an obituary published in 1921 for a Frederick Fields. I was sure he must have been the man who built Fieldcrest Manor. Tillie's great-grandfather and the gardener's employer.

For some reason that small success made me think there might be something else hidden in the pages of that novel, and I scanned each page carefully until near the end I was stopped by this passage: "It was strange to feel everything slipping away from one and to have no power to struggle, no right to complain. One had to sit with folded hands and see it all go." I felt the hair stand up on my arms. Those sentences had seemed to speak so directly to me, I felt almost afraid of the book and tucked the obituary back inside before quickly putting it back on the shelf.

The second thing I discovered after trying and failing to unpack Grandma's rolling pin and pie tins, those things I'd cherished since I was a teenager. I hadn't baked a pie in months, and when I opened the box, the sight of them made me feel so sick I couldn't make myself touch them. The box was still sitting on the kitchen counter in the late afternoon when I finally decided to put it out of sight in the coat closet by the front door. That's where I found the gardener's wooden toolbox. As I sorted through the old tools, I found among them a leather datebook. Its pages were stained and stank of mildew. It took me a while to figure out that the notes inside were shorthand reminders about important dates for gardening tasks at Fieldcrest Manor.

After a sneezing fit, I finally put everything away. I didn't think much about it until I tried to stand up and was brought up short by a feeling of vertigo so intense I had to lie down on the wood floor. I closed my eyes and waited for it to pass. It didn't pass but instead morphed into something else altogether, something emotional, rather than physical, an overpowering feeling of mournfulness. I couldn't stop thinking about the gardener, wondering about his life in this cottage, how he'd died, and if he'd died alone. It wasn't sadness I felt, but a chasm opened up inside of me, and I had a sense of dread so powerful it seemed to pull me down into it. It was disturbing the way a nightmare is disturbing, but it passed quickly and when it was over, I seemed fine. I told myself it was just exhaustion.

Much later that night, long after dark, when I'd finished making my bed with the new sheets I'd bought, once again I felt the same horrifying dread I'd felt earlier, except this time I also had the physical sensation of something tickling the back of my neck, like ants crawling across my skin. My skin prickled with hyperawareness, and I sensed someone was watching me. Who else could it be but the trolls? I couldn't believe how quickly they'd tracked me here. There had been a time not so long before this when I would have laughed if someone had told me such a thing was possible, but no more. In the past few months I'd discovered an entire cast of people who seemed to have unlimited time and resources to terrorize other people.

I knew if these people wanted to find you they would. Even in Nebraska. They seemed almost supernatural to me. So that night, when I realized what I was feeling wasn't someone watching me from outside, but from *inside*, I panicked. This was a new level of crazy even for the trolls. I'd thought there was nothing they could do to shock me anymore. I was shaking as I picked up the only sharp knife out of the utensil drawer. I don't know what I thought I would do with that knife if I found someone there, but it made me feel a little safer having it. I was almost hyperventilating as I checked under the bed, and inside the closets, and behind every door, each time bracing myself to face an attacker. When I didn't find anyone, I went through it all again. Still no one, and yet I felt there was someone else in the house with me.

Maybe this was what my mother had meant about me having a "good old-fashioned nervous breakdown," or what the doctor had meant by a severe panic attack. For a few minutes it comforted me to think it was only a state of mind and not an intruder, but that didn't last long before once again that night I felt the hair rise on my arms, not with fear, but with some new emotion: an irrational reverence, an urge to perform a ritual of some kind, to appease in some way.

I've never been a spiritual adventurer; I don't like altered states, to the point that I don't even like smoking pot. Unlike a lot of the people I know, I don't like speculative fiction. I don't even relate that well to fairy tales or myths. For me, imagining there might be life on other planets has always seemed silly, a little immature. But that night I didn't seem to have a choice but to look closely at what was happening to me, to admit it didn't feel like an encounter with a person but rather with a presence that was permeating the cottage.

Even with three floor fans running at full speed, the cottage grew so quiet I could hear the ticking of the clock on the kitchen wall and the bathroom faucet dripping. I felt as if the cottage itself was holding its breath, listening. I'd cleaned earlier that day, but the smell of lemon was replaced now by the strong smell of old dust, old leather. Herbicide.

I'd never believed in ghosts in my life, but as troubling as it seemed, that night I preferred to think I'd encountered a ghost rather than believe I was unhinged. And then I remembered how I'd created an imaginary family when I was a little girl, afraid and alone those long nights after my mother left for what she called "adult fun." My imaginary family was never particularly distinct, and I didn't talk to them like other kids did their imaginary friends, but I liked the feeling that there was someone else with me in those empty houses.

I decided to think of the gardener—for I was sure it was his presence I was sensing—as a member of the family I'd imagined as a child. There was no ghost, but rather the invention of my exhausted, fearful mind. I chose to believe the gardener was welcoming me, and I accepted him—the way I had my imaginary family—as part of the interior atmosphere of the cottage.

CHAPTER 8

Brain Fog

First thing every morning I still reached for my phone like I had for years. Throughout the day I was startled every time I reached for it and found it wasn't there. The first two days in Nebraska the hours stretched ahead of me like a prison sentence, an incomprehensible, impossible assignment. I had no idea how to fill them. I was in a fog, without direction. I couldn't seem to figure out how to move forward, how to live at all. Boredom was a new form of torture. Jittery, I paced the floors of the stifling cottage, obsessing about my situation. I felt waves of dread, desperate to know how things were going at PIE, and in the world at large, until finally the heat drove me to seek out cool places. I wandered around the Target on North Forty-Eighth Street, looking at every shelf to kill time. I wandered the aisles of the nearby Super Saver grocery. I wasn't a cook, so I had no real interest in shopping for food, but I lingered in every aisle, paying particular attention to the freezer sections, where I opened doors just to feel a blast of frigid air as if storing it up for later when I had to go back to the hot cottage.

I'd never before had to think about how to organize a formless day. For years, my days were shaped by the demands of PIE. As I wandered the aisles of Best Buy on the other side of Forty-Eighth Street, I wondered if this was how I was going to spend the next year, shopping block by block in every store in Lincoln. I couldn't bring myself to buy a TV. I wasn't a network TV watcher. I still resisted buying a CD player or CDs when I had a phone and a laptop in California with all the music I wanted. I hadn't freed myself from my mother's disdain for "crap dragging."

I still felt blank, erased, not quite real, the way I had on the drive from California. This feeling of disconnection was pierced now and then by a stab of guilt about Kylie. It had been wrong of me, vindictive, to leave without talking to her. Over and over I soothed myself with any number of excuses for my pettiness.

Finally, on the morning of my fourth day in the cottage I decided to draw up a set of rules for the year:

1. wake up at a decent hour
2. do yoga
3. get dressed
4. make the bed
5. straighten the house
6. make coffee and breakfast
7. make plans for the day/ the week/ the month

When I'd finished and looked over this list, I couldn't believe I'd needed to make actual rules for the most basic functions of life. Despite how pathetic it was, though, the list was a start toward accounting for my days, even if it meant I was in a holding pattern for the year.

My new plan for getting out of the heat each day was to go on long drives, taking advantage of the car's air-conditioner. I drove for hours that first week, acquainting myself with Lincoln. I drove all the major streets downtown first, making my way on the one-ways north and south before tackling the east–west streets. From there, I drove the streets around the university. To the west of downtown, I drove through the Haymarket District. It had changed in the fifteen years since I'd last been there. Condos and national franchises. An ice-skating rink and a convention center and arena across from the football stadium where the Cornhuskers played, which even as a kid I'd thought was a dumb name for a sports team.

From there, I drove down the long north–south streets bisecting the city, followed by the east–west streets on either side of O. After I'd established these parameters, I wandered slowly up and down side streets just as I'd wandered the aisles of the big-box stores. I drove through neighborhoods rich and poor, discovered community gardens, and boutiques, and ethnic stores—including the Asian grocery where I remembered Grandma buying me sweet-and-spicy tamarind seeds—schools and libraries, bars and restaurants, big shopping malls, and everywhere parking lots, parking garages, and endless strip malls. I discovered neighborhood parks and the Children's Zoo, which had doubled in size since I was a kid, though I was happy to see the little train I remembered riding on was still there. Within walking distance of the cottage, I discovered the swimming pool at Eden Park. Also near the cottage, Holmes Lake, and in the historic district south of downtown, a little pocket park called Hazel Abel. East of the university, Trago Park and its splash park where I pulled over for a few minutes and watched little kids play. I noted the places I'd return to: movie theaters, bars, restaurants, libraries, Holmes Lake, the pool at Eden Park.

When I spotted the Nebraska Tourism office across from the state capitol, I parked and went inside. The woman behind the desk was on the phone. She smiled and nodded at me. No one else was there, and I looked through a bank of brochures where I found a free map of Nebraska, for all the good it'd do me, and a map of bike trails in and around the city, even though I didn't have a bike. There were postcards in a kiosk, but just as I didn't have phone numbers, I didn't have addresses and couldn't imagine who I'd send a postcard to anyway. There were touristy gift things like T-shirts and mugs. One T-shirt made me laugh: "Nebraska. Honestly, It's Not for Everyone." The woman behind the desk hung up the phone and asked if there was anything in particular I was looking for.

"Not really," I said. "I guess there is something. I used to come visit my grandmother here when I was little, and I have a vague memory of a big park with an Indian statue, and buffalo. Real buffalo. Is that just something in my imagination?"

"You're talking about Pioneers Park." She reached under her desk and brought out a city map. "Here, I'll show you where it is." She circled the park with a red marker. "Pioneers Park has a nice nature center, and yes, live buffalo. You weren't imagining that." She glanced up with a little smile as she said this. The woman circled another park near the same area. "If you like hiking, you might also enjoy Wilderness Park," she said as she handed me the map. "Is there anything else I can help you with today?"

I shook my head but thought I'd be back before I left at the end of the year to buy some of those T-shirts. The marketing managers at PIE would love them.

When I got back to the cottage that evening, I took out the city map and studied it. It seemed to mirror the flatness of the city, and I thought of it like a game board, my car, a game piece, driving along the streets. Was this how other people read maps?

After my second day of driving around Lincoln, having used my new map to find Pioneers Park—which didn't disappoint—I remembered the guidebook I'd bought outside Omaha, still in the glove box where I'd put it. I decided I'd use it to start planning longer trips. And if I got tired of being a tourist in Nebraska, which seemed entirely likely, I'd buy guidebooks for nearby states. I wasn't trapped in Nebraska. I'd been overwhelmed by freedom, that was all. I bought a new swimsuit and went to Eden pool.

CHAPTER 9

You'd Be So Pretty If Only

From across the lane, Bridget saw me getting out of my car that evening after my swim. "You've been swimming."

"Yes. At Eden Park."

She walked to the front of their property so we didn't have to shout at each other. "Oh, don't pay to go swimming. Next time, come here. I'll be in the pool all tomorrow afternoon." Something about the way she said this told me she was a little offended that I'd gone swimming somewhere else, and I knew I had to accept her invitation.

The next afternoon she saw me before I reached the back gate and yelled from inside the fence, "Come on in, Vivi!" She was floating on an inflatable raft in the middle of a large kidney-shaped pool, her dark tan set off by a hot-pink bikini. The only other neighbor there was Moss who tossed a beach ball back and forth with Bridget's two teenagers in the shallow end of the pool. The kids waved at me when Bridget introduced them: Roger and Sophie.

Bridget pointed to another inflatable chair on the patio, and I joined her in the pool. The water was lovely, and I had to admit it was nice not to have to share it with hordes of little kids. As I floated, I looked around. Tucked into one end of the large patio were several stackable chairs. An industrial-sized grill took up most of the space outside the sliding glass door leading into the house. I wasn't surprised when

Bridget told me about the big pool parties they had when Chuck wasn't traveling for work.

The sun was hot, but a large willow tree shaded one end of the pool, and I hugged the shade. I looked up into the blank blue sky. The only clouds were high and thin. The air was still. Even the insects and birds were silent in the heat.

While we floated together, Bridget chattered about whatever popped into her head, frequently interrupting herself to change the subject. I didn't mind. Half asleep, I let her voice wash over me. I was startled into wakefulness when she threw her arms out wide and exclaimed, "I just love water!" She grabbed my arm and pulled my chair closer to her to say with an urgency that puzzled me, "One of the things I insisted on when we moved here was that we had to have a backyard pool. It was the least Chuck could do for me, making me leave my friends and my old house. But I got myself a beautiful pool, didn't I?"

One of the reasons she'd wanted a pool, she told me, was to keep the kids home during the summer. After she said this, she leaned in close and whispered hoarsely, "Isn't it funny about Moss and Harmony, how downright plain she is?" Harmony had since joined the other teenagers in the pool, and I looked at her as Bridget was talking. "They're twins, you know. It's weird, though. She has the same coloring, the same features as Moss, but instead of being delicious like he is, she's dowdy as all get out. Don't get me wrong, she's a sweet girl, the sweetest really, but," Bridget paused a second before continuing, "well, she must feel so bad about herself. And how unfair is that?"

Bridget wasn't looking for a response from me, but had she been, I would have disagreed with her description of Harmony, who I thought was unusual looking, exotic even, but certainly not dowdy. Nor did I think Harmony felt bad about herself. In fact, she seemed like the most grounded and sane person I'd met in the neighborhood.

I came back to the conversation as Bridget was telling me how she liked to invite her friends over when she knew Moss would be at the pool. She liked to watch their jaws drop the first time they saw him. "He just oozes self-confidence, doesn't he? He isn't arrogant. It isn't that. He's just—well, you can see it. He's a very *confident* man, if you know what I mean." I was a little uncomfortable with her lack of discretion, talking this way when the kids were almost close enough to hear, but of course I knew what she meant. Who wouldn't? Moss was the kind of boy (*boy*, being the operative word here) I'd fallen for in high school. Handsome, unattainable. By the time I got to college, I'd learned my lesson. I'd never liked it about my mother the way she always needed a man in her life, and I'd made up my mind to be selective. It hadn't been a struggle to keep true to that promise since my work for PIE had left me almost no time for relationships.

Bridget abruptly changed the subject again, "I'm always hungry! Don't you just love a tater tot? Slim Jims? Donut holes? Twinkies? I love them all, but if I gave into my temptations, I'd be big as a house, and Chuck would kill me dead. He takes a woman's appearance personally." I'd been laughing at her list of taboo foods, but I grew sober when she turned toward me with an appraising expression I recognized as the "you could look so much better if" look, and I guessed she was thinking about a makeover for me. I'm a plain Jane, and there's no point trying to make myself look better when I know from past efforts makeovers don't make any difference. I felt myself withdraw under her scrutiny. The truth is, I don't mind how I look, but I'd been roughed up badly by the trolls for everything, including my appearance, and I didn't like being reminded of it now.

I was relieved when Bridget returned to listing her favorite taboo foods. She was irrepressible, a little silly and easy to be around. As I laughed with her in the pool that day, my earlier hesitation about having neighbors was redeemed by the possibility of a new friendship.

"Nobody tells you how hard it is to maintain your looks once you're past thirty," she said at one point. "I'm dreading the big 4-o. My friends are all teasing about how they're going to throw me a funeral party for my birthday—which isn't for three years yet—since I'll be the first of us to make it that far."

"If things start sagging or falling too much, I'm having work done, no question about it. I don't care what anyone thinks. I even have a special savings account. I call it the Saving Face Fund. Sometimes Chuck teases and says we need the money for something else like a new truck, or a new driveway, just giving me a hard time, you know, trying to get a rise out of me."

With this, she abruptly steered her raft to the side of the pool and got out. "All this talk about food is making me hungry. I'll be back with snacks." She turned down my offer to help, and while she was gone, I moved to the other side of the pool where the teenagers were discussing the neighborhood musical coming up in a few weeks. They were just telling me how they were called the Attic Theatre Troupe when Bridget came back with a tray of soft drinks for the kids and margaritas for us. She returned to the kitchen several times to bring out trays of the snacks she'd been talking about earlier. Later, I noticed she limited herself to baby carrots and celery, though she watched each bite I took of one of her taboo foods with undisguised longing.

She'd overheard the kids talking earlier about the musical and said to me now, "You'll come, of course. You won't be able to avoid it if this year is anything like the past three. There will be hundreds of people here." I stopped chewing the mini taco I'd been eating, unable to hide my surprise.

Across the pool from where we were sitting, the Clarks' dog—a white Lab named Bill—lifted his head. He was on the large side, a bit overweight. Until then, I hadn't really noticed him, but now, as Bridget kept going on about the musical, his eyes met mine, and I swear I felt that dog was as embarrassed as I was by all of Bridget's inflated talk.

I'd always liked dogs, but I'd never had a pet; our vagabond life much too erratic and my mother too focused on traveling light to commit to taking care of an animal, but until my eyes met Bill's that day, I hadn't understood why people loved their animals so much. In that instant I felt an immediate connection with him. Now, as if to acknowledge our mutual bond, Bill lumbered to his feet and padded across the patio toward me.

"Bill!" Bridget said when she noticed he'd made his way to my chair, had in fact laid his head on my lap. "Get!" Bridget snapped her fingers. Bill hesitated a second, sighed—or groaned—I wasn't sure which, before slowly returning to his place on the other side of the pool. "That stinking dog," Bridget complained as he walked away. "Chuck's *hunting* dog," she snorted. "He's never hunted for anything in his life but handouts."

From across the pool, Bill watched Bridget. He seemed to understand her disparagement of him, his face as sympathetic as that of a maligned human being's, as mournful as a long-suffering medieval saint. While I was watching Bill, Bridget's phone vibrated on the small table between us. Until then, I hadn't noticed it there, but at the sound, I felt a rush of adrenaline, not unlike that I might have felt if I'd seen a rattlesnake on the table. I warily eyed the phone and hoped Bridget hadn't noticed my reaction, thankful when she finally picked it up, looked at it quickly, and set it on the other side of her.

I couldn't comprehend this new phobia for something I'd loved, and still love, so much. Even before I'd seen an iPhone or knew what it was called, I'd had an early heads-up about it. This was in December of 2006, a couple weeks before anyone knew about this big thing that would change the world, and Kylie had invited me to come home with her to San Francisco for the Christmas break.

It was my first time visiting her family. At the time, they were still living in the middle unit of a three-story near Telegraph Hill. I remember Kylie's dad, who's eccentric under the best of circumstances, was more hyper than usual on Christmas morning. After we'd opened all of the gifts, he jumped up like a squirrely little kid and handed Kylie, her brother, and her mom each an empty envelope.

"This is your Christmas present from me, but I'm not going to tell you anything about it. Not yet. You'll have to wait until January 7." It was obvious he was dying to tell them what it was, but only Kylie's brother asked any questions. Kylie's dad finally got impatient with him. "Stop. Just stop. I can't talk about it right now."

We'd all forgotten about his gift until the day before Kylie and I were set to go back to school when he made all of us sit down and listen to Steve Jobs's announcement about this revolutionary new thing, the iPhone. He didn't have the actual phones yet, but they'd each get one soon. It turned out her dad was one of the engineers in Project Purple, the division that developed the iPhone, and I don't think even he realized how much their lives were about to change because of it.

I admit, the day Kylie got that phone is the only time I was ever envious of her. The first time I saw it I fell for that perfect little machine. I loved its sleekness, the weight of it in my hand, but more than anything, I loved everything it could do, the way it connected me to the world. Kylie and I played with it for hours, getting to know all of its features together. That's a happy memory; it's important to remember those good times. And it reminds me her dad was, and probably still is, in spite of everything, a good guy.

Chuck was out of town that night and as afternoon became evening, things grew even more relaxed as we lingered around the pool. It seemed pretty clear that at least when Chuck was away things were ad hoc at the Clarks' house. In lieu of a meal there were more snacks. Bridget put on some music, something Moss had recommended to her. I recognized Gilberto Gil.

The four kids eventually went back to the opposite side of the pool. A few times they erupted into laughter, but otherwise I forgot they were there. Bridget was as generous keeping my wine glass full as she'd been earlier with trays of food. She talked, and I was happy to listen since it kept her from asking me questions about myself. She told me that night how she and Chuck had both been athletes at Concordia College in Seward, Nebraska, how she'd gone there on a swimming scholarship and Chuck on a football scholarship. He'd been her first real love, she said, though more than once she expressed regret about how quickly time had gone by, repeating it with such sadness she seemed like someone facing a bad diagnosis.

They'd gotten married when she was nineteen and he was twenty. She wasn't shy about admitting she'd been pregnant when they got married, or as she put it, they *had to get married*, which sounded weirdly old-fashioned to me. She was proud of herself for not having taken a break from any of her classes before Roger was born and finishing her degree two years later, a week before Sophie came. As she was talking, I realized she was only eight years older than me, but she seemed to be from another generation.

She'd worked as a bank teller for years and was now an associate in the loan department at Union Bank. Chuck worked in what she called "the grain industry," an expert in corn oil exports. They'd moved to Lincoln four years earlier from a little town in the middle of the state when Chuck was offered a job in Omaha. She'd refused to move to Omaha—too big—so they'd compromised on Lincoln.

"When Chuck told me he'd found a house for us on a private street— which he described as a dead-end street the city didn't maintain—it sounded trashy to me. I pictured a dirt road and trailer houses." She gestured then with a sweeping motion that took in the entire house and yard, "But really, he did a good job finding this place, don't you think? It's a custom-built home—only two years old when we bought it—everything top of the line, and I just love that they kept the old willow tree and the oaks and evergreens when they built the house. It's my dream house really." She went on to say she liked Fieldcrest Drive because *the bad guys can't find us here*. I hoped she was right about that.

Chuck had told her she didn't need to work. "But," she said, "I'd go nuts sitting around the house all day."

As soon as she said this, I worried about what she'd make of me and decided I'd better come up with a better explanation for what I was doing here than I had with Mary Garlic and Tillie, since it was already clear nothing escaped Bridget's notice. I guessed she was the neighbor most likely to spread rumors.

As if she'd read my thoughts, Bridget turned to me with a piercing gaze. "So, I hear you're only planning to stay for a year in Lincoln."

"I'm just taking a break to restart my creative batteries."

Bridget nodded. "And what *is* it you do exactly?"

"Marketing," I said, telling a half truth. "Content development mostly. I love the work, but I was really burnt out after an intense few years, so I decided to recharge for a while. It's just temporary."

I was surprised by how easily this satisfied her, so satisfied in fact that she proposed taking a selfie of the two of us to post on Facebook. She'd already scooted toward me to take the photo when I reacted as if I was having a seizure.

"Oh no, no. No!" I said, making ridiculous swatting motions with both hands and hoping she wouldn't pick up on how panicked I was. "I look terrible. Please." This appeal seemed to make perfect sense to her, and she snapped a selfie of herself instead. A burst of laughter from the teenagers distracted me. I glanced across the pool. Bill was sitting near them, and I caught his eye but looked away quickly, not wanting him to get any ideas that would get him into trouble with Bridget again.

Bridget noticed me watching the kids and told me Moss, Harmony, and Roger were all going into their senior year that fall. "Moss and Harmony are a year older than Roger because Tillie held them back from kindergarten until they were almost seven," she said with disapproval. The kids were all good friends, but Bridget fretted under her breath that she didn't want them "getting too tangled up with Tillie's family."

She sighed. "Mary Garlic—isn't that the dumbest name you've ever heard?—and Tillie never come to our parties. We run into each other, of course, but Chuck and I don't understand their relationship at all. We can't tell if they're roommates or friends, or what. Chuck says they're 'muff sniffers'—he can be terrible sometimes—but I have to wonder myself. It isn't something you can ask about." Her hair had come loose from its clip, and she rearranged it into a loose bun before going on. "Nobody ever answers the door over there, so you end up just walking in, and then when you finally run into Tillie she acts like it's completely normal that you're wandering around in their house. I just want to slap her sometimes. Plus, the house is filthy."

It seemed Bridget was just getting warmed up as she switched her attention from Tillie and Mary Garlic to Audra and Jim, who, despite being "real oddballs," were, by her estimation, good neighbors. In the same way Audra had welcomed me to the neighborhood, she and Jim had shown up at Bridget and Chuck's door first thing after the moving van pulled into the driveway. "Audra brought us sandwiches and lemonade. Chuck worried they'd become pests, but they've turned out to be anything but pests. Audra's good about watching our place when we're gone, letting repairmen in if I'm at work. She's saved me a few times."

I hadn't talked to Audra again since that first day, though she waved if she saw me as she left her house every afternoon. Bridget told me how Audra went every day to the nursing home to visit Jim who was in the last stages of Lou Gehrig's disease, confirming my first impression that she was someone whose life had been derailed.

"Audra's nice as the day is long, I'm not saying she isn't, but oh my god is she uptight. And Jim is . . . *was*? a total tight-ass. He's about as charming as a box of rocks." Bridget smiled at me. "It's mean of me to say that now that he's basically a vegetable—which Chuck tells me isn't actually true since there's still brain activity, but he's like a zombie or something. Audra's an angel to go sit with him every day like she does. It'd give me the heebie-jeebies to watch somebody die like that. Chuck told me if anything like that ever happens to him, he wants me to suffocate him with a pillow."

Bridget grinned then. "Now, whenever he complains about not feeling good, I offer to put him out of his misery. We're terrible, I know, but sometimes we can't help ourselves, even after Audra told us about how Jim had wanted her to help him end his life after he was first diagnosed. He'd been mad at her when she wouldn't do it, but it was probably just his disease talking, treating her that way."

As fun as it had been to spend the day at Bridget's house, as I walked back to the cottage late that night, it was obvious Bridget was a gossip, and though I had nothing to hide, not really, my old habit of secrecy warned me she'd pry and would make a story out of nothing. Plus, she'd spent a lot of time through the day posting on Facebook, and I knew if I hung out there too much, it would only be a matter of time before she'd post something about me that could alert the trolls.

Gazetteer Nebraska

I stayed up late that night and stared at the state map spread out on the kitchen table. I untangled the highways, roads, rivers, and county lines. I marked the entries in my guidebook that sounded the littlest bit interesting, found all of them on the map, and made a list of day trips starting with Homestead National Monument outside of Beatrice.

The next morning I did what my grandma would have done and made myself a lunch before I set out. I detoured, driving through little towns along Highway 77. Some seemed to be dried up while others were bustling. The bustling towns had little grocery stores or farm supply stores, a few restaurants or small take-out places, maybe a store selling clothes or household stuff. Some had town squares with old trees and benches, small bandshells, county buildings. The roads and highways were so quiet in the middle of a work day I almost forgot I was driving. When I did meet another car, or truck, if it was a man alone, he almost always lifted one index finger off the steering wheel in greeting. I started lifting my finger in reply like I'd been doing it all my life.

Alongside the highway sprawled pastures dotted with cows or huge fields of tall corn and soybeans. The irrigated fields were green, while the grass in the ditches beside the road was dry and brown. I was mystified by several long white metal buildings in the distance until I noticed semis full of chickens.

When I finally found Homestead National Monument, it was a more impressive place than I'd expected. It housed a digitized archive of every homestead claim filed during the Homestead Act and a small museum. Before I left, I browsed through the books in the gift shop. There were books about Indians and pioneers by writers I'd never heard of: Mari Sandoz, Bess Streeter Aldrich, Joe Starita, David Wishart, John Neihardt. There were books about the Lewis and Clark expedition and a book of Solomon Butcher's photographs of homesteaders, books by and about Willa Cather. I was briefly tempted by a biography before putting it back on the shelf.

It was already late afternoon by the time I left Homestead, but I decided to drive the short distance to Fairbury, and once I was there, since it was so close, I drove across the Kansas state line just to say I'd done it.

It was dusk by the time I got back to the cottage. Crossing the state line into Kansas had given me an odd sense of accomplishment, and—like a simpleton—I made it one of my goals to drive to all the states bordering Nebraska, states I'd never thought about in my life, I made plans to drive north to South Dakota, and eventually across the state west to Wyoming, and southwest to Colorado.

When the neighbors on Fieldcrest Drive heard I was sightseeing across Nebraska, all of them had suggestions for places I must see, a reminder of how closely they were watching and listening to me. I'd never had anyone—least of all my own mother—pay such close attention to my comings and goings, but each day my smiling jailers reminded me they saw all.

It wasn't until Audra gave me Jim's gazetteer of Nebraska, though, that I began to plan my routes to avoid the interstate and major highways. I put hundreds of miles on my Honda Fit as I meandered across the state, no road or small town or historical marker too insignificant. If the guidebook mentioned it, I went: state parks and national monuments, rivers and lakes, art museums, historical museums. I visited every dusty historical society I saw until I finally decided I'd learned more than I'd ever wanted to about pioneers and their dugouts and their sod houses, their endless problems with blizzards and locusts and drought, but I never got over my fascination with the history of the Plains Indians. The stories of their resistance to westward expansion were as shocking and stirring as the stories I'd learned in sixth grade about the California tribes. Those stories of massacres and murders and betrayals and broken treaties made my own trouble with the trolls seem minor by comparison.

There were so many roads in Nebraska, none of them interrupted by mountains or big lakes (with the exception of Lake McConaughy) or large forests. I'd expected Nebraska to be flat like Lincoln mostly was, but instead I discovered hills everywhere, bluffs along the river in Omaha, steep hills outside of Wayne and Wakefield, rolling hills in Ponca and Winnebego, loaf-shaped green hills outside of Garland and Dwight that the locals called the Bohemian Alps, hills around Pawnee City and Eustace. Rugged hills in Peru, Falls City, and Auburn. Gently rolling fields of corn and soybeans around Ceresco, Wahoo, Bee, and Valparaiso. Deep, dry canyons on the outskirts of North Platte and the back roads to Calloway and Arnold. There were red bluffs outside of Scottsbluff and Valentine, dry buttes around Crawford, rocky cedar-covered hills outside Chadron. And for miles and miles I drove through the dry sandhills finding no landmarks, rarely seeing a house, or encountering another vehicle. And all of it, everywhere I looked—except for irrigated fields and watered lawns—was depleted in the heat and drought of late summer.

I went to rodeos and county fairs where I ate deep-fried cheese and deep-fried snickers bars, deep-fried eggs and deep-fried pickles. I ate at diners with names like Deb's and Barb's and Donna's and Mel's, and in all of them, I discovered the dessert of choice was pie, usually a choice of three, most kept in glass pie cases on the counter. They were almost always homemade, with flaky crusts. Sky-high meringues topped silky custards or second crust covered fruit pies. I could never face actually trying any of them, but I guessed they'd be about as good as Grandma's. If everything were normal, I would have been sending photos of all those gorgeous pies to my social media team: #prairiepies #countrydinerpies.

I liked being alone on these trips, but I was never invisible. In every small town some old man (almost always an old man), noticing my license plates, joked about me being a long way from home. He had no idea.

CHAPTER II

Tillie's Wonderland

A couple weeks later, Tillie caught me getting out of my car one evening after one of my trips to ask if I could help her the next morning. "Mary Garlic has to work," she said with a look of sympathy that I assumed was meant for Mary Garlic, "and the kids, well, the kids . . ." she gestured dismissively.

The next morning no one answered my knock, and I remembered Bridget's outrage at their habit of leaving their doors unlocked. I tentatively opened the door. I called out, but the house was quiet. I wandered through several rooms until I found the three little kids playing with clay at the dining room table. Tillie hadn't needed to tell me that first night the three little kids were adopted. They were as different from one another as they could be. Lake seemed tall for an eight-year-old. Her long thin arms and legs were almost as white as her hair, her eyes so pale blue she seemed a little otherworldly. Kettle was very small for six. His black eyes were bright and watchful. He had a pointed chin, olive skin, and long dark bangs that partially hid one of his eyes, making him look like a miniature member of a boy band. Five-year-old Spur had a round freckled face and a round body. His auburn hair stuck up in two cowlicks like wings on either side of his head. I'd seen that first night that he was quick to smile but just as quick to anger.

None of them bothered to look up when I came into the room. "Where's your mom?" I asked. Unfazed, they looked at me in silence before Lake finally said, "Til's in the attic."

"And how do I find the attic?"

Kettle jumped down from his chair and motioned for me to follow him. He ran up the big staircase. Organized around two halls, one a bit longer than the other, the second floor was as messy and meandering as the first floor. The two upstairs halls met to form a large common space where a leather couch with sagging springs and a group of mismatched chairs—one of them repaired with duct tape—were scattered around an old TV. A large oak rolltop desk sat against one wall, every surface covered with teetering stacks of books and papers. Beside it, an open chest spilled toys across the floor.

At one end of the intersecting hallway, I caught a glimpse of French doors, and at the other end I saw, with a pang of nostalgia, a window seat in a large bay window. I had another vivid memory of Ruth's house, which also had a window seat. Her house had smelled like ginger tea and slightly burned potatoes, and I remembered long, quiet afternoons, the light filtering through the bushes outside the windows, slanting across Persian rugs and dusty wood floors. I remembered how as the sun went down and the library where I was reading grew dark, Ruth would come in without disturbing me to turn on the lamp above my head. It had been years since I'd read in that engrossed way. I couldn't remember the last time I'd read a book, and I decided that day in Tillie's house I was going to start reading again.

At the end of the other hallway Kettle was waiting for me. When I finally caught up to him, he opened a mahogany door and yelled up the stairs, "Til, that girl's here." With that he seemed to feel his work was done and ran down a small servant's stairway I hadn't noticed until then.

The walls of the stairwell were covered with dark green wallpaper, and the stuffy air smelled like old dust and crumbling plaster. Dust motes shimmered in a column of light coming through a window on the landing. Past the landing, I climbed another set of stairs before finally reaching the third floor, a large open attic with multiple windows on three sides and a high painted ceiling, its once elaborate pattern now faded. I guessed it might have been once used as a ballroom. The windows were all open, and a brisk cross breeze made the attic space surprisingly comfortable despite the heat.

I finally saw Tillie in the southeast corner separated from the rest of the room by a long wooden table. An old Singer sewing machine in a wrought iron frame sat beside the table, and across from it two dressmaker's dummies faced each other. Against the adjacent wall an open ironing board stood in front of narrow shelves holding folded fabric. Near where I stood at the top of the stairs I saw a metal roller rack filled with strange-looking garments.

"We're up with the sun today, aren't we, Gigi?" Tillie gestured toward the rack. "That's what we have to get downstairs. The cast is coming over this afternoon for a final fitting before the dress rehearsal." Noticing my confusion, she seemed impatient. "The musical. Tomorrow. The musical?" Seeing I still didn't understand, she said, "You *have* to come tonight. You *have* to come to the Break-a-Leg party. All the neighbors come, even Audra." When I didn't respond, she drew her thick eyebrows down in concern. "It's bad luck for anyone in the neighborhood to stay away." She got up from behind the table as she said this and came across the room. She took hold of my arm for emphasis. "I mean it, Gigi. You have to be there."

Then, as if the matter had been settled, she abruptly dropped my arm. "I need a few minutes to get myself organized," she said and returned to her workspace. She ignored me for so long I finally wandered over to the far side of the room. From here, facing west, I could see the streets surrounding Fieldcrest Drive. The rooftops of distant houses peeked above the trees. Much closer, I saw the roof of Audra's house, the whole of my own little cottage, the Clarks' pool, and a few feet into their kitchen through the large sliding glass doors off their patio.

I turned away from the window when I heard Tillie stirring. "Did your mother teach you how to sew?"

"Lady Anne?" This was accompanied by a sharp laugh. "I wish she could hear you say that." Tillie smiled and swept her long hair off her neck. "No, I learned from a maid at a hotel where we were staying in Seville the summer I was twelve. Shall we?" she said brusquely, explaining as she started to remove the costumes from the rack, "This contraption is hard enough to move without the costumes. We'll come back for them later."

I helped her remove the rest of the costumes, and together we awkwardly rolled and pushed and lifted the heavy rack down the first set of stairs. While we stopped on the landing to catch our breath, Tillie said, "Lady Anne always told me I have a taste for mud—it's a French saying. It means to like the underbelly. You see, I liked the people she thought of as 'the help' better than the people I was supposed to like."

She nodded then, and we began to move the rack down the next set of stairs, both of us perspiring heavily and needing to take frequent breaks as we maneuvered down each step. Once we reached the main stairway, the little kids were there to help guide us down the steps and through the first floor of the house, running ahead of and behind us, chattering and laughing and mostly getting in the way.

We made several trips back and forth from the attic to bring down the costumes. On our third trip up the stairs, Tillie, for no reason I understood, mentioned something about how Mary Garlic had been homeless when she'd first met her. "Mary Garlic's problem wasn't drugs; Mary Garlic's problem was that she was raised by wolves."

"The twins were babies, and I needed help with them, so she came to live with me," she said this like it was the only sensible thing to do. I didn't understand quite why she was telling me this, but after we'd loaded our arms again with costumes and had started back down the stairs, she added, "Mary Garlic wasn't really that much help at first. The truth is, she was like having a teenager in the house."

Really? I thought, panting with the heat and the exertion of carrying costumes. Really? *A homeless teenager raised by wolves is no help to you and your infant twins?* I concluded this was an example of what Mary Garlic had once referred to as "Tillie logic."

We didn't talk as we hung the costumes on the rack: tight black pants and tops. Black capes. Gingham dresses, white shirts and dark gray pants, and suspenders. One flowing gray dress made of chiffon. Hats and bonnets. Once we were finished we pushed the rack along the rough brick walkway beside the house to the patio. We were still a little out of breath when Tillie poured each of us a large glass of water, and we sat down to rest for a few minutes at the kitchen table. As we drank our water, Tillie said, as if there had been no break in our previous conversation, "Mary Garlic's the one who holds everything together. She's the one who remembers the kids have to go to school."

It turned out Tillie had never gone to school a day in her life. Her mother had *seen to her education.* Her philosophy, "The unrestrained child knows best. The child eats when she's hungry, sleeps when she's tired, wakes when she's rested. She seeks and finds what she needs. She learns by living," Tillie said, all the while mimicking a voice of high snobbishness before adding with a smile, "Mary Garlic has opinions about this." Even knowing Mary Garlic the little I did, this made me laugh.

Later, as I was pinning tags to each costume according to Tillie's instructions, I asked about the little kids. She didn't answer until she'd finished making a note for herself. "I wanted more kids, but I didn't want go through the whole pregnant thing again, so I decided to adopt." She concentrated to write something on one of the little tags before adding casually, "When I adopted Lake, I wanted to adopt Mary Garlic too."

I thought I hadn't heard her right and looked up quickly.

She shrugged, "How else could she be next of kin if something happened? I tried to adopt her, but it was too much trouble. Besides,

Mary Garlic's like a wild animal. She lets you be part of her life, but she isn't tame." She looked into the middle distance then and pursed her lips before reconsidering. "Or maybe she's like a guard dog with really strong instincts. Yes, it's more like that I think. She's the German shepherd at the door."

By this time, we'd finished tagging the costumes, and she was making an adjustment to a pair of gray pants. She concentrated to rethread her needle before saying, "When I met her, Mary Garlic's name was Marian Garelick." She looked up at me to gauge my reaction before going on, "It's a nice enough name, I suppose, but it wasn't right for her." She admitted then she'd heard it wrong the first time, "But I trust things like that," she said. "I always liked how all the Catholic girls had names like Mary Katherine, Mary Carol, Mary Louise, Mary Anne. Why not Mary Garlic?"

Before I left, Tillie asked if I'd do one last big favor and help her set up tables for the potluck. We worked together in the hot sun in a kind of trance moving tables onto the edge of the patio, and as if we couldn't stop ourselves, I went on to help her set up a couple dozen chairs for the orchestra. When I commented on the size of the orchestra, she said, "Oh the musical is really about the music."

Harmony called to us from the back door, "I've made some lunch. Come inside and try to cool off." The kitchen felt cool after the hot sun. "Sit down, you two," Harmony said, and only after I sat down did I realize how tired I was. She'd made a pitcher of iced tea and tuna salad sandwiches.

"How did you end up living in this house?" I asked before taking a bite of the sandwich, thinking as I did that I'd never tasted anything so good in my life.

Tillie, who was eating like she was starving, seemed a little startled by the question. I had expected a simple answer, but she launched into a long backstory about how she'd been kicking around Southeast Asia for years and had decided she was becoming a version of her mother. "I wanted to change, but I didn't know how," she said. "And then, just like that, the answer came. My great-great-aunt Matilda died and left me Fieldcrest Manor." Neither Tillie nor her mother had ever met Aunt Matilda, and they guessed the only reason she'd left the house to Tillie was because she was her namesake.

Harmony seemed to like listening to her mother's stories, though she'd obviously heard them before. As she cleared away the dishes, Harmony told me, "Matilda was 102 when she died, and she'd never lived anywhere her entire life except in this house that our great-great-great-great-grandfather built."

Tillie said dismissively, "He invented some kind of farm tool, some whirligig or other that made him rich."

"It was a type of wrench," Harmony said, clearly the family archivist.

"I needed something to fill all these rooms," Tillie said. "I had a bunch of animals and that helped a little, but I thought there should be lots of kids running around, too, so I went through all that in vitro thing with the twins." She smiled up at Harmony then, and I saw the look of mutual affection that passed between them.

After lunch, I made one last trip to the attic to help Tillie bring down a few props she'd forgotten. While she was putting things into boxes, I was distracted by a noise outside. When I looked out the west-facing windows, I saw Bridget standing on her patio loudly taunting Bill, calling him a "stinking old thing" before pushing him into the pool.

Tillie had come to stand beside me at the window, and we watched together in silence for a few minutes before I finally glanced over at her, surprised by the serious expression on her face. "It's true what they say, Gigi." She looked at me. "No life bears too much scrutiny."

CHAPTER 12

Give-Me-a-Break Potluck

I was so wiped out after helping Tillie, I showered and lay down for what I'd thought would be a short nap only to wake up at 5:00 when I heard a brisk knock at front door. Bridget was there holding a huge tray of fruit. She gestured with her head to the bag of chips sitting on top of the fruit. "I figured you wouldn't have thought to get something for tonight. These chips can be your contribution." I was still groggy, and for a few seconds I was confused until I remembered the Break-a-Leg potluck. I started to make an excuse about why I couldn't go that night, but Bridget's expression hardened, and without saying a word she made it clear she'd wait at my door for as long as it took me to get my butt in gear to go with her.

A few minutes later as we left the cottage, Bridget nudged me to take the bag of chips. Her insistence seemed strange until we met Mary Garlic at the entrance to their backyard. She brusquely looked over our contributions to the potluck before finally gesturing for me to leave the chips at a table to her left and instructing Bridget to set the fruit tray on another table.

I noticed several teenagers scattered around the meadow, some setting up music stands, others tuning instruments, while in the distance a group of kids were practicing a scene. Since I'd left Tillie's around 2:00, someone had mowed a circular track in the meadow and along this track were scattered refrigerator boxes painted to look like buildings in a frontier town. Four kids wearing papier-mâché horse heads practiced pulling a crude prairie schooner around the mowed track, stopping and starting as they worked out their cadence.

A guy too old to be a teenager tinkered with an elaborate sound system, causing the large speakers dotted across the meadow to screech now and then as he adjusted the volume to mitigate feedback. Now that they were on, I appreciated how clever the costumes were, especially compared to the crudeness of the set. When the prairie schooner came a little closer, I saw it was carrying four actors dressed as a pioneer family.

Farther across the meadow I watched as actors in black leotards and capes performed a mystifying choreography. Bridget's daughter, Sophie, was among this group in black, though over her black leotard she wore a gray diaphanous pioneer dress that flew around her as she executed a number of athletic kicks and turns. I didn't know how any of them could stand to be wearing these costumes in the heat, let alone exerting such energy.

Nothing I saw made any sense, and I was thinking about sneaking away when Tillie rushed over to me, her face full of excitement.

"The costumes look great," I said, and she smiled. "So what exactly . . . ? What's the play about?"

Tillie looked at me with surprise, as though it should have been obvious. "It's *Buffy the Vampire Slayer on the Oregon Trail*," she said. "Can you come help me with some adjustments?" I followed her to the tent they'd set up as a changing room.

The rehearsal felt like a disorganized disaster to me as Moss and the older guy—who I guessed was a former participant returning in a directorial role—kept stopping the actors and giving directions. All I could hear was the orchestra stopping and starting. The teenagers were more than ten years younger than me, but still, way too old to be doing this kind of thing.

During the rehearsal, parents of cast and orchestra members began to arrive, bringing yet more dishes for the potluck, and then, abruptly, the rehearsal was over and everyone descended at once on the food tables. Behind two grills, Mary Garlic and Chuck turned out endless hamburgers, veggie burgers, and brats.

Tillie had changed clothes and was now wearing the same chiffony gray dress I'd seen her in the day I arrived, what I now realized was a prototype for Sophie's costume. Tillie seemed to float around the yard pointing people to the tables we'd set up earlier that day and blankets spread out on the meadow.

No one but me seemed worried about how the teenagers were headed for serious public humiliation the following night. Apparently, they thought it was normal, cute even, that their kids got together every summer to create a spectacle the way they might have in grade school. Then I noticed I had a far bigger problem to deal with than worrying about the neighbor kids' feelings. Everyone was recording and photographing and posting online. I had to make myself invisible. I stayed well in the background and, like an ethnologist, quietly observed the native culture. I'd known things would be different in Nebraska, but until that night I hadn't understood just *how* different things were *in the provinces.*

It was after dark by the time most of the parents and the performers left. I stayed to help Mary Garlic put away the tables and chairs. As we were finishing, I saw someone had built a bonfire in the trees along the creek. I liked the novelty of that little creek, the way it had been preserved as the town grew up around it. At first I thought it was just a group of kids, and I hesitated about joining them until I saw Bridget was there too. She was sitting between Moss and another boy I recognized from the orchestra. All of them, including Bridget, looked up warily when they saw me, and I soon saw the reason was a bottle of Jim Beam making the rounds. They visibly relaxed when they saw it was only me and not one of the parents.

It was far too hot to be sitting around a fire, but I sat down on a fallen log anyway. Across the fire, I watched Bridget take a long swig from the bottle before passing it to Moss, who smiled and nudged her with his shoulder before taking it from her. The talk around the fire wasn't about the musical but instead about something that had happened at Bridget's pool a few days earlier, something about an elaborate practical joke Moss had played on Bridget. Another boy, who'd been there, kept inserting comments that, each time, caused Bridget to throw her head back in laughter.

I finally stopped trying to figure out what they were talking about, ignoring them as they ignored me except to pass me the bottle as it made its way around the circle. I took an occasional swig and enjoyed the fire in spite of the ungodly heat. Fireflies lifted out of the tall grass in the meadow and rose into the trees above us. The moon, diffused through the humid night air, cast everything, including the tiny yellow lights of those fireflies, in a yellowish haze. I heard first one cello— Harmony maybe—and then another cellist. The two instruments played an intricate duet, moving together in complex runs before ending again with the soloist. It was a haunting piece, part of the score for the musical that I now realized I'd been hearing since the day I arrived when I'd overheard Moss on the guitar and Harmony on the cello.

I remembered being told at some point that day it was Roger who arranged all of the music for the orchestra once Moss and Harmony wrote the songs. When there was a little break in their inane conversation, I asked Bridget, "Where are Sophie and Roger tonight?"

I noticed Bridget's eyes narrowed a little, and I wasn't sure if was because of the smoke or because she was annoyed at the interruption. "They went home early," she finally said, adding, after a short pause, "they don't like fires," which caused Moss, who'd just taken a swig of whiskey, to choke with laughter. They returned to their earlier conversation, making it obvious it was time for me to leave.

I'd left a light on in the cottage, and I saw it now through the trees. I didn't feel afraid as I walked across the meadow in the dark. It wasn't until the front gate clicked shut, and I glanced back through the trees toward the bonfire, that I felt a little shard of fear pass through me. As soon as I opened the door to the cottage, though, I felt the gardener's welcoming presence, and my fear disappeared.

CHAPTER 13

Buffy the Vampire Slayer Kills on Fieldcrest Drive

While the fear had gone away, an uneasy feeling lingered and kept me awake half the night. I spent those restless hours reading Willa Cather's novel *Song of the Lark*. When I woke up around noon the next day, I was still thinking about the novel, not quite sure what to make of it. It was very different from the nineteenth-century English novels I loved. So far, the only thing I could say for sure was that I liked Cather's plain, well-made sentences and her descriptions. There wasn't a plot really, and I wasn't sure why the backstory about Thea Kronberg's growing up and figuring out she wanted to be a singer went on as long as it did, but I hadn't been able to stop reading the night before because of those sentences.

I needed to escape from the heat of the cottage, and I decided to try the little neighborhood coffee house I'd discovered on one of my walks. The Bean was close enough to walk to but because of the heat I drove. Inside, I found a long, narrow space with very high ceilings and two walls of exposed brick. The counter ran parallel to the longest of the outside walls, and there was space for three small tables across from it. Toward the back were more tables and a grouping of worn leather chairs and a couch.

The place was empty in the middle of the day, and after she made my iced coffee, the barista settled in behind the counter and studied her phone. The air-conditioning didn't quite cool the space, but it was better than the cottage, so I sought out one of the leather chairs in the back where I read about the endless sacrifices Thea Kronberg made for her career and the people (mostly men) who helped her along the way, and how, even after all that help and sacrifice, she still wasn't allowed to have everything she wanted, which, frankly, depressed the hell out of me.

Throughout the afternoon, a few people came in, ordered, and left. No one made me feel guilty about staying as long as I did, but I ordered another coffee and a sandwich and read until I finished the novel. I concluded by the end that Thea wasn't all that happy about how things had turned out with her life, even though she'd achieved her goal of becoming a famous opera singer. She was acclaimed, but it was obvious she'd been happiest during the week she'd spent with Fred, the man she loved and couldn't have, in the canyons of the Southwest, far away from the complications of his marriage to another woman and the rigid, obsessive discipline Thea's ambition demanded of her. I wondered if she ever sang while she was in those canyons? The novel doesn't say, but I thought she must have. How could she have resisted hearing the echo of her big voice? Cather had described the Southwest so beautifully I decided I was going to make a detour through it when I drove back to California.

I puzzled over the meaning of the novel, not sure what Cather was saying about art and ambition, as I drove back to the cottage a little after 5:00 when I noticed a small group of people sitting on the meadow, one guy in a folding chair sitting under a tree drinking what looked like a beer from the cooler at his feet.

Over the next hour, I watched out my kitchen window as a steady stream of people walked by. By 6:00, the meadow was almost full, and still more were arriving. I'd scoffed to myself the night before when Tillie promised to save me a seat up front, but by 6:30—when I encountered Mary Garlic standing sentry at the back gate, clicking the tiny counter she held when she saw me—I appreciated it. People sat on blankets and lawn chairs, many of them brought picnic dinners, some with candles and wine glasses. I didn't get it. How bored people in Nebraska must be for an amateur musical to attract this kind of attention.

I found Tillie in the costume tent helping actors get dressed. She was so fixated on what she was doing she barely acknowledged me. She pointed to a row of chairs and told me to sit there. A few minutes before 7:00, she joined me. The orchestra had already started playing when Mary Garlic slipped in on the other side of Tillie, and I overheard her say to Tillie, "I counted 347." Tillie only nodded, as if this wasn't surprising.

The size of the audience was unexpected, but the performance itself was a revelation. Moss, Harmony, and Roger may have been the talent behind the script, lyrics, and score, but Sophie was the star. Quiet Sophie was transformed in the character of Buffy. She gracefully executed kicks and karate chops as she took down vampires and delivered her silly lines with impeccable timing, keeping everyone laughing. But most remarkable of all, she could sing. She sang those ridiculous, campy, somewhat predictable but also at times surprisingly haunting songs with a passion and pathos that transcended talent. And as Tillie had promised, the musicians in the orchestra played the score with a high seriousness that in contrast to the absurdity of the play, made for something inspired, at times almost sublime.

If Cather's story of Thea Kronberg cultivating and methodically sacrificing for her talent, seeking success and immortality through art, told one kind of story about an artist, here was a very different story altogether—Buffy, as a reluctant Christ figure, the vampire slayer tormented by her calling, desperate to be released from the burden of her gift. Buffy wants nothing more than to be a normal high school girl. She doesn't want to save the world; she wants to go to the high school dance, to hang out with her friends. Between vigorously kicking vampire ass, Sophie's Buffy begs the universe to spare her this destiny.

The morning after, when I saw Sophie on the street, she smiled politely as if nothing had happened. "Sophie," I said and went on to gush about her performance. She shrugged, betraying no hint of the charismatic performer I'd seen the night before. Nothing now suggested the way through sheer force of talent and personality, she'd captivated a huge crowd, in less than perfect outdoor conditions, for almost two hours. She was back to being a somewhat self-conscious sixteen-year-old, seemingly the normal girl Buffy dreamt of being.

Sophie started to shift a little, obviously uncomfortable, as I talked about every detail of her performance. I couldn't seem to stop myself, though, even asking at one point about her plans after high school. Expecting her to say she was headed to LA or New York, like so many other talented girls from the middle of the country, I couldn't hide my surprise when she told me about her modest ambitions.

"I'm looking at Hastings College. They have a good music program—and the University of Nebraska. I'd like to teach high school music, maybe, but I'm not sure. My dad really wants me to major in business."

"But your voice!" I finally interrupted her. "You have such talent, *real* talent, Sophie." I heard myself pleading with her, but she was impatient, only smiling uncomfortably before finally saying she needed to go.

Her nonchalance unnerved me. I couldn't get past her unwillingness to even entertain my ambitions for her, wondering aloud before she turned away if they would at least be posting some of the songs on YouTube.

She shrugged. "I'm sure Moss will post something. It's no big deal."

No big deal? She ended the conversation by saying, "Singing is fun and all, but I can't see doing *that* with my life." *That.* How contemptuous she was of her talent. And how overeager was I? I'd gone from being the biggest doubter of the teenagers on Fieldcrest Drive to their biggest fan, wanting to help them market and exploit their talent. Until Sophie had delivered her dismissive closing statement, I'd been brainstorming strategies to market and promote her talent. I knew exactly the approach I'd take with social media and had begun to formulate a strategy in my mind, to think through every little detail of how I would execute the plan: I'd set up social media accounts for her and develop her brand, and from there, I'd enlist a team to start posting on her behalf. I'd send video clips of her work to major influencers on Twitter and Instagram. If interest didn't grow organically, I'd pull in every favor I had with all my contacts, finding out who knew someone who knew someone in the music industry who might comment and repost.

In spite of Sophie's disinterest, it had felt good that day to be engaged, the first real glimpse I'd had of my old self in months. All day I kept thinking about how exhilarating it had been to start something new, to see my efforts gain traction and take off, to watch as the germ of an idea grew into reality. I'd been so caught up in the details of the day-to-day operations supporting that success, I'd almost forgotten how much fun it had been at the beginning when Kylie and I were still renting the house on Vermont Street after we moved out of the dorm our junior year. Kylie's parents had bought the house, so our rent was low, but it was too big for us so we advertised for two roommates. We ended up with two sophomore girls from Redlands U: Jill and Rory. Kylie and I liked both of them, but it turned out they couldn't stand each other. We thought they'd work it out, but they didn't. It got so disruptive we finally decided we had to get rid of one of them, but which one?

Everything changed one night near the end of the first semester while we were all studying for finals. I was taking an astronomy class that was kicking my butt, and I decided to procrastinate that night in the best way I knew how by baking a pie. The smell of it finally brought all of them into the kitchen, and even though we were all stressed about exams and paper deadlines, we sat down together at the table and ate that lemon meringue pie, feeling like we were breaking the rules, enjoying ourselves instead of cramming for tests.

When I was younger, it never failed to impress people that I could bake a pie, my one reliable party trick. Mystified, Jill asked me that night, "Were you, like, a Girl Scout or something?" God knows why this comment struck Kylie so funny, but she insisted I tell them about how I'd grown up, living in houses without electricity, for periods of time without bathrooms. I should have been mad at her for outing me like that, but for some reason I wasn't. Something about my descriptions of those situations made all of us slap happy. We laughed our asses off. And then we got serious. We started telling one another about the worst things that had happened to us—a sort of girl bonding ritual I wasn't accustomed to—Jill and Rory ended up crying and hugging each other.

I suspected it was a temporary truce, but the next morning they were still friends, and they stayed friends for the four months they lived with us. Later, Kylie joked, "What did you put in that pie?" For weeks afterward every time there was a problem that needed to be solved, she'd suggest I bake a pie. Just like my grandma: *When in doubt, bake a pie.*

Earlier that fall I'd started a short-lived blog. Blogging never became my thing, but it was the start of the 2008 recession, and like every other college kid that year, I was freaked out about what I was going to do after graduation. The way I wrote about it, we'd all been set up by our parents' generation, who, instead of blaming themselves, blamed us for being lazy and soft. I wasn't the only one who felt like a loser at the time, and my whole intention with the blog was to try out different ideas (most of them intentionally wacko) about what an adult life might look like post-recession, and most of all not to accept the blame game foisted on us by the feckless older generation. The upshot was that we were all screwed.

The Gen Xers were all DIY, and we'd started to worry we were all going to have go even further than they had and learn to live off the land or become foragers. The blog was mostly an outlet for me to think up solutions to worst-case scenarios. No surprise, I didn't have many followers.

After the pie incident, though, I wrote a blog post titled "Pie Action for Peace." It was never meant to be taken seriously, but weirdly, it touched a nerve with my readers and was by far the most successful of all my blog posts, not the part about how my housemates became friends—that didn't interest anyone much—but the part about baking a lemon meringue pie. It turned out a lot of my readers were into baking pie, too, and it seemed like all of them had a story about pie. They ended up sharing recipes and advice. It was a spontaneous thing, and I questioned what was really going on until one of my blog readers said, "All this talk about pie is the surest sign of denial about our terrible, rotten, horrible future."

That spring, after the university provost changed graduation requirements, Kylie joked that we should do a "pie-in" to protest, an idea nobody took seriously until eight girls volunteered to storm the provost's office with homemade pies. One of the girls knew a photographer for the student newspaper, and she convinced him to tag along to record the protest in hopes it might get attention and embarrass the college.

I agreed to bake nine pies, but I didn't go along with them to the provost's office that Monday. I'd thought it was a silly stunt even on Tuesday morning when Kylie ran home after class waving a copy of the school paper, on the front-page a photo of her and the other eight girls surprising the provost with their pies. We died laughing at the unflattering picture of the provost. Likely nothing more would have come from it except the next day the *Redlands Daily Facts* ran the same photos and an article about the protest, creating a major embarrassment for the administration. Within a few days the provost made a statement correcting an earlier "misunderstanding about the policy."

The night of the provost's reversal, Kylie and I were sitting on the back patio laughing about what had happened when she said, "You know, Vivi. This could be your thing."

I knew immediately what she meant. I'd been stumped about what to do for my senior project, the last hoop before graduating with a degree in marketing. Kylie's suggestion got me thinking. Social media platforms were just starting to take off, and I wondered how such a platform could support information sharing around pie.

"You could call it Pies for Progress," Kylie said.

"How about peace? Peaceable Pies."

"Peace? As in pies that are peaceable? What does that even mean, peaceable pies?"

We laughed. The sun had gone down by then, and we'd started to feel a little chilly sitting outside. The conversation ended there, but for the next few days I thought about how the project might work.

"How's this for a mission statement?" I finally asked Kylie the next weekend. "Where there's conflict: in the family, at work, among *housemates*, in the neighborhood, the school, the town, the world . . ."

She smiled and said sarcastically, "Pies for World Peace."

I wasn't the least bit serious as I later made the pitch to my advisor, but I knew I'd need a high-minded statement in order to get him to sign off. I finally settled on this: Pies4Peace will be a social media platform built around pie as a social and cultural phenomenon, a ubiquitous domestic product reconsidered as a subversive agent for change.

Later, I threw around a few ideas about feminism and the family, the neighborhood, as the center, or *locus* as Kylie suggested, of power. We came up with all kinds of crazy shit. I focused my pitch on the way recipe sharing was a perfect vehicle for a social media platform. There were always more recipes, more stories, more advice. I already had anecdotal evidence from my earlier blog post that there were a lot of opinions when it came to pie. Everything was theoretical then; I was only thinking about satisfying the requirements for graduation so I could start my promising future as an underemployed college graduate.

CHAPTER 14

One Little Life

After the musical, Mary Garlic rolled the makeshift prairie schooner onto the private way where for the next week Lake, Kettle, and Spur pushed it up and down the street. Lake obsessively sang the catchy little section of Buffy's theme song that got stuck in my head. For days I caught myself mindlessly humming over and over again:

I want to be a girl
a normal girl
a girl who goes dancing
a girl who gets kissed
by a regular boy.
I don't want to be a hero.
I don't want to save the world.
I only want to live my one
little life.

I'd been so taken at first by Sophie's performance that I hadn't given much thought to what the other teenagers had accomplished. Now, though, I wondered how Harmony and Moss had come up with the concept, how they'd conveyed its campy smartness. The music, too, had at times been pretty great, a tribute to all of their talents. Together this little group of teenagers had made something much greater than the sum of its parts, turning a profane subject into something at times almost profound.

I thought for days about the difference between a Thea Kronberg and a Sophie Clark. I'd always thought talent was everything, but Cather seemed to have a different theory. At least in this novel, she made it clear she didn't think it was talent that mattered as much as *desire*. Sophie was exhibit A in support of this argument. The question of desire stuck with me, and I inevitably turned the question to myself. Had I lacked desire? Had I walked away because I couldn't cut it when things got tough? I didn't think that was the case, but how could I be sure? I kept hearing Kylie's voice scolding me. This wasn't a good loop for me.

There had been something deeply, mysteriously impenetrable in Sophie's response to my questions about her future plans, something that went well beyond indifference. True, I'd had no idea what I wanted from life when I was sixteen. I understood that confusion. But I'd known I wanted something bigger than my mother had. I was all over the map with ideas about where I could see myself in the future. Sophie's goals seemed so modest, so circumspect and cautious, so *practical* about life before she'd even started to live. What teenager is that practical? Everything I'd worked so hard for had been violently, unfairly threatened. I couldn't comprehend someone who couldn't at least dream about living more fully.

These thoughts about Sophie's indifference were maddening to me. Yet how could I possibly understand the mysteries of other people's lives when I was so mystified by my own. I was tempted for a while to say fuck it and buy a new phone and laptop, to abort this whole contrived thing I was doing. My own retreat from life seemed every bit as maddening as Sophie's indifference.

School started for the kids soon after the musical, and the days started to get cooler. When I wasn't driving to some out-of-town destination, I took long walks, sometimes spending hours walking each day. I walked miles in adjacent neighborhoods, avoiding the busy main streets. I rarely met anyone else walking on the sidewalks; sometimes I'd notice someone working in their yard. Almost always, they waved when they saw me. I consulted my city map and drove to other neighborhoods where I'd walk for a few hours.

I listened to the birds and the insects, their sounds more frenzied now that the weather was changing. The grass that had been stressed by the heat grew green again. I smelled something earthy and pungent in the air, and I thought it must be the leaves beginning to die.

Mary Garlic, who couldn't understand why anyone would walk when they could drive, mentioned one day that they had several old bikes no one was using, and I could use one if I wanted. "Beats walking," she added. I followed her into their ancient garage used for storing everything *except* their cars. "We keep all the old bikes back there." She pointed toward the back wall, and left me to climb over old lawnmowers, unused patio furniture, boxes of yard tools, and other castoffs from previous generations until I finally found a stash of bikes. As I sorted through them, I wasn't optimistic I'd find anything until I saw the vintage one-speed hanging on the wall: The blue paint was faded, its white leather seat torn and rust stained, and the handlebars pocked with corrosion, but I liked the shape of its heavy frame.

Later, when I pointed it out to Mary Garlic, she looked at me to make sure I was serious before she climbed up on the workbench and stretched precariously to take it down from the hooks. She strained a bit with its weight as she handed it down to me.

"This isn't one of ours," she said after she'd dismounted from the workbench. She looked at it critically, wiping her dusty hands on her pants. "Must have belonged to Tillie's aunt Matilda. You sure you want this old thing?"

The tires were shot, the rims were bent, but as I stood astride it, I saw if I raised the seat a bit, it would be a good fit for me. "I think with a little work, it'll be perfect."

Mary Garlic raised her eyebrows and pursed her lips. "To each his own, man."

A couple days later at the bike shop Moss had recommended, the bearded guy behind the counter looked over the bike and said in that bored way they must all learn in bike mechanic school that he could fix it, sure, but making it clear he thought I'd be nuts to pay for work on such a stupid bike. I told him to go ahead. A few days later when I went to pick it up, he'd not only straightened the rims, replaced the tires, and worked on the chain and the hub, he'd replaced the seat and "thrown in" a new pair of handle grips. Still not giving away too much, he seemed to warm up a little when I thanked him for all the extra work he'd done. "Take it for a spin while you're here," he said, "just to be sure everything's good." He adjusted the seat for me, and I hopped on.

I must have been smiling when I got back to the shop, because that too-cool-to-care bike mechanic actually turned up the corners of his mouth into something that resembled a smile when he saw me. As he handed me my receipt, he said, "This'll be a nice little commuter for you."

I found a spot for the bike under the eaves along the east side of the cottage. I planned to ride it as much as possible. I'd been noticing all the bike lanes around the city, and I'd gone back to the Nebraska tourism place to pick up one of the bike trail maps. There were train routes converted to trails going in all directions from Lincoln to Iowa, Missouri, and Kansas. Once the weather got a little cooler, I was going to explore those trails.

On my walks through various neighborhoods, I'd started noticing signs for the 2016 presidential campaign. I'd been so distracted before leaving California, I hadn't paid much attention to it. It had been a long time since I'd heard any news, but when I started listening to the little radio I'd bought at Best Buy, I was irritated by the coverage of the campaign. Why were the journalists so shocked and outraged when the real estate man from New York said something intended to shock and outrage? I couldn't take it seriously. I listened to NPR's evening edition while I heated up whatever frozen thing I was making for dinner, but as soon as the news was over, the Lincoln station reverted to its playlist of all classical all the time. Not a fan.

Some nights I listened to the college radio station, KRNU, and some nights I listened to KZUM, the community radio station where some of the volunteer DJS hosted decent programs, most of them knowledgeable, if a bit quirky. Late one Friday night when I was listening to KZUM I heard a familiar voice. The host of a program featuring old-style country music. She said at one point, while on air, "I don't play any of that new shit that passes for country." And I knew for sure it was Mary Garlic.

It was mid-September when I finally started biking on those long trails. The trail to Bennet was lined with tall sunflowers, their huge heads leaning over the path. The blue sky so brilliant and opaque it seemed I was inside a painting. The wind was still those days, and the frenzy of insects I'd noticed in the city was much more intense in the countryside. The trails cut away from the highways through quiet woods and tall grass. South of the city, the trail going toward Cortland and on toward Kansas, hugged Wilderness Park before plunging into the trees. I felt exhilarated those days, and after returning from my bike trips, I walked for miles each evening. The trees had started to turn by then. Russets, yellows, and oranges. I never spoke to anyone on these walks, even crossing the street sometimes to avoid people.

As I biked and walked on those golden days, my mind was often empty. Long periods went by where I couldn't account for myself. Unapologetic about my mindlessness, I sometimes worried about how satisfied I was to wander aimlessly. During the daylight hours, if I started to feel lonely or anxious or worried or overly critical of myself, I simply took another walk or wandered down to the creek where I sat on the bank and watched the water flow until I was lulled back into mindless contentment.

Biking, walking, and creek-sitting were only a few of my mindless activities, though. As day turned into evening—what I'd heard was referred to as the golden hour and what my mother called cocktail hour—I couldn't resist being outside to watch the day drop behind the trees to the west of the private way. I sat in the old lounge chair in the backyard and watched the birds fly overheard, listening closely to the sounds of day transitioning to night. I'd never paid attention to nature, surprised now by my stupid fascination. I'd become as dull-witted as a sheep, content to absorb the world through my senses: listening, watching, smelling.

Each evening, intending to be more productive, I took a book outside with me, but I was invariably distracted by a birdcall or the droning of insects, finally dropping the book into my lap to watch the clouds instead, my mind drifting along with them, as afternoon melted into evening. I lost track of time, only coming back to myself when I was stiff from sitting so long in one position. In this trancelike state I never worried or felt anxious about anything. I was like a single-celled creature, floating without purpose or direction, suspended in nothingness.

In brief moments of lucidity, I questioned this state of mind and wondered, as I had before, if maybe I'd suffered brain damage. Could emotional trauma result in actual brain injury? I'd resolved to take a year off, but I hadn't signed on for mental torpor. Truthfully, though, most days I was past thinking or caring—let alone judging myself—about anything except what was right in front of me. The world outside felt very far away. The past seemed like something I'd imagined, and, like a vegetable, I was listlessly satisfied with my lot on those golden fall days.

On one of those afternoons, I read a passage in *My Ántonia* that seemed to describe my current condition in its most positive light. The narrator, Jim Burden, is lying on the prairie, under the autumn sun, beside a pumpkin patch: "I kept as still as I could. Nothing happened. I did not expect anything to happen. I was something that lay under the sun and felt it, like the pumpkins, and I did not want to be anything more. I was entirely happy. Perhaps we feel like that when we die and become a part of something entire, whether it is sun and air, or goodness and knowledge. At any rate, that is happiness; to be dissolved into something complete and great. When it comes to one, it comes as naturally as sleep."

That is happiness; to be dissolved into something complete and great. I took inordinate comfort from that passage and read it again and again as if to soothe myself in my predicament. Only later did I think to question if maybe Cather hadn't been critical, describing something insidious, maybe something about the plains, about Nebraska itself, something contagious in the environment, that had afflicted Jim, and now afflicted me. Maybe this same affliction explained Sophie's complacency.

In all those weeks, no one ever came to my cottage, except Bill. The first time he escaped from the Clarks' backyard and I heard him scratching at the cottage door, I returned him immediately, scolding him a little as I walked him back across the street, even as I was secretly thrilled by his visit. A few days later, when he showed up again, I didn't return him immediately but instead took him with me into the backyard where he lay down beside the lounge chair, the perfect companion, quietly watching, and listening, and smelling along with me.

I'd justified keeping him for a couple hours that evening because no one was home at the Clarks' house at the time. But when a week or so later, he ran away for the third time, Bridget caught me crossing the street with him as she was pulling into the driveway.

"Bill just came for a little visit," I said when she met me at the back gate, still hanging open from his earlier escape. Bridget frowned as she looked from the open gate to Bill before reacting with a suddenness that startled me. She grabbed Bill roughly by the collar and drug him into the yard, ignoring me as she closed the gate. From where I stood outside the fence, I heard her berate Bill before administering some punishment that made him yelp. I ran back to my cottage then, filled with an unaccountable rage, feeling Bill's punishment as if it were my own.

That afternoon instead of passing the golden hour in my usual contentment, I played over and over again the encounter with Bridget, each time feeling the same irrational rage. If these two extremes were the only choices in my new reality, I much preferred to be practically brain dead than to be consumed by so much anger. I didn't know why I was taking things so personally, except, I guessed, because I felt Bill was being blamed for Bridget's negligence. Still, my rage felt disproportionate to the offense.

My days and early evenings were fine as long as I kept busy and engaged, but late at night, alone in the cottage, my mind turned to the same dark obsessions that had plagued me in California. A few times I was sure I heard someone creeping outside under the living room window, and I huddled in bed with the kitchen knife. The mornings after the worst of these nights, I'd go outside and search the ground to make sure no one had been there. Mornings, my fears felt silly and unfounded, but come night, reason fled again.

The only thing that consoled me was the gardener's presence, and in the darkness, I clung to my idea of him, making him into a savior of sorts, pleading, as if in prayer, to save me from whomever might be lurking outside. If the gardener had been a real person, he would have gotten sick of me, but he was my benign, trustworthy—all right just say it, imaginary—friend, a long-suffering, patient source of solace, in much the way my phone had once been.

CHAPTER 15

The Storm That Was a Mother to Me

I.

After weeks of perfect weather, one day early in the second week of October, it rained all day. At first, it was a soft rain, welcome after all those days of sunshine, but in the late afternoon a cold wind swept in, and the cottage felt damp and cold. The neighbors had told me not to expect cold weather until late October at the earliest, and I'd taken them at their word. I still wasn't prepared for winter. I didn't have blankets; I didn't even have a sweater. I'd been looking forward to the cold, though, imagining long walks in the snow.

Once I figured out how to turn on the furnace, and the house warmed up, I started a list of the winter things I needed to get the next day. While making my list, I heard what sounded like hundreds of fingernails tapping on the windows. I stepped outside and tiny pieces of ice pelted me. So this was sleet. I loved that word: *sleet*. The cottage felt even toastier when I went back inside. The cold was a new adventure.

I woke up late that night and listened as the wind gusted around the cottage, rattling the windows and shaking the walls. Outside, thick ice had coated tree branches and power lines. It coated every blade of grass and every dried stem still standing in the garden around the cottage. The next time I woke up, I could barely see that it was snowing outside for the thick coat of ice covering the windows. I watched, mesmerized, until I noticed how cold the cottage was. The furnace had stopped running, and the clock beside the bed indicated the electricity had gone off at 1:37.

I put on all the clothes I had and wrapped myself in bathroom towels to wait for morning to come. By dawn, the snow had drifted so high in the front yard it blocked the front door and covered the lower half of the front windows. The wind howled and shook the windows like an intruder trying to break in.

First thing that morning, the neighbors arrived, starting with Roger and Moss who, working together, shoveled out the front walk. Knowing I wasn't prepared for winter yet, the women came with provisions. They brought blankets and fleece jackets, sweaters, and waterproof pants. They brought down coats and snow boots. They showered me with mufflers and mittens, hats and socks. They gave me flashlights and coolers for the food I had in the fridge. They brought food. Throughout the day, they kept an eye on me, checking in periodically to make sure I was all right.

I watched as all day Roger and Moss worked to keep everyone's walks clear of snow, shoveling almost constantly, starting with their own walks and meeting in the middle of the street to clear Audra's walk and then mine. It seemed like a competition. If so, the snow was the clear winner. As soon as they finished one pass, the wind blew the walks closed, forcing them to begin again.

Roger finally left the snow shovel he'd been using outside of my door, shouting into the wind that they had extra shovels at home and this was mine for the duration. *Duration.* I felt my stomach sink at this word even though everyone had assured me throughout the day this was a freak storm, that it would blow over quickly, the snow would melt by the next day, and the power would be on again soon.

2.

The neighbors were wrong. The snow didn't stop that day. Instead, the storm grew worse. The power was still off when in the late afternoon Tillie and Mary Garlic sent Moss to invite me over for chili. I surprised myself by welcoming the idea of being around other people. All day I'd been thinking about a passage from Cyril Connolly's book *The Unquiet Grave* I'd had to read for a class at the university. He describes how we seek out nature for restoration but soon find it inhospitable, the cold, the wet, the dark forcing us to seek the comfort of home and civilization as a protection from nature, which is, in the end, entirely indifferent to us. More than any time in my life, that day, watching the storm from inside my cold, dark cottage, I felt the complete, dangerous, indifference of nature.

I put on the winter gear everyone had brought for me earlier, finally ready to face the weather. It was only 4:30 when I headed out, but the storm had created its own strange twilight. The wind howled and the snow pelted me. It was much colder than I'd expected.

When Tillie saw me at the door, she said, "Oh, Gigi, come in! You look like a snowman. Don't worry about your boots. Just get inside." She held Mr. Shipley by his collar as he panted and lunged at me, his tail wagging furiously, obviously part mad with being cooped up all day. Behind them, I watched as The Lord skulked across the dark hallway, stopping only long enough to glare at me as if I'd come to kill him.

Once I was inside, Tillie drug Mr. Shipley into the entryway where he finally settled down, resting his big head on his paws, even though his eyes monitored my every move, watching as I unwrapped myself from all the layers of winter clothes, hanging them to dry on the built-in coat valet in the hall.

"Mary Garlic made chili on the camp stove," Tillie said, "and we're singing around the campfire."

I had smelled smoke when I'd first come inside, but now as I entered the living room I found Mary Garlic tending a fire in the living room's ancient fireplace. The house was full of smoke, whether from the fireplace or from the dozens of candles they'd lit, their flames wicking in the drafty room.

"Gigi!" Spur called out when he saw me. "Come sing with us." Moss was playing the guitar, and Harmony was leading the little ones in a sing-along. It was a silly song about an aardvark, and Kettle laughed so hard each time they got to the chorus he could barely sing.

"We haven't used this fireplace for a long time," Mary Garlic said with a tinge of worry when I came to stand beside her. "I hope there isn't too much creosote built up. That would be bad." She looked up at the chimney, as though she might be able to see through the bricks, and then looked at me with a meaningful smile. "I knocked some stuff out of there earlier this fall, though, so it should be okay."

"Sit down, Gigi," Tillie interrupted. "I'm going to get you a bowl of Mary Garlic's chili. It's the best chili you'll ever eat."

Without interrupting the song, Harmony pulled a chair closer to the fire for me, and within seconds Tillie reappeared with a bowl of chili. She was right. It was the best chili I'd ever eaten, but I couldn't be sure my assessment wasn't influenced by my gratitude for being in their company.

After the sing-along, the adults watched a play—made up by Spur, Lake told me—about three little mice who've been left alone and are looking for their mothers. Moss and Harmony had improvised costumes for the little kids out of pipe cleaners, tissue paper, face paint, and mittens.

Later, there was hot cocoa for everyone, with a dash of peppermint schnapps for the adults and Moss and Harmony. While we sipped our cocoa, we quietly watched out the windows as the snow continued to fall.

"If the wind doesn't die down tonight, we'll be snowed in solid by morning," Mary Garlic said before assuring me again that the power was always back on the day after a storm. There had already been an announcement that the schools would be closed in the morning, and when Moss went to the basement to get out their sleds and cross-country skis for the next day, I took it as a sign that it was time for me to go. As I thanked them for inviting me over, Tillie looked at me with an expression of surprised hurt. "But you have to stay overnight, Gigi. We're going to camp by the fire tonight," and as if to underscore the point, Moss returned from a second trip to the basement having brought up sleeping bags for everyone, including an extra one for me. A few minutes later Harmony handed me a pillow from among those she'd brought down from their beds upstairs.

I was shy about imposing on them, but I couldn't resist the comfort of being around other people as I felt the storm raging outside. I rolled out my sleeping bag in a far corner of the room, a bit away from where the family had all clustered together around the fireplace.

Late in the night, I woke once to see Moss throwing more logs on the fire. The fire wasn't doing anything to heat the house, but its light was comforting. I watched him, beautiful boy, and allowed myself to imagine briefly that he'd looked in my direction. It was enough to fuel a fantasy that became a dream, that he crossed the room and crawled into my sleeping bag with me.

I woke again to what sounded like loud gunshots. The noise woke everyone else too. "Oh, shit," Mary Garlic said, sitting up in her sleeping bag across the room. In the firelight, I saw her short hair standing on end. "I was worried this would happen. It's the trees," she said to the room. "They hadn't lost their leaves and this heavy snow is bringing down the big branches." At this news, the little kids jumped from their sleeping bags to look out the windows, though it was too dark for anyone to see what was happening outside.

The following morning, we saw it was more than branches the storm had brought down in the night. Entire trees had been uprooted. I'd never seen anything like it, and from their reactions neither had Tillie or Mary Garlic. It was the scene of a disaster, a chaotic mixture of drifted snow, blocked driveways, and downed trees and power lines. Mary Garlic expressed relief that nothing had come down on their cars or the roof of the house, though the crown of a large tree hanging over the side of the garage led her to speculate they might have to replace the garage roof. Until she'd pointed them out, these weren't hazards I'd known enough to worry about.

For the first time I thought about possible damage to my car and the roof of the cottage.

They had seemed calm when discussing the storm, but while Mary Garlic made bacon and eggs in a cast iron skillet over the camp stove, and the little kids clambered to go sledding, I intercepted the glance she exchanged with Tillie. They seemed concerned about something as they gently discouraged the kids from sledding that day.

As if she'd guessed my earlier worries, while she plated my eggs and bacon, Mary Garlic said, "I'm sure your car's all right, Vivi. The only big tree on that side of the street is the maple behind the cottage, and the prevailing winds are in your favor. You're welcome to stay with us until the power comes back on. What's one more mouth to feed with this gang?" I knew she'd meant it kindly, but her joke emphasized my awareness that I was a fifth wheel, and even if I'd been tempted to stay, I knew it was time to go.

When I walked back to the cottage after breakfast, the sky was a milky gray. Snow spewed thick as smoke. The wind whipped and churned it as it fell. I clambered over downed trees and branches, and dodged downed power lines, understanding then why Tillie and Mary Garlic had discouraged the kids from being outside.

By the time I reached the cottage, I felt like I'd been on an expedition. I was so relieved to find my car and the roof of the cottage intact that I almost didn't mind that the house was dark and cold inside, glad in fact that I'd made it home safely. *Home.* The word had come to me without hesitation.

Audra had brought me a battery-operated lamp and a portable propane heater. It seemed fitting to be reading *Shadows on the Rock* with its descriptions of the struggles of the tough early settlers in Quebec City, the ways they managed their hardships and created order out of chaos, created comfort in spite of mud and snow and cold and dark, in spite of being cut off from everything they'd known and loved in France.

3.

I had spent a contented day reading under the blankets, eating peanut butter sandwiches and apples in bed when around the same time as the previous afternoon, I heard a muffled knock at the door. Expecting it to be Moss again, I was surprised to see Roger instead. He'd trudged through the thigh deep snow to my fence, where he'd then had to shovel to reach my door. I hadn't heard him for the roar of the wind.

"My mother sent me." He was breathing heavily from his exertions. "She figured you wouldn't be prepared for being alone in this kind of storm."

"No worries. I'm fine. Thank her for me, though."

During the brief time we'd been talking, snow had blown into the kitchen, forming a little drift on the floor beside me. Roger looked at that little drift with a glum expression I took to be concern about the drift, until he said, "Mom told me to invite you over for spaghetti. It's our tradition whenever it storms. Don't ask." Through all his winter gear, I saw him roll his eyes at this, making me laugh. He added in a pleading voice, "Please don't say no. You can't say no to my mom. If I come back without you, she'll send me out again." He looked so miserable, his cap and coat covered with snow, his teeth chattering with the cold that I finally said, "Oh, all right." I gestured for him to come inside while I put on my winter things.

"Do you have a flashlight?" he asked as I pulled on a pair of gloves Bridget had given me. "It's dark on the street, and it's crazy walking with the power lines down." I had the flashlight Audra had brought for me. Only then did I realize she had brought me several sources of light.

Roger and I leaned hard into the wind, struggling to walk the short distance across the street. In several places, the snowdrifts were so high we had to find a way around them. We didn't try to talk, but now and then Roger wordlessly took my arm to help me over a drift or a downed limb. Visibility was so poor it wasn't until we were almost to their house that I saw it was lit up as if nothing had happened.

"Oh, you didn't lose your power?" I said, when we finally reached their back door, feeling an odd sense of injustice about this.

"We did," Roger shouted, "but my dad turned on the generators. We have three, and between them we have enough power to keep most things running for several days."

Bridget was there to meet us at the back door; her long, expressive arms reached out to pull us both inside, as if saving us from drowning. "Get in here and get warmed up," she said, while she took my things. "You must be frozen over there in that drafty little hovel."

"What's your poison, Vivi," Chuck asked. "I'm drinking Maker's Mark. You want a bump? Or would you prefer a glass of wine? A martini? Beer? Just name it."

I noted Bridget was drinking red wine. "I'll take whatever Bridget's having."

"Will do."

I'd never been inside their house, having kept only to the backyard pool and patio those last weeks of summer. Through the patio door I'd glimpsed the large entry room I was now standing in. In summer it had served as a poolroom, but it was now transformed into a mudroom. The hooks that only a short time before had held beach towels and swimsuits were now hung with coats, and where there had been flip-flops, snow boots now lined the floor beneath them.

Bill, who I knew was kept confined to this room when he was inside, thumped his tail on the tile floor when he saw me, and I stooped to give his belly a quick rub before I finished taking off my boots.

Bridget grabbed my arm and escorted me into a large central living room, its vaulted ceiling opening up to the second floor. The large arched window in the front spanned the height of both floors and looked over the drive below. Without seeing it, I guessed my cottage—my little hovel—was in full view from this room.

White leather couches were grouped around a gas fireplace burning cheerfully. Above the fireplace, Fox News was muted on a large, flat screen TV. The clownlike reality-show star was speaking somewhere, and the banner tape across the bottom of the screen said he was now a serious candidate for the presidency.

The house was so toasty that once I was in the living room I took off the thick outer sweater I'd been wearing. Roger was half sitting, half reclining on the thick taupe rug in front of the fireplace. Sophie was nowhere to be seen.

"Sit, sit," Bridget said as Chuck appeared with a glass of wine before he disappeared and returned again a few seconds later with two bowls of popcorn. "I recommend the chocolate salted caramel," he said, gesturing with his head to the bowl in his left hand.

"Sophie, come down and say hello to our guest," Bridget hollered up to the second floor as I reached for a handful of popcorn. A few seconds later, Sophie appeared on the loft above us. She was wearing glasses I'd never seen before, and I guessed she'd been watching TV in her room. Without smiling, she silently looked down at us over the railing.

"Say hi to Vivi," Bridget instructed. Sophie blushed and said in an ironic tone of voice, "Hi, Vivi."

"Come on down and join us, Soph. It's a storm!" Bridget said, before turning to me. "Chuck and I just love a good storm. Our first date turned into a storm—didn't it, honey?—and we've loved storms ever since. The kids like storms too. Or they used to anyway. Now, they act like it's a bother to have to be stuck at home with us old fogies."

Sophie had come downstairs and was now sitting on the arm of Bridget's chair. She idly took a handful of cheese popcorn. "You want a cup of cocoa, Soph? There's hot water on the stove."

Sophie shook her head.

"So, Vivi, we're curious about you? Do you have family in California?"

"My mother."

"Oh. It's just the two of you?"

"Yep." I felt my teeth clench slightly and forced myself to answer cheerfully.

There was an odd pause, as all of them grew alert. I felt a silent calculation take place. I hadn't realized I'd been put on a scale until I felt this information land, like a weight on the side of something disagreeable to them.

And then, as if nothing had happened, they moved on.

"So, how do you manage to fill time every day?" Chuck said.

"I've been getting acquainted with the area—by the way, thanks, Bridget, for all your good recommendations." She'd told me about the kitschy Pioneer Village and the more sedate Stuhr Museum. "And I've been reading a lot. Cather mostly. I'm maybe becoming a little obsessed with Cather." I laughed, hoping my attempt at self-denigration might lighten the mood.

Chuck and Bridget exchanged a quick glance of confusion before Chuck's face cleared. "Well, isn't that a coincidence. Willa Cather, right? Sophie loves her books." He looked toward Sophie for affirmation, but she gave away nothing.

"Oh, *that* Cather," Bridget interrupted. "I used to be something of a reader, but I don't have time for that kind of thing anymore."

From previous visits to the pool, I knew how things worked when Chuck wasn't home, but that night I saw a different dynamic in the family. Whenever he was in the room, Bridget and the kids seemed to be a little on edge with each other, their conversation a bit forced, a bit too cheerful. I noticed how each of them glanced quickly at Chuck before they said anything, even if they weren't talking to him. It wasn't the easy back and forth I'd witnessed on those summer nights when it was just Bridget and the kids bantering together around the pool.

After about a half an hour, Chuck stood up and said he needed to check on the spaghetti sauce. Before leaving, he asked Bridget if she preferred to eat at the dining room table or in front of the fire. In the few seconds he waited for her answer, he paused and awkwardly mimicked the swinging of a golf club. "The fire," she finally said.

He returned twice with plates of spaghetti for all of us, explaining to me that spaghetti sauce was the one thing he knew how to make, and that whenever there was a storm, if he wasn't traveling, he did the cooking.

We'd been eating for only a few minutes when Bridget said in a slightly wheedling tone, "Honey, could you please grate some more Parmesan?" Chuck made a little grunting noise that I took to be a signal of impatience before setting his plate aside and leaving the room. Bridget and the kids watched him closely, and as soon as he'd rounded the corner to the kitchen, Roger and Bridget hastily took helpings of spaghetti from Sophie's plate and put it onto theirs. They were fast and focused in their work.

Once Sophie's plate was clean, Bridget whispered to me, "Sophie hates Chuck's spaghetti sauce."

"Thank you, honey," Bridget said when Chuck came back into the living room with the Parmesan. He started to sit down when he noticed Sophie's empty plate and caught himself. "Soph. Geez. You must have been starved, kiddo. You really snarfed your spaghetti."

Sophie laughed. "I know. It's so good I couldn't stop myself."

"Here, I'll get you a second helping while I'm up." He reached for her plate.

"Thanks, Dad, but I'm stuffed. It was great, as usual."

Chuck smiled and settled down again in his chair. During this exchange Bridget had kept her head lowered over her plate, but I'd felt her watching closely, noticing she only relaxed again once Chuck had started to eat.

After dinner, Chuck insisted on taking our plates and doing the dishes. His waiting on us seemed to make Bridget and the kids jittery, and once he'd left the room, we were all quiet as we watched the fire. We were all startled when Chuck shouted above the sound of water running in the kitchen sink, "Mother, Bill really wants to come out and say hello to our guest." He must have been rubbing Bill's belly as he spoke, because we heard the sound of Bill's tail rhythmically hitting the floor in the kitchen, where Chuck must have invited him in spite of Bridget's strict rules against it.

Bridget didn't respond, and Chuck said in a high-pitched voice meant to channel Bill, "Please, please, please, Mommy. Please." Chuck paused and then added, "Did you hear that, Mother?"

Bridget frowned but said nothing. A few seconds later Bill bounded into the room, a big doggy grin on his face, knowing enough to stay away from Bridget. Chuck had followed him into the room. He seemed to enjoy making Bridget uncomfortable even more than he enjoyed indulging the dog. Still avoiding Bridget, Bill made the rounds, starting with Sophie who pushed him away when he tried to lick her face and moving on to Roger who absently scratched between his ears, before he finally reached my chair.

I hadn't seen Bill since he'd been punished for running away a few weeks earlier. He stopped beside me now and looked into my eyes before he laid his heavy head on my lap the way he had that first day at the pool. He looked up at me with an expression of such devotion it made Chuck laugh.

"Would you look at that? Bill's in love with Vivi."

Bill's head felt warm in my lap and the weight of it so comforting I didn't want him to move, but I saw Bridget watching me with an expression of such disgust and distrust I knew not to show my pleasure, suspecting that although she didn't like Bill, she disliked even more that he liked me.

"That's enough. Bill." Bridget stood up. "Get off this carpet right now. Come on." She snapped her fingers, and Bill slowly lifted his head from my lap to follow her back to the mudroom. When Bridget returned she frowned and muttered at Chuck, "I don't understand why you always have to push" before switching roles, once again the cheerful hostess. "Ice cream?" she said as if nothing had happened, clapping her hands twice before taking everyone's order.

We ate our ice cream in complete silence, and I had the distinct impression this was what life was like at the Clarks most of the time when Chuck was home.

"The whole town'll be shut down again tomorrow," Chuck said once the ice cream dishes had been cleared away. He'd been drinking throughout the evening, and his words were a little slurred. "I've been tracking the storm on radar," he continued, "and it's a bad one. There are trees and power lines down all across the city. It's going to be a long time before they get a crew out here to Fieldcrest, plus it'll cost all of us an arm and a leg to find someone willing to clear the trees out of here. Mark my words, it'll be at least a week before we get power back, and none of us are going anywhere with that big elm blocking us from the street."

I was horrified by this news. I wasn't sure—despite all my earlier resolve to be as strong as Cather's characters—I could handle such a long time by myself in the cottage, perversely deciding at that moment it was time for me to leave.

"Thank you so much for your hospitality, but I'd better be getting back."

Like Tillie had the night before, Bridget looked at me with alarm. "Oh no. Absolutely not, Vivi," she said. "You can't go back there tonight. I've already made up the bed in the guest room. You have to stay."

As much as the idea of staying in their warm house appealed to me, I knew I didn't want to wake up there the next morning.

"You're so sweet, but I'll be fine. Really."

Bridget looked very serious as she shook her head. "I'm not being sweet, Vivi. This kind of cold is dangerous. I promise we'll let you go home first thing tomorrow morning. We'll send more blankets and candles and food. We know you weren't prepared. Well, none of us could have predicted it."

Chuck perked up. "So it's settled then. Come on. I'll show you around the house before we show you the guest room." I trailed after him through room after room, listening to details of all the bargains they'd made, everything "top of the line." Among the rooms he showed me was a den full of hunting and fishing themes: pictures of Chuck with various kills or catches, taxidermy trophies of numerous conquests mounted on the dark green walls, an oak gun cabinet filled with rifles. I'd never seen so many guns in my life. He started to open the cabinet to show me a new rifle when Bridget interrupted him to say I was probably tired and could see it another time. We finally made it to the guest room where I slept better than I'd imagined I would.

I was surprised the next morning by how natural it felt to wake up in the Clarks' house, as natural as it had been to wake up in Tillie and Mary Garlic's house the day before, as if staying the night was a kind of initiation.

They all saw me off after a breakfast of waffles with instructions to come back again that night if the power was still out. "We mean it, Vivi," Bridget said again before I left. Roger helped me carry all the extra things Bridget had gathered for me, and together we trudged back to the cottage through the snow and the wind. I looked back at their house once to see it lit up the way it had been the night before. In the room I'd just left, I glimpsed Bridget and Chuck sitting together in front of the fire. I didn't know why that tableau seemed so sad to me.

4.

As if the neighbors had prearranged it, on the third day of the storm, Audra crossed the street to invite me to come to her house. It had stopped snowing that morning, but the temperature had fallen, and it was now very cold in the cottage. By then, all of us knew it would be many days until the power was restored to our little street.

I thanked Audra but declined her offer. I couldn't face spending that much time with her. I preferred the cold and the dark to that, thanking her again for all the things she'd brought for me earlier, mentioning specifically that she'd been right to guess Jim's boots would fit me. While I hadn't known at first how I felt about wearing her husband's boots, I'd quickly gotten over my squeamishness as they'd come in so handy the previous two days.

"I'm glad to hear they're working out for you." As she said this, she looked past the threshold of the door and into my cold, dark kitchen. "You can't stay here like this," she finally said.

"I'm fine. I've got everything I need."

She shook her head, and I noticed a stubborn set to her jaw. "I have a big house. I'm alone over there, and you're alone here. I have everything we need to get through this, but it'll be better for both of us if we're together." She went on to tell me she had a generator that provided enough power to keep her furnace, refrigerator, and freezer running, adding, "Jim always made sure we were prepared for every sort of disaster. You've seen for yourself, we have enough food in our basement to survive a six-month siege."

All the time she was talking she continued to step farther into the doorway, until she now blocked the door, a subtle aggression that surprised me. She took another step inside. "I have a fire going in the fireplace, and it's cozy over there. I have an extra bedroom with its own bath. We'll help keep one another company." She paused, her eyes once again sweeping the dark rooms behind me. "Plus, it's too lonely over there for me."

By this time, she'd made her way into the kitchen, and she now shut the door behind her. "Why don't you go get the things you'll need to stay for a few days, Vivi." I was impressed with her willfulness, while also realizing the problem with the invitations from the other neighbors was the way I was inconveniencing them. By appealing to my generosity, Audra had made it almost impossible for me not to accept. Still, I equivocated. I'd go with her, but only for one night. I didn't want to get trapped into staying at her place.

I don't know why I'd taken such a dislike to Audra my first day in the neighborhood, but when I woke up the next morning in her house I felt at home. Where before her house had seemed stuffy and formal, I now found its open floor plan inviting. The furniture was simple and spare, not uncomfortable at all, and I quickly saw how every piece had its use. It was elegant and understated. Unpretentious. And, unlike Bridget, I *liked* the quiet of Audra's house. It was familiar to me. The truth was, I wasn't used to being around a family, having to deal with more than one other person at a time. The relationships between those couples made me uneasy. There were tensions in partner dynamics I couldn't quite grasp.

In the eight nights I stayed with Audra we established an uncomplicated routine. Yoga in the morning, hot tea and oatmeal for breakfast while we listened to NPR, a few housekeeping chores before strapping on snowshoes and walking: first to the nursing home where Audra checked in with Jim and later around the city. It was exhilarating to be out, especially those first few days when we agreed it was like being among the survivors of a postapocalyptic world. We watched as the city slowly emerged and returned to an orderly, normal world. Each time we returned to our dark, snow-covered private way it was like returning to an abandoned scene of violence, a place forgotten by the outside world. It took several days of Mary Garlic and Chuck working together to finally find someone to remove the big elm blocking our entrance.

After our morning walks, Audra and I read in front of the fireplace for as long as we had light through the afternoon. Jim had a large collection of vinyl records, mostly jazz, but some early rock and folk, and each afternoon Audra put on a smattering of records: Bill Evans, Wes Montgomery, John Coltrane, and Miles Davis. She had to tell me who these people were since I didn't know anything about jazz. She and Jim had kept their old turntable and speakers from the late '70s, and Audra admitted they'd never migrated to CDs or MP3s. She was surprised when I told her turntables had made a comeback.

Except to bake a pie, I didn't know anything about cooking, but that week helping Audra make our simple dinners I learned some things. After dinner we cleaned the kitchen and then sat in front of the fire and talked until bedtime. As we performed those small domestic tasks throughout the day, I often thought about Cather's Cecile Auclair, the little girl left behind to carry forward her mother's domestic values, and through them create comfort and order in the wilderness of eighteenth-century Quebec. I'd brought the book with me to Audra's house, and one night I read this passage for her as we sat by the fire: "These coppers, big and little, these brooms and clouts and brushes were tools; and with them one made not shoes or cabinet-work, but life itself. One made a climate within a climate; one made the days, the complexion, the special flavor, the special happiness of each day as it passed; one made life."

When I finished I looked up to see that Audra's face had fallen slightly. As soon as she saw I was watching her, she brightened artificially. I didn't press her about what she was feeling. As I'd gotten to know her better, it was clear she'd created an isolated life for herself. I knew from what she'd told me that she'd been enlisted from the start of their relationship to serve Jim's career, and part of that training had made her distrustful of herself and others. She told me how Jim warned her before every college gathering they hosted, "These people aren't our friends. They're my colleagues. Don't say anything that I'll have to pay for later." In other words, she told me, "Don't be yourself. Don't ever be yourself." Our backgrounds couldn't have been more different, but I saw in her my same habits of secrecy and solitude.

The only thing I didn't enjoy about those days was going to the nursing home every morning. The first day we went, Audra insisted on introducing me to Jim. I hadn't known how to dissuade her. What could our meeting possibly mean to either of us? I knew from Audra that Jim had ALS, which meant he was trapped inside himself. Until a few weeks ago, he'd still been able to signal by blinking, but now even that small communication had been lost. The doctors told her Jim's mind was still alive and encouraged her to keep talking to him. She admitted to me it was hard to talk to someone when there was no response at all.

Seeing him was worse than I imagined it would be. He was lying under a sheet, his body rigid and corpselike. The worst part, though, was the way his face was frozen in a rictus of pain.

Audra went to the side of the bed and said to him, "I've brought you a visitor today, Jim." Without looking, she gestured for me to come closer. I didn't know where to look as I came to stand beside her. "This is Vivi," Audra said. "She's renting the little garden shed across from us. Mary Garlic and Tillie worked wonders and made it into the sweetest little house. Can you believe that? They finally fixed up that place." She smiled. "Maybe they heard all your grumbling."

She looked at me then, inviting me to say something. I made a futile waving motion with my left hand. "Hi, Jim. I've heard a lot about you." I cringed as I said this, but Audra smiled at me. A nurse came into the room and briskly opened the curtains.

"Here, we'll make things a little more cheerful for your visitors, Mr. Bell."

"Thank you," Audra said before turning back to Jim. "That's better, isn't it?"

After the nurse left, I motioned to Audra that I was going to wait for her in the lobby. "Nice meeting you, Jim," I said.

I sat in the lobby in a chair nearest the front door. I hated it here. The cloying, sweet smell amplifying the foul smells it was meant to mask. From then on, I resisted all of Audra's invitations to visit Jim in his room and waited for her in the lobby, reading while she did god knows what for that hour she spent with him each day. I squeamishly avoided looking at anyone, fearful the entire time one of the residents would stop and want to talk to me.

That week, as we listened to the news, we kept hearing about the discovery of emails found on a private server that Hillary Clinton had used when she was secretary of state. There was outrage that these emails hadn't been turned over to the congressional committee investigating what had gone wrong at the embassy in Benghazi. I hadn't been following the presidential campaign until then, so Audra had to fill in a lot of the backstory to help me make sense of what was going on. She was sure that in spite of this setback Hillary would be the Democratic candidate. We tried to picture how it would be to have a woman president, something Audra hadn't believed, until now, could happen in the United States. The news was also full of the antics of the real estate man from New York. We regularly shook our heads in disbelief, and on a few occasions had to laugh outright at the ridiculousness of it all.

One night, during a conversation about strong women, Audra said, "My dad always said 'only the strong can be kind.' Jim thought that was pure hokum, but then, he never thought much of my family— 'Arkansas hillbillies' he always called them." Her laugh surprised me, but I laughed, too, a little uneasy that it might seem I was going along with such a harsh judgment of her family.

"We were a mismatch from the beginning, Jim and I. I was just a little hick girl on scholarship at the University of Arkansas, the first person in my family to ever go to college. The first woman in my family to graduate high school, and here he was a tenured professor."

We'd carried this conversation into the basement where we gathered things for that night's dinner from among the canned goods on the shelves. Like every other night, each of us wore a headlamp to navigate through the dark. I wasn't surprised when Audra had told me Jim always insisted the headlamps be kept in good working order. On our nightly forays into the basement, I'd noticed the numerous laminated lists Jim had made, instructions for every possible emergency: fire, flood, tornado, intruders, power outages. By now, I'd gotten used to how silly we looked wearing those headlamps and found them useful.

We were rummaging among the jars of canned goods when Audra said, "There was a big dust-up in my family when I went away to the big city of Fayetteville. My grandpa said they'd fill my head with no good." She turned her headlamp toward me, and though I couldn't see her face for the light in my eyes, I guessed she was smiling. "Jim always liked to tell that story at faculty gatherings," she said as she turned away. "It was a reliable way to get a laugh." As she said this, I wordlessly held up a bag of dried apricots for her approval. She nodded. "We could use that in some sort of chicken, nut, fruit, rice dish," she said.

That night, we were savoring the dish she'd created when I asked, "How did you meet Jim anyway?"

Before answering, she took another bite of the dish, a Middle East–inspired rice concoction. Nodding, she said, "We did good with this one." She set her plate on the coffee table. "He was my classics professor. First class, first semester of my freshman year."

"He was your professor?" I didn't disguise my surprise. "How did you end up marrying your professor?"

"Oh, things like that happened then. It was a different time in the early '70s. Male professors had affairs with their students all the time." My mouth dropped in shock, and as if she thought it would help, she said, "No one thought anything about it. Jim decided to start an affair with me the first day he laid eyes on me in that class. I was so dumb I didn't have a clue until he asked me to stop by his office for a *talk*. Like I said, things were different in those days."

Audra sat back against the couch. After a long pause, she said, "Jim was married at the time we met. I always felt bad about that, but since they didn't have any children it seemed a little less . . . oh, I don't know." She looked up at me. "We all have ways of telling ourselves what we're doing isn't really as bad as we know it is."

We kept the fire going a little longer than usual that night as she told me how the University of Arkansas had been Jim's first teaching job after he'd gotten his PhD at the University of Pennsylvania. "I've never told Jim this," she said, "but the thing I remember most from the class I took with him isn't anything to do with the classics, but rather how he made it clear to all of us that we were from a low-class state, and we were attending a third-rate university, and all of it was beneath him." She smiled when she said this, but I thought I saw a little shadow cross behind her eyes.

Wanting to lighten the mood, I teased her a little. "He couldn't keep saying that about Arkansas after meeting you, though, right?"

"Oh, you'd be surprised, Vivi, how enduring a low opinion can be." I expected her to laugh at this, but she changed the subject instead. "I'm going to make a cup of tea. You want one?"

"Yes, but I'll make it." While I made the tea, she told me how Jim had ignored his faculty colleagues who scoffed at him when he decided to move up the administrative ladder. Then she went on to rattle off a list of jobs: chair of the Classics Department at U of Arkansas, dean of students at Kansas State, dean at Simmons College in Boston, associate vice president for academic affairs at Murray State, vice provost at Southeastern Missouri State, and past that, I couldn't keep track of the list of associate this and vice president that before he was finally offered his last job as provost at Nebraska Wesleyan.

I brought the teapot and two mugs to the coffee table and turned up the gas on the fire a little, before sitting down again in the armchair that had quickly become my favorite. "Did Jim feel like he'd achieved his goals before he got sick?" I asked idly, a little bored by the story of Jim's career.

"He was sixty-eight when he took the job at Nebraska Wesleyan; his plan was to become a college president by the time he was seventy, and I don't doubt he would have found a way to achieve that goal if fate hadn't had other plans for him." She shifted on the couch and smoothed the cashmere throw she was using to cover her legs. "Jim, of course, hated—hates—when I talk like that. He doesn't believe in fate." She looked down at the throw again and made a show of picking off a piece of lint. "But really, what else can you call it but fate?" She asked this in a deadpan voice, combined with a mock dumb expression I'd become familiar with and which reliably made me laugh.

Until those days I stayed with Audra, I'd never talked to anybody so much in my life, not even with Kylie. Sitting around talking to people wasn't something I did. I could never have expected this relationship with Audra. The last night before the power returned, I feared I may have jeopardized the trust we'd established when she asked me in a way that felt sincere and concerned rather than snoopy, what had brought me to Nebraska?

She was the only person on the private way I felt I could trust with the story, and I wanted to tell her everything. I knew she wouldn't judge me, that she'd be nothing but supportive, but for some reason I couldn't do it. For one thing, I didn't know where to start. She'd told me she didn't know anything about social media. She wasn't on Facebook or Twitter and wasn't curious about those platforms. I figured she wouldn't understand how something like PIE could even be a thing, let alone be so successful. Plus, until now, faced with telling someone new about it, I'd never had to think about how silly the name PIE was, how stupid the whole thing would sound to someone who wasn't a part of it. There was too much to explain, and I didn't want to focus on the pathetic saga of the past year, so I did what I'd been doing with everyone since I'd arrived. I dodged the question by joking about how I had an outlaw past I needed to hide. I saw a little flash of bewilderment in her eyes before she adjusted her expression, lowered her expectations, put up her guard a little. I knew she was hurt by my withholding but was too polite to confront me. I felt like I was making a mistake not to say something. This was my opportunity after all. What else was there to do except tell one another long stories.

"The truth is, Audra," I finally said, "I'm not quite ready to talk about it yet, but when I am, you're the first person I'll tell."

She smiled a closed-mouth smile and nodded. "Whenever you're ready."

CHAPTER 16

Go-To Neighbor

Everything changed after the storm. I was fully accepted by the neighbors into the rhythms of the private way, first by Audra whose house and habits I'd gotten to know well during the days we'd shared together, and next by Tillie and Mary Garlic, whose boundaries were more porous than most. I quickly adapted to their open-door policy, their low expectations for privacy, and their standing invitation to Sunday morning brunch and Wednesday night movies at their house.

After Mary Garlic made an offhand comment one day about how stressful her mornings were getting the little kids ready for school, I asked why no one helped her. Turned out Harmony left early for school, while Moss, who had opted out of taking college prep courses, had a late start time and slept in on school days. And Tillie? Well, no one expected Tillie to be reliable in that way. Mary Garlic turned the question back on me.

"So why aren't you over here helping me? It's not like you have anything else to do."

By then, I knew not to take this personally. "Well, sure," I said. "I could come help you. What time would you need me?"

She looked at me closely as if testing me. "7:00. Breakfast."

"Okay."

"I'll pay you. Five an hour. Cash. I get paid on Fridays. End of the week okay?"

I started to protest that I didn't need the money but stopped myself. Knowing Mary Garlic, any suggestion that I didn't need to make money would only be a cause for confusion and resentment. "It's a deal," I said.

She nodded without a smile and stuck out her hand to seal the agreement.

If, as Tillie had said, Mary Garlic was the German shepherd at their door, it appeared she was a pretty chill German shepherd. On those busy mornings, once I'd figured out their routine, I found a way to be of help. I, who had never been part of a big family, accepted the role I was assigned within theirs—a sort of auntie, or an older sister, it wasn't entirely clear. I was privy to their squabbles, their inside jokes, their pranks, their loving, and their constant group teasing of Tillie.

Even the Clarks relaxed with me after the storm. I still wouldn't have gone into their house without knocking, but Bridget lowered her boundaries enough to show me where they hid the spare key and began to ask me to help out in ways I assumed she'd once assigned to Audra. I became the go-to neighbor to let in the repairman, to double-check that the iron was unplugged, to rummage in the freezer for something Bridget wanted thawed for dinner, or to take to school whatever one of the kids might have forgotten that morning.

That fall I came to know my neighbors through the most intimate details of their lives: I knew their basements, their laundry rooms, their closets and junk drawers, their medicine cabinets, their garages, their car trunks and outbuildings. I knew what kind of mail they received, the meds they took, and what sort of consumers they were. I knew their parenting styles, their habits, and their pet peeves. There seemed to be little they didn't allow me to see or hear. Whatever their reasons, all of them except Audra (and I only include the women because they were the ones I interacted with most) seemed to have concluded I had nothing to hide, no past, no regrets, no secrets, and certainly no means or motives to hurt them. The others accepted me as a kind of blank slate, a kind of communal pet, someone reliably handy for company, support, help, or confession.

They willingly, even eagerly, confessed to me things I felt sure they had never told one another and, in some cases, had perhaps never told anyone before. I knew when Tillie was sixteen she fell in love with an Albanian boy who worked as the doorman of an apartment her mother was renting in Paris; he was an immigrant who dreamt of being a doctor, until her mother, offended by the relationship, had him fired. I tried to hide my shock when she admitted to me after telling this story, that if Agron, that was his name, showed up at their front door, she wasn't sure she could resist running off with him, even now after all these years.

Bridget admitted she didn't like her oldest brother and had, when they were kids, once prayed that he would die. She said she was still worried that God might punish her for that prayer. I wondered what her brother could have done that had made her hate him so much.

And Mary Garlic told me once that she'd always wanted to learn to fly a plane. It hadn't seemed like that big of a thing to me, her having a dream like that, but she seemed to regret having said it and asked me not say anything to Tillie. "She'll try to make it happen if she knows, and that's not what I want."

And while I was soothed by the simplicity of these relationships, relieved not to be scrutinized, there were times when I resented their lack of curiosity. I felt there was something self-satisfied, even smug in the way they'd so quickly dismissed me. If I was feeling sorry for myself, it felt downright disrespectful. All except Audra had no idea who I was, and they didn't find this imbalance odd. Maybe it was my being a young, single woman. Maybe they had good instincts and knew I was worthy of their trust. Or, as I suspected, maybe they'd decided I was of so little consequence it didn't really matter who I was.

CHAPTER 17

Ivan the Czech Guy

The Bean had a brisk morning take-out business, but afternoons I was often the only person there for long stretches of time. It had become my go-to place to hang out and read. I had a favorite table by the big front window. In the weeks since visiting Homestead, I'd bought books about homesteaders and Native Americans. They'd disturbed me, complicating the ideas I'd formed about the opening of the West. Sandoz's homesteader father, Jules, was not a heroic pioneer. While he had a brutish intelligence as a farmer, he was cruel and obsessive, demanding of his daughter, and literally working multiple wives to death. His story forever undermined my romantic ideas about pioneers. And the stories I read about the treatment of Indians during western expansion left me shaken. It wasn't just that individuals on both sides had been savage, it was the perverse role played by the U.S. military and the U.S. government and their adoption of policies designed not only to subdue resistance but to systematically destroy Native culture, regularly breaking treaties, and lying to create situations where Indians could be massacred with impunity. Even what I'd learned about the genocide of the California tribes, these stories still shocked me. I'd somehow thought California was an exception when I now suspected it was simply part of a much bigger plan.

So I returned to Cather to soothe me in part, seeking out her perfect prose, her ability to elide those dark stories of early settlement within the mythic. I had enough problems of my own. I couldn't seem to absorb too many horrors from the past.

The barista those late afternoons was a tall, skinny guy with unruly black hair and a sparse beard. He had a lot of nervous energy, and when there wasn't a customer, I was sometimes distracted by his jangling around behind the counter. He played good music, though, Beach House, Radiohead, Fiona Apple, and some older stuff, Frank Black, Wilco, Roxy Music, Bowie. He was friendly in a way I thought of as Nebraska-nice, smiling and saying hello when I came in but not talkative. I was glad for it. I couldn't have kept going there if he'd been *that* guy. I was definitely not interested in guys right then. I'd seen a side of men during the past year that had shocked me to my core.

One afternoon in mid-October when the snow from the storm still hadn't quite melted, as I was tucking *My Ántonia* into my bag before I left, the barista caught my eye.

"You liking that book?"

"Yes. Have you read it?"

"Lots of times." He said this as though it should have been apparent.

"Why?" I said without thinking.

He shrugged. "Because I like Willa Cather." And then a goofy, disarming grin sprawled across his face that made him look impish and a little silly. "And because my great-great-grandmother, Annie Pavelka, was the real-life Ántonia."

"There was a real Ántonia?" I felt oddly disappointed to learn a novel could cross over with reality in such a personal way.

"Of course. If you google it, you'll see."

"You know, you're a little bit like the kid in grade school who tells the other kids there's no Santa."

He grimaced and dipped his head shyly at this characterization before smiling again. "Shoot. Sorry. But, yeah, there was definitely a real Ántonia. Besides, everybody knows Cather based a lot of her characters on real people."

"*Everybody?*"

He chuckled. "It got her into trouble sometimes, but in the case of *My Ántonia*, everyone says that Grandma Annie was happy with the story."

I'd just finished rereading the novel that afternoon, still full of its grand ending, Ántonia emerging from the fruit cellar, her many children spilling out behind her. "And why wouldn't she have been happy? Cather makes her a goddess in the end?" I said.

"True." He hesitated a second. "But there's all that other stuff too. About her family, you know, and the thing with Wick Cutter, and the bit about the illegitimate baby, the shame of all that. I mean, most people wouldn't like their personal lives tangled up with a made-up story that way."

I couldn't remember another time in my life when I'd talked about a book in this way, a conversation framed by how the book had been received by a reader so intimate with the sources of the writer's inspiration. Truth was, I'd really never talked to other people about books at all, except in class discussions. Maybe he mistook my confusion for friendliness, because he came around from behind the counter and stuck out his hand.

"My name's Ivan. Ivan Sedlacek."

I shifted my bag to take his hand. "I'm Vivi Marx"

"Vivi? Short for . . ."

I hesitated, and for reasons I still don't understand I told him my full name, a name no one has ever used. "Vivienne. It's short for Vivienne."

He smiled his goofy smile again and repeated "Vivienne," almost in a whisper. "That's a beautiful name. Do you mind if I call you that?"

I felt my face grow hot, embarrassed but not sure why, except that I didn't want anyone to be paying this much attention to me. The only reason I wasn't weirded out by him was that he seemed so childlike, so harmless, so downright dorky I couldn't see him ever being a threat. He noticed my reaction and sensed he'd crossed a line. "Oh, gosh. I'm sorry," he said in a rush. "Wow. That was rude of me. I mean, it's your name. Geez. Not cool. Me putting you on the spot like that."

The entire time he was talking, I'd been slowly working my way toward the door, but now, before I opened it to go, I relented, maybe just so I could get out of there. "It's fine," I said. "I mean, you'd be the only person in the entire world to call me that, but hey, like you said, it's my name."

In the space of the time it took me to say this, something passed between us, some transaction, that left both of us deeply embarrassed, and to get past the awkwardness, we silently agreed to pretend nothing had happened. Still rattled, I turned to leave, and if I'd left then, I'm sure I would never have gone back.

"Hey, Vivi," Ivan said then, in a warm, neutral tone, the way a friend says your name, "it was really nice to meet you."

His doing that, acting normal, gave me the little bit of space I needed to recover. "It was nice to meet you, too, Ivan."

"You know," he added before I left, "if you like Cather, you might like to visit her home town of Red Cloud. There's a museum and the house where she grew up. It's not that far away, and it's pretty country over there, especially this time of year."

"Thanks, I might do that." How was it possible the guidebook I'd bought outside Omaha hadn't mentioned anything about Red Cloud? What else hadn't it mentioned?

"See you soon." he said, before the door closed, his tone so casual, I knew it'd be okay to come back.

After that, if Ivan was there when I came in, we greeted each other but otherwise he left me alone to read until I got up to leave. In those short conversations, I learned he taught Life Skills at North Star High School and was working afternoon shifts at the coffee house to help pay off his student loans. He told me he was part of a working group giving input on a bill that he and a few other teachers hoped would be taken up by the state legislature, something about kids with autism and expanded medical benefits. He seemed to take it for granted that I was as interested in the bill as he was, and most days he gave me a rundown about their progress.

Unlike the neighbors, though, Ivan's curiosity about me wasn't so easily satisfied by my vague answers or my dismissive line that it was a long story. He wasn't convinced by these evasions and saw me in a way the neighbors didn't. I wondered if maybe the ladies, as I'd taken to calling the neighbor women to myself, simply *couldn't* see me. Maybe it had something to do with Ivan being close to my age. He recognized something was off where they couldn't. Could I honestly say I understood everything about what concerned the ladies on Fieldcrest? Maybe it was true what Cather said, that those who were of different ages occupied different planes of a shared reality. Or, as she put it, "The dead might as well try to speak to the living as the old to the young."

I liked Ivan, but I also knew his curiosity would inevitably lead him to search for information about me. I distracted him by giving him tidbits. I told him about growing up in California, even telling him that my mother flipped houses for a living without giving him too many details.

He never bought my lie about de-gridding in order to recharge. No one completely unplugs for an entire year just to enhance creativity. He teased me sometimes, and once jokingly asked who I was hiding from? He was smiling when he said it, but when I didn't respond immediately, he looked a little stricken. "Hey, I was just joking, Vivi, but if you're really afraid of someone . . ."

"It's nothing like that," I said, thinking it wasn't technically a lie since I was afraid of thousands of someones. It was a mistake on my part, though, not to be more forceful in countering his concerns, because the next time I came into the Bean, he said, "I did a little sleuthing about you, Vivi Marx."

I felt my heart race. "Oh?" I waited, not breathing, to hear what he'd learned.

"So, what's with this pie-baking, feminist, activist thing? Is it some kind of not-for-profit?" My initial response to his question was relief. I smiled at his characterization of PIE, but I was also puzzled by his superficial search.

My first thought was a moment of self-congratulation for how successfully we'd managed to scrub PIE of any evidence of the trolls, but this was followed by a darker realization. Scrubbing evidence of the trolls wouldn't have erased me from PIE. Anyone doing even the most superficial search would have quickly found my connection to the platform. Unless? Unless, in my absence, Kylie, with the backing of her father, and the board had formally distanced the site *itself* from me, leaving only the residue of the earliest incarnation of PIE when it was still based on my senior project—Pies4Peace—at Redlands University.

As soon as I thought this, I knew it was true. I felt the psychic wound of the betrayal in almost the same way I would have a physical wound, stunned by the vindictiveness of it. I was angry with Kylie, but I was also angry with myself. Why had I imagined PIE would remain in stasis for a year while I was gone? This enormous, dynamic business? Why had I been so naïve about the repercussions, thinking Kylie would understand and simply shrug off my disappearing without even talking to her?

Ivan watched me closely. He seemed to miss nothing as I churned through all these emotions, finally turning my face away from him and staggering to my usual table before turning to him and saying, with as genuine a smile as I could fake, "It was just something I did in college. My senior project. I'm embarrassed it's still up on the web."

He knew I was lying, but being Nebraska-nice, he didn't push me. I only pretended to read that afternoon. Instead, I plotted as I sat in the front window of the Bean about how I could repair the damage, how I could stop what was happening, forced that day to see what I'd been trying to ignore, how deeply troubled I was. Everything I needed to do to fight back involved being online. But even after this many months, just the thought of opening a laptop or picking up a phone made my skin itch and my breathing grow shallow and ragged. The anxiety attacks hadn't diminished; they'd become an actual phobia. I took advantage of another customer at the counter to sneak out of the Bean without having to face Ivan.

CHAPTER 18

Road Trip to Catherland

By the end of October, I'd convinced myself the situation with PIE was only temporary and that whatever was happening there could be made right after I returned. I'd been helping Mary Garlic with the little kids for two weeks, going over early each weekday morning to oversee breakfast. After my shift on Friday, I felt like I'd been freed from jail. I decided to take Ivan's advice and make a trip to Red Cloud.

The only things that remained as evidence from the storm in Lincoln were the damaged and now missing trees. As I drove out of the city, I felt sick with sadness at seeing street after street of those disfigured trees. Once I was on the highway, though, I felt almost joyful as I drove through the countryside, green again with a last burst of life before winter. The fields of corn and soybeans lay unharvested under a cloudless, blue sky, though I'd heard reports the soybeans had been damaged in the storm and the harvest would be lower this year because of it.

Like most other small towns in Nebraska, Red Cloud had a modest main street lined with mostly one-story buildings, a few two- and three-story brick buildings left over from the town's heyday in the late nineteenth century. Among them was the restored opera house that had contributed to shaping Cather's aesthetic. Her early exposure to opera played a major role in her brief career as an influential music and theater critic beginning when she was only nineteen. I'd learned this and other surprising things about her in the biography I'd read. A small grid of residential streets surrounded the downtown, but from what I could see, the only game in town appeared to be the Cather industry.

As I parked on the main street, near the Cather Museum, I noticed several other out-of-state license plates, making my own California plates less of a novelty than they usually were on my visits to small towns. A group of people milling around the entrance finally headed into the gift shop. I guessed they were all associated with the tour bus I'd seen on an adjacent street.

If I hadn't read Cather's biography before going to the museum, I would have had no idea how unusual she'd been. Even then I was still surprised to see photographs of her as a teenager with a shaved head, cross-dressed, during the period when she called herself William Cather and sometimes signed her name Dr. William Cather. The biography softened this somehow, but now as I thought about it, it seemed radical for a girl growing up in the 1880s in a little town in Nebraska. The biography hadn't mentioned anything about how her straight-laced, Virginia-born Victorian mother had handled it, though it seemed clear she hadn't tried to stop it. As I wandered through the museum, I wasn't sure my own relatively open, downright disinterested mother would have been all that cool with me cross-dressing when I was fourteen.

My earlier conversation with Ivan had prepared me for what turned out to be the weirdest part of the day, a tour of Red Cloud. The guide in our van pointed out house after house once lived in by the actual people who'd inspired some of Cather's most memorable characters. Some people on the tour actually hissed when the guide pointed out the house in which the prototype for Wick Cutter, Ántonia's would-be rapist, had lived.

While I'd started reading Cather's novels out of boredom in August, I'd since decided her commitment to documenting what was required of a civilized society was a kind of medicine. Despite seeming a little sugar coated, her novels felt sane to me. At the time I desperately needed to believe there was sanity in the world. I'd begun to think of her at times as a sort of guide—a life coach—for surviving the year in Nebraska, a good sidekick for this hiatus from my real life. Her novels were full of life, scattered with nuggets of what I took for wisdom, much of which I dutifully recorded in my journal. Even when I disagreed with her, I felt she saw a lot of things clearly.

It became obvious that day in Red Cloud that my feelings about Cather were very different from those of the "Catherites." What I observed in those diehard fans was a kind of worship. They seemed to be making a pilgrimage, not simply visiting an author's home. Fandom of any kind brings out something perverse and rebellious in me, an instinct to distance myself or to detract from the adored object. Despite this tendency, I knew not to make any joking comments with the group of fanatics in Red Cloud that day. These were true believers, theirs a devotion to the point of obsession.

The details of Cather's life were hard to disguise, and the tour guide worked hard to tease out every biographical detail. I'd reread *The Song of the Lark* and felt sure it was the key to understanding Cather's own journey as an artist. Thea, like Cather, was one of the older kids in a large family, though unlike Thea, it had been Cather's father, not her mother, who'd been supportive of her dreams. Otherwise, Cather's story mirrored that of Thea's, the guide pointing out the importance of the educated and sophisticated immigrant men of Red Cloud in helping Cather focus her talent outward. These men were the first to recognize her gifts, to see she had passion (the all-important desire) and talent. They'd encouraged her and helped with her education. And like Thea, Cather had experienced a symbolic rebirth in the cliff dwellings of the Southwest.

What I hadn't anticipated was how moved I'd be when I actually saw Cather's small attic bedroom, recognizing it immediately from her description of Thea's room. I was glad to be alone in the room for a few minutes, because as soon as I climbed those attic stairs and stepped into that space, I was overcome with emotion, in much the way I had been when I first felt the gardener's presence in the cottage. In Cather's attic room that day I was engulfed by the spirit of the strong-willed, remarkable girl who'd once inhabited it.

I was still in this exalted mood when I left Cather's house. I'd stopped wondering by then if I was losing my mind. It seemed certain I had, and I'd decided there was nothing to be done but to sink into it. The mellow, late afternoon sun, the crystalline blue sky, the muted chatter of insects and birds created a glowing radius around all the common little things in that common little town and conspired with my feelings to create a state near ecstasy. I might have wandered to my car in this delirium and driven straight home if I hadn't encountered the memorial to a fallen World War I officer. The guide had pointed it out to us earlier, but I hadn't paid much attention. Now, though, I stopped to read the inscription to G. P. Cather.

This artifact pierced through my dreamy state, and I was strangely shaken by the understanding that here was a tribute to the cousin who had inspired the character of Claude Wheeler, the dissatisfied, idealistic young protagonist of *One of Ours*. All day I'd been put off by how the tour guide and the museum exhibits insisted on reading Cather's work in this biographical way. I'd wondered why the sources of her inspiration mattered so much to some of her readers when for me it took away from her artistry, made light of the worlds she'd worked so hard to create, as though she'd been merely the town scribe.

In spite of myself, though, as I stood before this memorial marker, I was forced to revise my reading of that novel. I thought about the passage at the end of the book where Claude's mother thinks about his dying, how "he died believing his own country better than it is, and France better than any country can ever be. And those were beautiful beliefs to die with." But it was her conclusion that, "Perhaps it was as well to see that vision, and then see no more," that made the passage such a dark comfort. I recalled then something I'd all but skipped over before, how Claude's mother went on to describe the returning soldiers as having survived the war but not surviving their disappointment in an unworthy, disinterested, self-absorbed country.

I sensed someone hovering just outside my peripheral vision and glanced up to see an older woman watching me. She wore faded blue jeans and the kind of black lace-up shoes my grandma wore for her bunions. The woman's skin was clear except for a sprinkling of little cinnamon-colored freckles across her nose; her cheeks were pink and full. She wore her curly gray hair short. When she saw I'd noticed her, she smiled and came to stand beside me.

"Sad, isn't it?" she said. "That was her own cousin, G. P."

We were both quiet for a few seconds before she said with a note of personal pride, "She won the Pulitzer Prize for that book." She paused briefly, her face darkening as she said, "Oh, the way they beat up on her after that. Well . . ." She shook her head with a stern expression. "Mencken and that gang, Hemingway, and the rest of them . . ." I had no idea what she was talking about, but I didn't interrupt. "It was just jealousy, plain and simple. Those men were jealous of her, that's all it was. But name-calling like that? Calling her an old lady when she was only fifty. Old lady," she repeated with a scoffing sound, as though it was obvious that fifty wasn't old, when it sounded very old to me.

The woman seemed pleased to have found an audience and went on to tell me she was a Cather "groupie," a categorization I wouldn't have appreciated if I hadn't just witnessed it. She told me scholars had learned the source for Cather's insights about World War I were the interviews she'd conducted with veterans. "Folks never want to listen to what returning vets have to say, and like most, those World War I vets clammed up about what they'd been through. Willa"— I'd noticed this familiarity among her fans, using her first name like she was a friend or a family member—"was good at listening, good at getting those fellas to open up." The woman went on to tell me how scholars were persuaded Cather's methods of digesting these firsthand accounts was part of what gave her work the feeling of lived experience. "But those critics," she said, "they were so mean to her, said she had no right to write about war because she was a woman and had never gone over there. They were just bullies, that's all." As she delivered her final verdict against Cather's long-dead assailants, her face flushed with anger as if they were still at it, still trying to destroy her reputation.

She drew herself up a little before slumping again. "You'll have to pardon me. I get myself worked up sometimes. But you know, that hurt Willa something awful." She shifted and held her hand up to shade the sun from her eyes as she looked directly at me. "Willa said around that time the 'world cracked in two,' and she didn't say it like it was a good thing." I couldn't imagine a time when the "world cracking in two" would ever be a good thing, but she went on, "After that, you feel her discouragement about life. You see it for sure in *The Professor's House*" (an observation she wouldn't have needed to make, since it's clearly about a flirtation with suicide). She went on as if thinking out loud. "True, it might not only have been those men, of course. There were personal losses around that same time. Another war and the deaths of her father and her dearest brother." She said this with a kind of delicacy, not wanting to betray Cather's well-established insistence on privacy, as if by now Cather's life hadn't been mined for every last detail. "Such viciousness," she said, returning to her earlier critique of the men who'd dissed Cather. "Even if they were only words, it was still hurtful. It really was." She interrupted herself then to look at her watch. "Oh look at that. I need to get home before Eldon starts complaining about my gallivanting."

I watched her hurry away and get into a pickup truck parked a block away. She waved and smiled as she drove past as though we were old friends, and I waved back, feeling a little the same way.

I took one last look at Red Cloud through my rearview mirror and watched it recede, the buildings casting long shadows across the prairie, everything enlarged by the setting sun, like the plow against the horizon in *My Ántonia*. And as I drove through the hills away from the town, the intensity of the sun made every blade of grass, every detail of every cow in all those herds lumbering toward home, every fencepost, and every bird in flight vivid and distinct against the deep blue of the sky and the technicolor green hills. It was breathtaking, but even the beauty of the late afternoon couldn't distract me from my brooding about those brutal men and their casual ganging up on Cather. I couldn't stop thinking about their cruelty, their dismissiveness, their misogyny, the way they'd seemed to despise her. It hadn't been enough to dismiss her work, they'd made it personal, ridiculing her appearance, her age, her gender.

Rather than dissipating, my anger only grew as I drove, far out of proportion to my investment in Cather. By the time I'd reached the outskirts of Lincoln, I'd worked myself into a rage before I grasped what was happening and why. Over the past few weeks, I'd successfully distracted myself from my anger, but now that I'd been reminded of it again, I seethed. There'd been a time when I'd believed there was justice in the world, when I'd naïvely trusted the rule of law, and trusted that, with time, things came right. But I didn't think I believed that any more, not since my own life had been so casually blown up. Oh, I was damaged. It was clear that afternoon just how damaged I'd been by the impunity of vile and violent men, by the betrayal of my closest friend. My faith in the world wasn't simply shaken; I'd lost my trust in life altogether. Like Cather's, my world had cracked in two.

CHAPTER 19

Thanksgiving in the Czech
Capital of the USA

The days grew shorter and colder in November as autumn gave way to winter. I walked less and drove more. I watched as the tall prairie grass and the leaves of the sumac reddened along the banks and the bluffs of the Platte River. As the days grew shorter and the nights longer, even the radio was no remedy for my boredom. I was irritated by so much talk about the maverick Republican candidate whose every controversial utterance was repeated and debated.

I forced myself to get out of the cottage at night. I went to a few public lectures at the university where scholars talked about their scientific research or various studies. Some were interesting, but most were too technical for me and I eventually lost interest. I went to openings of new exhibits at the Sheldon Art Museum. I went to a few movies. Ivan had recommended a few restaurants and a music venue he thought I might like. One day in passing, he told me that Lincoln was an immigrant resettlement community and there were seventy languages represented in Lincoln High's English Language Learner program, which helped explain all the ethnic restaurants I'd found on my drives and walks around the city.

Ivan was such a Lincoln booster I'd assumed he was from Lincoln until, in the days leading up to Thanksgiving, he kept talking about how excited he was about going home to Wilbur, the little town where he grew up, for the holiday. Always polite, he asked me about my plans for the holiday. He didn't try to hide his shock when I told him I was spending the day alone. I wasn't feeling sorry for myself. My mother and I didn't celebrate holidays. Thanksgiving was just another day for me, but for a guy like Ivan—who, I came to realize, thought spending time with family was the most important thing in his life—my indifference was inconceivable. He seemed personally offended that no one on Fieldcrest had invited me for Thanksgiving dinner, forcing me to explain that, like me, Tillie and Mary Garlic didn't celebrate the holiday; the Clarks were going to Minnesota to spend the day with Bridget's family; and Audra was planning to spend the day with Jim, eating the dinner prepared by the staff at the care center. She'd invited me to join her, but I couldn't think of anything more revolting than eating turkey and dressing with Jim in that place.

I was firm in declining Ivan's invitation to go with him to Wilbur for the day, but he was persistent, asking me every day if I'd had "a change of heart" until he finally wore me down. I told myself I wasn't caving in to him but was taking advantage of an opportunity to observe small town life.

Thanksgiving morning Ivan picked me up in his old Honda Civic. It wasn't until I'd settled into the passenger seat—determined to be a good guest despite my dread for the ordeal—that I realized if I hadn't been going with him, Ivan would have spent the long weekend at home. I didn't like to think he was depriving himself to include me, but I kept it to myself.

It was very cold that morning, the first day below freezing since the October storm. In the ditches lining the roads, the red prairie grass was stiff and white with frost. Gray, saggy clouds hung udder-like over the gray landscape. In fields along the highway, cattle crowded against the fences, heads turned away from the bitter wind gusting out of the north.

While he drove, Ivan told me he was a sixth-generation Czech. Wilbur, he said without irony, was the Czech capital of the United States. His great-great-great-grandparents had settled there. Czech had been his parents' and his grandparents' first language. I didn't say anything, but my expression must have made it clear I didn't believe him.

"I know it sounds strange," he said, "but we're a tight-knit community and keeping the language alive is important to us." He flashed one of his goofy smiles at me and turned his attention back to the road. "Granted, it's a nineteenth-century version of Czech," he said. "People from Wilbur who visit Czechoslovakia are always surprised that the Czechs they meet there don't understand a word they say." He laughed, and I had to laugh with him.

He went on to tell me how every year since he was a kid he'd taken part in the annual Wilber Czech Days celebration in July, performing traditional Czech dances in folk costumes with other kids when he was little, which, like the language, had been passed down through the generations. These days, though, he played accordion with the Wilbur accordion orchestra. As if he thought I might not believe this, he leaned to his left and removed his billfold from his back pocket. He opened it with one hand and not taking his eyes off the road held it out to me. I liked that about him, that he could talk and watch the road at the same time. I couldn't make out any faces in the tiny photo, even when he told me he was in the second row. They were all dressed in traditional embroidered Czech vests over billowy white shirts. Imagining the cacophony of an accordion orchestra, I couldn't stop myself from laughing again. Ivan, prepared for every possible slight to accordion players, told a few self-deprecating accordion jokes. After joking he grew serious. "Mark your calendar for the third weekend in July, and you can hear the accordion orchestra for yourself."

We pulled into Wilbur a little before noon. There was no traffic on the streets of the little town. He'd told me in the car that his huge extended family always gathered at his grandmother's house for dinner. Some of them coming from long distances. Even with this prior warning, I wasn't prepared for the crush of so many people crowded into every available space in the house. Tables were set up everywhere.

Kids yelled. Babies cried. Adults yelled over all of it. The older people moved easily between Czech and English, and his grandparents—third-generation Czechs—spoke English with a heavy accent.

Ivan's great-grandmother, a tiny woman perched in a chair in the corner of the living room, was deaf and nearly blind. She was folded in on herself assuming the posture of a tiny shrimp. I thought I had more in common with that old lady than I did with anyone else in that crowd, though, since neither of us could fully engage with the events around us. Later, I watched as they served her dinner on a TV tray, and one of Ivan's aunts fed her like a baby.

Ivan's grandma was tall and formidable, especially when compared to his grandfather, who, like his mother slumped in his wheelchair. I noticed how throughout dinner Ivan's grandma matter-of-factly cut Grandpa's turkey into small bites. Grandma was clearly the matriarch of the rambunctious, opinionated family, and everyone at the table deferred to her. She was kind but not particularly friendly to me. I think she suspected Ivan and I were dating, and I guessed she didn't approve because I wasn't Czech. Ivan's mother, on the other hand, was friendly and talkative, while Ivan's father, who seemed to take after his mother, was quiet and a little stern. Ivan clearly took after his mother.

The meal itself was over the top ridiculous. In addition to the traditional Thanksgiving dishes were Bohemian favorites. Ivan pointed out for me sweetish Czech dumplings, Czech sausages in fennel sauce, and for dessert Ivan's mother and grandmother had baked dozens of kolaches, a Czech pastry they all swooned over. I took one of each kind—poppyseed, apricot, and lemon curd. There were pies too. So many pies. Thanksgiving was always when PIE saw peak traffic. I admired the homemade pies, similar to those my grandma had made and those I'd seen in diners across the state, but there were three pies that stood out from the rest, a coconut cream—its meringue not spread by a knife but pipetted into roses that were not oven browned but browned by a kitchen torch; a pecan pie topped by a gyre of pecans placed so perfectly it looked like a cephalopod fossil; and most surprising of all a blackberry-ginger galette that looked very much like one of my own creations. Whoever had made these pies was almost certainly a PIE member. I felt myself sink a little deeper into my chair. I listened as others around the table exclaimed and pegged the baker as one of Ivan's aunts who'd driven up from Kansas City. Unlike my grandma's pie tins, I didn't feel phobic about pie—my favorite thing in the world—but seeing them made me so sad I couldn't imagine ever eating pie again. I couldn't even get excited about the pics I might have sent to my Twitter team.

The bedlam never let up as five generations of Sedlaceks—old people, little kids, teenagers, young adults, middle-aged adults—laughed and argued, teased, and pitched in to help. Ivan had told me his family descended from the "famous" Bohemian Freethinkers and not the Catholic Czechs. They were all outspoken about politics, clearly engaged with the election coming up the following year. I was surprised by how many of them were Bernie Sanders supporters. Several planned to caucus for him in February, including Ivan. Many were vociferous in their general dislike for Republicans, some specific in their distaste stressing *conservative* Republicans. Ivan's grandma was a Hillary supporter, while Grandpa rallied himself once to speak up for Kasich. Although the conversation was spirited, everyone speaking up without reservations, I never heard anyone make a disparaging remark about someone else's opinion, except twice, once when one of Ivan's cousins mentioned liking Ted Cruz—for which he was roundly put down, and later when an aunt by marriage mentioned liking it that a businessman—by which she meant the real estate guy from New York—was running. Ivan's grandma responded to this with a withering look. "He's a con-man and a grifter. Voting for that man isn't simply a political choice; it goes to character." There was dead silence for two beats after she spoke before Ivan said, "Tell us what you really think, Grams."

Everyone laughed boisterously at this, except Ivan's grandma. Instead, she seemed to be taking the measure of every family member around the table and finding a few of them wanting. She was one of the most formidable women I'd ever met.

I'd never experienced anything like this family gathering. At times, it was almost unbearable. I vacillated wildly between loving it and hating it.

After dinner, Ivan's mother insisted we all watch a video she'd taken during Czech Days the previous summer. Everyone teased about her inability to hold her iPhone still during the filming as we watched first a video of little kids dressed in traditional costumes dancing to Czech folk tunes. Ivan's nieces and nephews and younger cousins squealed with delight whenever they saw themselves on the erratic video footage. Their dancing was accompanied by the accordion orchestra, which wasn't as bad as I'd imagined. I recognized one of Ivan's uncles playing in the front row before spotting Ivan himself. He played with concentration, his expression so comical, I nudged him with my elbow making him laugh. As they watched the video, everyone talked at once. I couldn't hear a thing except laughter as they gave one another a bad time.

Once the dishes had been washed, the men dozed or watched football on TV, and the women talked in various knots around the house. I excused myself to go for a walk. The little town was absolutely silent that gray afternoon, not a single car on the streets, every sidewalk empty. Most of the houses were modest, and through the lighted windows I saw families gathered inside.

The only sign of life on the street besides me were a couple of dogs lying unchained in their front yards and a solitary cat sauntering down the middle of the abandoned street. The quiet felt eerie to me, like a town in a fairy tale enchantment.

I thought about all the people in this little town who still spoke antiquated Czech, still preserved the songs and dances their ancestors had brought with them to Nebraska over a hundred years before. I couldn't decide if their commitment to Czech culture was admirable or maniacal. Either way, it seemed as exotic as anything I'd ever encountered.

It was well past dark by the time we finally headed back to Lincoln, the car full of leftovers Ivan's grandma had sent for both of us. Somehow, like the neighbors on Fieldcrest Drive, Ivan had slipped through my defenses. I'd wanted to keep my distance from people, but I'd failed. Meeting Ivan's family had been a big step outside my comfort zone, and, I thought, a big mistake. Still, here I was, comfortably chatting away with him as we drove through the darkness.

The sky was still overcast, the stars hidden, the moon a yellow smudge behind the clouds. It softly illuminated the fields around us. If I looked too deeply into them, those dark fields felt menacing and inhospitable, and each time I turned away from the darkness, I was grateful to find Ivan there beside me.

As I'd walked around Wilbur earlier that day, I'd sometimes had a hard time separating the history of Ivan's family from the history of the fictional Shimerda family—which was, after all, based on his great-great-grandmother. I couldn't help feeling on that drive back to Lincoln that Ivan had somehow escaped a treacherous past, that his being born at all was a kind of miracle, given the family's tough pioneer origins. I conflated his history with Ántonia's and couldn't seem to shake the details of her immigrant parents living in their horrible dirt dugout—her brutish peasant mother; her strange, violent brothers; her sad, sensitive father, his rusty black suit, his violin—and his gun. *The gun.* As miserable as things were for the poor man, I hadn't been prepared for that gun. I hadn't seen it coming.

At times, like the drive back to Lincoln on Thanksgiving night, if I started to feel like maybe things were returning to normal, like I was returning to my old self, I would entertain thoughts about going back to California earlier than planned, only to feel my heart seize with anxiety. Three and a half months in Nebraska, and things were different. I didn't long for my phone the way I had at first or feel as frustrated about not being able to research something on my computer. But all was not well.

On the Saturday night after Thanksgiving I was up late reading in the living room when I heard a sound at my front door like someone trying to get in. I turned off the lamp and waited, my breathing shallow and quick. I finally grabbed the only weapon I had, the sharp kitchen knife I'd armed myself with that first night in the cottage. I hesitated a few seconds before I looked out the kitchen window. When I didn't see anyone, I took a deep breath and flung open the door, hoping the surprise would give me an advantage. What I found was Bill laying on the stoop. I was so relieved to see him, I dropped to my knees and hugged him. I glanced up the street to the Clarks' dark house before I decided to bring him inside.

I'd intended to let him stay only long enough to warm up before taking him back home, but it was so nice to have him lying on the rag rug beside the chair while I read that I lost track of time. By the time I thought about returning him, it was very late and the Clarks' house was still dark. It was much too cold for a dog to be left outside. I promised myself I'd return him early the next morning.

Until I met Bill, I had no idea what it meant to love an animal. I couldn't understand why the Clarks didn't treasure him, why they didn't take better care of him. From what I'd observed, they were sometimes negligent. I lay awake that night plotting various scenarios where I might convince them to let me keep Bill, but the next morning, before dawn, as I walked Bill back home, all my scheming to keep him—so logical the night before—now seemed ridiculous.

As I let Bill in through the back gate, I told myself the Clarks probably wouldn't even have noticed he was missing, but Bridget was awake and opened the backdoor. "Vivi! Thank god. Where did you find him? We were just getting ready to call the Humane Society. We've been so worried about him out in this bitter cold all night. Chuck and the kids went out again early this morning to search for him." This dedication to Bill surprised me. When I didn't answer, she asked again, "So, where *did* you find him?"

She'd been scrutinizing Bill, and when I didn't answer a second time, both of us watching as he settled himself contentedly on the floor of the mudroom and making it obvious he wasn't traumatized by having spent the night outside, I saw suspicion gather in her eyes. "You kept him all night, didn't you?" I couldn't refute it. "Really, Vivi? How could you? We were up half the night worrying. We're responsible for him. Bill is *our* responsibility. Didn't you think we needed to know he was safe?"

I stammered an apology, explaining that since their house had been dark I'd thought they were gone. I was truly sorry to have caused them worry, but I was also a little defiant. It was Bridget's use of the word *responsible* to describe her relationship with Bill that bothered me. I wanted to tell her, "But don't you understand? I *love* Bill. I don't see him as a *responsibility*." Wisely, I kept silent, relieved when Bridget didn't seem inclined to punish Bill again the way she had before. She waved away my apology and looked at Bill, now asleep on his dog bed.

"Bill's big adventure," she said, sounding almost affectionate toward him. And then, as if to explain away his behavior. "I worried when we were out so late last night. We shouldn't have left him in the yard. Serves us right. Who wouldn't go looking for a warm place on such a night?"

In her version of things, Bill had simply been cold and went to the first house he encountered. She seemed to need to erase me from the story, not admitting any preference he might have for me. I knew I was overdramatizing my role, but that morning I resolved that when the time came for me to leave Lincoln, I would find a way to take Bill with me.

CHAPTER 20

Where Ivan Outs Me

After Thanksgiving, Ivan invited me to his apartment on the second floor of an old house on G Street near Hazel Abel, the little pocket park I'd discovered in July. He told me he'd moved in a few months earlier. It was the first time he'd had his own place since coming to Lincoln for college ten years earlier. He'd furnished the apartment with castoffs he'd found on the street and from thrift stores. His newest "booty-dig" was a tile-topped coffee table. I'd brought a bottle of wine, and he set out crackers and cheese on a serving platter his mother had given him as a housewarming gift.

I wandered around looking at the art on his walls—some clearly also found in thrift stores, some, he told me, made by his friends—framed pictures of his family, books overflowing the bookshelves into stacks on the floor. He had an expensive turntable and a small collection of vinyl records. When I commented that I hadn't heard any live music for a long time, he smiled. "You need to get out more."

"I suppose . . ."

"No, really. I'd be glad to show you around Lincoln."

For the next two weeks, Ivan seemed to see it as his assignment to show me the parts of Lincoln that I hadn't found in my tourist guide. He took me bowling at the Hollywood Bowl and to the ice cream store on the university's east campus, and he took me barhopping.

He seemed to feel obliged to take me first to the famous Zoo Bar downtown, followed by Barrymore's, and Duffy's, and a speakeasy called The Other Room with its celebrity mixologist. And just to change things up a little, he took me to the taproom at the Zipline brewery where we met the cool owners Tom and Heather. I wasn't sure if he was testing me in some way, or trying to assure me Lincoln had its sophisticated side, but finally he took me to the dive bars he really loved: Bob's and Arnold's in Havelock, WC's South, and the Tack Room. He took me to diners and taverns outside of Lincoln, too, in Roca and Bennet and Cortland and Emerald. He liked what he called grandpa drinks—whiskey sours and old-fashioneds and Pabst beer.

I learned a few things about Ivan those nights, as he talked about his friends—still loyal to a group of guys he'd known since grade school—and his family. His father owned an insurance agency and his mother taught third grade. He had two older sisters, both married and living in Colorado (neither of whom had been able to come back for Thanksgiving). His dad had hoped Ivan would follow him into the business, and Ivan had gone along with that plan until the war in Iraq. Like me, he'd been a teenager at the time, and he said something snapped in him after that. He vowed he wanted to do as little harm as possible in the world and decided the best way to do that was to help vulnerable kids.

He didn't say much about his work beyond that until one night when we were at Duffy's. The live band wasn't very good, and we'd gone to sit in the back. We watched as a few people danced. While we watched them, Ivan said, "My favorite thing about teaching is the Friday dance party for the special ed kids."

"How's that look?"

"You'd be surprised. They can dance! On Friday afternoons, I'm the student and they're the teachers. They try to help me with my moves, but I'm useless. They love to tease me."

His story inspired me to tell a remarkable kid story of my own. After I'd finished telling him about the kids in my neighborhood and the Attic Theater, he said, "Do they have an accordion player?"

"No, Ivan. It's a normal orchestra."

I could see his mind working. "Would you introduce me to Moss and Harmony? I think I could contribute."

I thought he was joking, but he looked so eager for an answer, I said, "Sure." After that, every time we got together, he asked about a meeting until finally, in mid-December, I invited him to come along with me to a Wednesday movie night.

Mary Garlic had kept their old VCR working, and on Wednesday nights they rotated movies from their large stash of vintage videos. The night Ivan joined me, *Swiss Family Robinson* was up in the rotation.

I'd asked Mary Garlic if it was all right to bring Ivan, but apparently she hadn't mentioned it to the rest of the family. When we showed up that night, the little kids came running to hug me but stopped short when they saw Ivan. They stood silent in the dim hallway and stared at Ivan, who glanced at me with a questioning expression. After spending weekday mornings with them, I knew the little kids approached things in their own way, and I knew to wait awhile before introducing Ivan.

Finally, Lake said suspiciously, "Who are you?"

"This is my friend Ivan," I said. "He's going to watch the movie with us tonight." The kids still held back a little until Ivan knelt down to their level making them laugh by shaking hands with each of them. After Spur grabbed his hand and started to lead him upstairs, Ivan turned back to smile at me, never having doubted he'd find a way to fit in. Later, when I introduced him to the rest of the clan, I was certain Mary Garlic would grill him the way she had me; instead, she took one look at him and seemed to decide he was fine. I felt a little sting of envy as the rest of them quickly accepted him as well. I watched him comfortably settle in. How had I not noticed before how handsome Ivan was? As if he'd read my mind, he looked at me, his glance lingering a little longer than usual before he smiled and turned away.

Once the movie had ended and the little kids went off to bed, Moss and Harmony hung around, something they wouldn't have done if Ivan hadn't been there. It had been obvious during the film that Ivan and Moss shared the same irreverent sense of humor. When I mentioned that Ivan played accordion, Moss and Harmony exchanged a quick glance before nodding at one another.

"We've been throwing around ideas for the next musical," Moss told Ivan before turning back to Harmony. Ivan and I listened as, rapid-fire, Harmony and Moss suggested one outrageous idea after another: Pee Wee Herman's Big Adventure in the Mexican Revolution; War and Peace and Duck Dynasty; an Appalachian feud between the Palins and the Kardashians. It was a side of them I'd never seen before, this free-for-all creative process, and judging by the expression on Ivan's face, he was smitten. Before we left that night, Moss invited Ivan to join in their next planning meeting the following Tuesday.

I'd forgotten all about the meeting until 9:00 on Tuesday night when I heard a soft tap on the door of the cottage. The meeting was over, and Ivan held up a six-pack of Pabst he'd brought to celebrate. It was his first time inside my cottage, and while I scavenged in the kitchen for a few snacks to share, he wandered through the rooms.

"Your place . . . ," he finally said, "it's. . . . well, it's not what I expected. It's so spartan."

"What do you mean?" I said, oddly hurt by the comment.

Ivan, sensing my defensiveness, smiled at me, but his forehead was still creased in puzzlement. "Spartan isn't the right word. It's so . . ." he flung his arms out to include the whole place, "it's so low-tech, man. I mean, all you have is a radio." He looked at me then. "Geez, Vivi. You didn't just de-grid, you fell off the face of the earth." He laughed after he said this, and while I knew he hadn't meant to accuse, I felt accused anyway. I hadn't told him anything about the way I'd grown up. I didn't think he'd understand my mother, and I didn't want him to judge her.

"What can I say? I'm just a low-tech kinda gal." He frowned at my dishonesty but didn't push. Instead, he grinned the goofy grin I'd come to count on as he opened a can of Pabst and held it out to me.

Once he'd left that night, though, I looked around the cottage and tried to see it through his eyes. Ivan was right. It was incredibly bare, and I had a feeling he'd learned something about me I hadn't wanted him to. Aside from the low-tech vibe of the cottage, which was easy to explain, I saw now how the sparseness of the cottage matched that of my condo in Echo Park. I'd never noticed it before, but both places now struck me as comfortless. Unlike Audra who knew how to create comfort in simplicity, I hadn't even been aware you should expect to be comfortable in your own home.

When I went to read at the Bean later that week, Ivan came over to my table and sat down, something he'd never done before. There was no one else there that day but it still surprised me.

"So, what's shakin'?" he said, the kind of thing he said all the time. I was rereading *The Professor's House*, and I started to tell him about the book until I saw he wasn't listening. He seemed agitated, distracted.

"Ivan?" He looked at me, his brown eyes boring into mine, and I was startled by the complex expression on his face—part confusion, part accusation, a little hurt. "What's wrong?"

He smiled. Not his usual smile, but a smile of resignation. "I'm just trying to make sense of you, Vivi Marx."

"Of me?" I kept my voice light even as I felt something grip my insides.

"I know it shouldn't be a big deal, right, keeping a few secrets from a friend. I mean, we're new friends after all, but I don't get your game at all, Vivi. I'm trying to understand what *exactly* it is you're up to? I mean, are you here spying on us?"

This was such an unexpected accusation I had to laugh, remembering Lake's crazy accusations my first night in Nebraska. I'd since learned this is how kids entertain themselves—getting worked up for fun—but Ivan's accusation mystified me.

"What on earth are you talking about?" A part of me wanted to believe it was a joke, but I couldn't ignore the edge I'd heard in his voice.

He didn't laugh with me. "I googled you again, Vivi, and this time I looked a little harder. That's how I found the whole PieGirl thing, the whole PIE—Pastry Innovations and Expertise," he said, spelling it out sarcastically. I felt a jolt of adrenaline, and like a drama queen, I brought my hand to my chest as if warding off a blow. I was embarrassed by the gesture and by my inability to play it cool. Ivan ignored me. "It was hard to track down, but I learned some surprising things about you, Vivi." The room spun. "Like how you're some kind of hotshot founder of some big social media site. PieGirl. That's what they call you, right?" I wanted to believe he wasn't making fun of me, but his tone told me otherwise. "So, PieGirl. Can I call you that? PieGirl?" He was killing me. I didn't know what he wanted from me, didn't know where this was going. Finally, I couldn't take it. I stuffed my book inside my bag and stood up to go.

He added a parting shot as I started toward the door, "So, why are you really here, Vivi? What's your game, lady? Are you planning some sort of ironic profile about the ignoramuses in Lincoln, Nebraska, because that's what you do, isn't it?"

The impersonal *lady*, the unfair depiction of my work, and the paranoid assumption that I'd been using all of them hurt me more than I would have expected. I wasn't prepared for this side of Ivan. Until then, we'd been buddies of a sort, friends who goofed around together. I'd assumed he saw our relationship the same way I did, one of convenience and circumstance. It hadn't occurred to me that he'd see it as lopsided until he said, "Here I take you to Wilbur, introduce you to my whole family, talk about my crappy little life all the time. I tell you *everything*, Vivi. You snoop around my apartment, know pretty much every nook and cranny. You know all about my jobs. You get me to open up like a jerk, like a complete fool. I've respected that you didn't want to talk too much about yourself, but it didn't really hit me how much I don't know about you until I started looking and found *all this stuff*. Then I see your place on Fieldcrest, and see how it's all . . . so provisional . . . like you don't really live there at all, like you're just on site, doing a job, slumming it, which is weird because you're rich, Vivi, you're very rich, and I can't make sense of any of it."

"I have no idea what you're talking about, Ivan." I was a little breathless and my voice strained. "You knew I was only staying for a year. It *is* provisional. I've been very up front about that. I'm sorry if you misunderstood."

He shook his head. "No, Vivi, a year is a long time. I'm not buying it that a year isn't time enough to settle into a place, but I guess that's me being stupid, a trusting idiot, because here's the thing. I thought we were going to be friends our whole lives. That's how stupid I am. And now I find out you're sort of famous in the world of . . . I don't know what . . . recipes, and pie, and politics, and ironic stuff, and I can't think of any reason why you'd need to keep that such a big secret—it just doesn't make sense to me—unless you're doing something undercover."

"That's truly insane, Ivan. You know that, right? Why would I do that? I'm sorry, but Nebraska just isn't interesting enough to merit this much focus, let alone the kind of elaborate deception you're describing. I mean, think about it."

"So, set me straight then, Vivi."

I've never been a great one for explaining myself verbally, and I definitely didn't want to be talking about any of this at all, but for the sake of my friendship with Ivan, which until that moment I hadn't realized was important to me, I tried to explain what had happened in California. Ivan didn't make it easy for me. His faced remained expressionless as I blathered. I heard myself saying things that sounded like nonsense, telling him about how my grandma had a bake-a-pie solution to all problems, how it had shaped my vision and helped to inspire a website, how from the beginning the website got the kind of response you can't ignore, the kind of response that sets the agenda for your whole life, but when it brings you into the limelight, draws attention to you, then the trolls come after you, and you try to get away, but you can't, and only then do you realize there's nowhere to hide, and you've become the subject du jour for people who love to hate, for people who devise unbelievably vile ways to threaten your life, and even worse than the trolls is your realization that you're a disappointment to millions of your so-called dedicated followers, whatever that is, people you don't know who love you until you're down and struggling, and then, in the process of dealing with the worst thing that's ever happened to you, when you fail to live up to their expectations, they just as quickly become your worst enemies and broadcast their disappointment in you so that people who didn't ever love you, or even know you, now hate you, too, and you realize even the people who said they loved you were strangers all along; they'd never loved you—how could they?—but you'd spent five years engaging with them all day every day, and your best friend, your business partner, the biggest disappointment of all, betrays your trust . . .

By the time I'd finished with this incoherent babble—and to this day I'm still not sure how much I actually said to him—Ivan was hugging me and saying over and over, "Okay, Vivi. It's okay."

"It is definitely *not* okay, Ivan." I pushed away from him and grabbed my things. I was almost out the door before I said, without turning around, "Please, just don't post anything about me, Ivan. At least do that for me, for the sake of whatever friendship we've had. I don't want those bastards finding me here. Will you at least do that for me?" I left then as fast as I could, in as much of a panic as I'd been in when I'd left California in July.

CHAPTER 21

Maybe It's a Ghost After All

My meltdown in front of Ivan had not been cathartic. It was, in fact, the opposite of cathartic. I felt like someone had ripped my skin off. Feelings I'd compartmentalized for months crashed down on me again, and that night, alone in the cottage, I felt my mind slip away from me. I felt hunted again. I felt the full impact of the loss of my work, my home, my identity, my safety, everything I thought I knew about who I was. This unmasking of my secret also meant the loss of my friendship with Ivan, since I couldn't imagine ever facing him again. I hadn't given much thought to how much I'd come to depend on his steadiness and his kindness, how nice it had been to have a friend in Nebraska. Now, though, I regretted introducing him to Moss and Harmony, regretted he knew where I lived, regretted I'd no longer be able to hang out at the Bean.

Of course, I couldn't sleep. I paced the three rooms of the cottage, too rattled to read, too anxious to sleep. I toyed with the idea of getting into the car and just driving, but there was nowhere to go. In the past, even when things were at their worst, I'd never seriously considered harming myself, but that night a chiding, evil little thought needled me: how easy it would be to simply blow out the pilot light in my old furnace and not wake up the next morning.

Around 3:00 a.m., I finally collapsed, exhausted, in the overstuffed chair in the living room. Until then, the noise in my head had been deafening, but as I grew quiet I felt the reassuring presence of the gardener, as much a part of that space as the lingering smell of herbicide and mildew. I didn't question the fact of his presence, even though I knew it wasn't something anyone else would understand or believe. I remembered how months before when I'd first read *Death Comes for the Archbishop*—the section where Archbishop Latour enters his home and has the "sense of a Presence awaiting him"—and feeling grateful to Cather for describing so well what I experienced each time I entered my little cottage.

I got up from the chair where I'd been sitting and opened *Death Comes for the Archbishop*, searching until I finally found the end of the passage. "The curtain of the arched doorway had scarcely fallen behind him when that feeling of personal loneliness was gone, and a sense of loss was replaced by a sense of restoration."

Like the archbishop, once I acknowledged it, the gardener's presence calmed me, and as if to console myself further, I had a strong urge to see the gardener's toolbox again, tangible evidence of a life separate from mine, yet accessible to me in some way. I retrieved the box from the coat closet and brought it back to the chair where I methodically removed all the tools and the little leather gardening journal, the same way I had when I'd first found it in July. It soothed me to turn the pages of his gardening journal and read his meticulous notes.

I felt drained of all emotion, and still holding the box on my lap, I closed my eyes. I may have slept. Time felt very strange to me, the past not something distant but simply a parallel dimension, my own past included. I felt the gardener there beside me, unseen but no less real for that.

I was so relaxed I might have gone to bed and slept then, except as I began to set the box on the floor, for the first time I noticed the box itself. Handmade I guessed and carved from what appeared to be a single piece of wood, a crude but remarkable thing. When I looked closer, though, I saw the bottom of the box seemed to be formed from a separate piece of wood held in place by small bent nails. Like the strange urge I'd had to take the toolbox from the closet in the first place, I now felt the urge to twist those little nails, and that's how I discovered the box's false bottom, and beneath it another journal, much slimmer than the gardening journal.

As soon as I saw that journal, I felt a frisson of some new emotion. Anything that needed to be this cleverly hidden had to be important in some way. I hesitated a few seconds, unsure if I really wanted to know its secrets, unsure if I had the right to them. I felt a fleeting fear that the journal could contain the gardener's confession of something terrible, a murder or a rape, and I wondered briefly what I'd do with that knowledge if it were the case. How could his presence still comfort me if I knew he'd been a monster? Wouldn't it haunt me instead?

Finally, I opened the journal's leather cover. By then, I was familiar with the gardener's tendency to record in code. Inside, I found only a few cryptic entries covering a period of three years. Some secrets, like the gardener's, say more about society than they do about the person. As I read, I felt sad for the way taboos of a past era had forced him to live a cramped, solitary life because he couldn't be honest about who he loved. This was the gardener's account of a very dangerous, furtive relationship. His crabbed handwriting communicated the terrible risk he'd taken, not only to continue the relationship for those three years, but also to record even these cryptic details. I wondered why, given that risk, he hadn't destroyed the journal instead of hiding it in this way.

I'd always thought of the gardener as an old man, but in the journal, he documented, in the barest of details, a passionate love affair he'd had when he was a very young man with a much older man he referred to only as F——. Despite the terse entries I eventually understood F—— must have been Tillie's great-great-grandfather—her great-aunt Matilda's father, Frederick Fields. The man whose obituary I'd found stuck between the pages of *Lucy Gayheart*. Frederick had hired the gardener around the turn of the century. Frederick was married, the father of three grown children, his unmarried daughter, Matilda, still living at home. He was a prominent citizen in the state and an important man in the city of Lincoln. Both men—the diary keeper and the powerful man who was his boss—appear to have been tormented by their love for one another, their stolen moments together deeply treasured but also deeply regretted. The entries ended with the death of F——, recorded in the journal's final line and written with such restraint, I felt the pathos of it across the years: "F—— is gone. It is very cold today. I'll never be warm again."

And yet, the gardener stayed and worked for Matilda for decades after that, his service so valued she'd built him this cottage and cared for him in his old age. I saw his staying as both a monument to his abiding love for F—and his inability to leave because of it.

I'd been so captivated by the gardener's life I'd forgotten my own. This connection was far beyond my usual escape into books. I felt sure I was the only other human being ever to have read this secret account of the gardener's lost love. Had he intended for someone in the future to discover the journal he'd so carefully preserved under the false bottom of his humble toolbox? Or had he simply needed to record what had happened, to document and honor that ephemeral passion as a way to make it more real?

Whatever it was, the discovery of his journal felt like a precious trust, and my dedication to respecting his secret a kind of sacrament. I knew as I tucked the journal beneath the false bottom of the toolbox again, I'd never tell anyone about it. The only thing I did differently was to put the toolbox under my bed instead of returning it to the closet, as though by keeping it close I could better guard its secret.

CHAPTER 22

The Part Where Ivan Brings a Pie

By the time Ivan appeared that Saturday, I'd regained my composure. I was sheepish, though, as I opened the door to him. The sun was a blurry disk behind a thin layer of pinkish clouds. A fine snow fell, melting as it hit the ground. Ivan held a pie out to me like an offering.

"I didn't make it, but it's homemade and, well . . ." He gestured with his head to a grocery bag hanging from his shoulder. "There's ice cream too."

In all the years of my pie obsession, no one had ever brought *me* a pie. I didn't tell him this as I stepped aside. Once he was inside, we were both silent while I took a knife from the drawer and held it out to him. Ivan cut the pie while I set out plates and forks. We sat down, across from one another, at the kitchen table. Ivan nodded toward my plate, and I held it up for him to serve me. While he served himself, I took a scoop of ice cream before I passed the carton to him. We conducted all of this in silence, as choreographed as a ritual, leading me to believe maybe there had been some truth in what I'd claimed all those years, that there was a kind of magic in the gift of pie, that it broke down barriers between people. I couldn't think of anything anyone had ever done in my life that was as kind as Ivan bringing me that pie.

I waited until he'd taken a scoop of ice cream before I took my first bite of pie in over ten months. It was a simple cherry pie. The cherries were tart and firm, contrasting nicely with the sweet, silky filling. The crust was flaky and flavorful, not as good as my grandma's but still good.

We continued to eat in silence, the only sound the scrape of our forks against the porcelain plates. Once we'd finished, I pushed my plate to the side and finally broke the silence. "Thank you, Ivan."

He picked up his fork and absently ran it through the leftover cherry filling on his plate before looking up at me, "Vivi, I want to apologize to you for what happened the other day. I was disappointed. I hope you understand."

"I do."

"Would it help you to talk about it?" I heard in this question Ivan the Life Skills teacher.

I shook my head. I wasn't one of his students.

We both sat in silence, a deep quiet settling over the room, like the snow still falling outside.

Finally, Ivan interrupted the stillness. "I found it all, Vivi. After you left the Bean the other day I searched again, and I found everything, the truth about what happened to you. PIE did a pretty good job, but they couldn't hide everything. I found enough of the residue of that shitstorm to know it was bad. I'm so sorry that happened to you."

I nodded but didn't say anything. Ivan smiled. "When I first searched and came upon PIE, I was so surprised by it. I didn't understand it and didn't understand why you were here in Nebraska. I got this idea—and I admit it sounds bizarre now—that maybe you weren't really unplugged, but that you'd come to Nebraska because you were doing reconnaissance, like you were maybe gathering information for a new series, like Bourdain, you know, going around the country like he did, only being ironic like you are, making fun of people, maybe even doing research about kolaches. I started to worry you might be planning to make a secret video about Czech Days, or something, and then you'd make fun of us. I don't know what I was thinking."

"Geez, Ivan. Neither do I. That's a pretty involved scheme you worked out there." I shook my head. "And besides, I don't even know what you're talking about, making fun of people. PIE could be irreverent, but I don't think we were ever making fun of anyone."

"But that's what I mean. It's clear the site has all these sincere users, but there are these other users, too, who get the irreverent, tongue-in-cheek aspects of the platform—mocking white-bread America. I mean, isn't that what the pie-actions are? Confrontations with who we think we are and who we really are?"

"Are we? Mocking white-bread America?"

"Aren't you?"

"I don't know. I suppose sometimes. Maybe. But not always."

"Okay." Ivan wiped his hand across his nose as he drew out the word. "You're telling me you weren't trying to be funny? 'When in doubt, bake a pie? That wasn't meant to be a little silly?"

"Of course, but not the way you're saying."

Ivan shook his head. "Okay. Jesus. Okay."

"And by the way, I don't even like kolaches." Ivan seemed confused, and I repeated, "I don't like kolaches."

He laughed. "Well, at least we're safe there."

"And they aren't pie, Ivan. Kolaches most definitely are not pie."

Before he left that afternoon, Ivan asked me one last question. After I'd told him about my differences with Kylie, how one of the pie-actions got out of hand, and how things had blown up before I left, he wanted to know if I trusted her with the platform? Of course I didn't trust her. I'd been telling myself for months that once I returned to work, with time, I'd reestablish myself in my former role. Once I was back, I could put my house in order again. Until then, I couldn't think about the ways Kylie and her dad had sidelined me, but I didn't say any of that to Ivan. Instead, I said, "Of course I trust her. The site's success is her success too."

He seemed to be pondering something. He furrowed his brow like he was going to speak, but instead he stood up, cleared our dishes from the table, and rinsed them in the sink.

When he came back to the table, he said, "When you think about the platform now, Vivi, what makes you most happy? What are you most proud of?"

I didn't hesitate. "The pie-actions. Without question."

He nodded. "That's what I heard as you were talking earlier."

"Yes, but Kylie's right. It isn't realistic. The stringers don't make the site profitable." He lifted his shoulders slightly, almost as if in irritation with my answer, and I felt I needed to explain further. "We have to make money, Ivan. Kylie's right about that. The stringers' action stories don't pay the bills."

"I'm sorry to be naïve here. Obviously, I'm not rich, so I don't think like a rich person, but why exactly do you need to keep making money when you've obviously already made far more money than you know what to do with." He reflexively looked around my cottage as if to make the point.

"But the money isn't about me. It's about commitments to the people who work for the business. PIE supports a lot of people, Ivan."

"True enough. But you're forgetting that you aren't PIE. It will go on with or without you," he said, and I wondered if he had his own suspicions about what it meant that Kylie had gone so far to erase me from the platform. "I mean, there's a whole world out there, Vivi. You aren't trapped, or at least you shouldn't be. You're free from the worries most people have about money. You can do whatever you want."

Until he'd said this, it had never occurred to me that I could step away from PIE, that I could redefine success for myself. The platform had always felt like a force of nature, something that had grown up around me and out of me, something organic, so much a part of my identity that leaving it had felt as impossible as leaving my own skin. Even now, it felt radical to think about it.

Ivan seemed to sense my discomfort. "I'm not trying to tell you what to do, Vivi. I'm just asking if you were genuinely happy at PIE? Even before everything got insane? Were you happy?"

"Not all the time, but most of the time. Yes. I guess. I wasn't always happy. I wasn't. But . . ." And here I caught myself.

Ivan, reading the confusion on my face, didn't push. "We've talked enough about this today." He abruptly changed the subject, then. "There's a film at the Ross right now about a sheep farmer. The reviews were good. It's one of those absurdist Scandinavian films you like so much. Do you feel like going tonight?"

I shrugged, and Ivan smiled ruefully. "Vivi, I don't want to leave you alone here tonight, not like this." We made dinner together and once the dishes were washed and put away, he followed me into the bedroom where we silently agreed to sleep fully clothed. The next morning, he left very early, and we never talked about that night again.

CHAPTER 23

Our Non-Traditions

Not long after we shared that cherry pie, Ivan told me about a part-time job at the Bean. He admitted he'd already talked to the owner about me, and the job was mine if I wanted it. Despite my suspicions that he'd pulled strings because he was worried about me, I took the job and a few days before Christmas I started working with Ivan three afternoons a week. Turned out, he did the scheduling.

I liked the challenge of learning how to make specialty drinks and the surprisingly physical aspects of some of the work. It got me out of the house and around people, which was fine as long as I didn't have to engage with them beyond taking their orders for mochas, vanilla chais, and Americanos.

The owner had decorated the place for Christmas. It was a little over the top, but the tiny white lights and sprays of evergreen made it feel cozy those afternoons when it got dark early. On my second day of the job, Ivan asked me about my Christmas traditions, even though he should have known, given our earlier conversation about Thanksgiving, there were no traditions.

"Are non-traditions traditions?" I said. "Because that's what my mom and I had, non-traditions." I knew my reticence about my mother bothered Ivan. For him, family was everything, and not having a family was among the worst things he could imagine in life. I sensed he hadn't believed me when I told him I was fine about my mother's non-involvement, my assurances that if I ever really needed her she'd be there for me, that she loved me in her way and I loved her. What I hadn't said was that I would find an overly involved family like his much harder to deal with than my mother's sometimes indifference.

I repeated my mother's philosophy that "holidays are corporate schemes to make people spend money they don't have." I suppose I shouldn't have been surprised when Ivan looked stricken by this. To appease him, I finally told him about our one Christmas tradition, going to Riverside to see the decorations at the Mission Inn. I tried to describe for him the life-sized mannequins singing carols in all the upstairs windows around the inn, lights everywhere, the inn's mascots— two parrots in a cage at the entrance—the enormous Christmas tree in the lobby, and the heavy boughs of evergreen on the mantels of all the blazing fireplaces burning in the lobby. I told him how each year my mother and I strolled around the plaza, looking into the shops decorated for Christmas and watching people ride in fancy horse-drawn carriages, how each year we bought candied almonds from the same nut roaster and ice cream cones from our favorite vendor. How we always stopped to listen to a guy who played jazz trumpet for tips, his old hound dog in sunglasses howling along.

As I was describing these happy memories, I felt them so viscerally I finally had to stop talking. This would be the first year in a lot of years that I wouldn't be going to the Mission Inn. I'd continued to go alone even after my mother seemed to have lost interest.

Ivan was quiet for a long time before he finally said, "I'm sorry, Vivi, but I don't think we have any hotels like that around here." I laughed, thinking he was being funny—of course, there weren't any hotels like that in Nebraska—but he didn't join my laughter. After a short pause, he said, "You at least put up a Christmas tree, didn't you?"

My god. What about this whole thing didn't he understand? Why couldn't he get his mind around the fact that not every family was exactly like his? When I finally told him I'd never had a Christmas tree in my life, he went silent. I could see he was trying to hide his shock. And I was trying to hide my irritation at his abject stupidity.

We stopped talking about Christmas then, but our conversation haunted me. All afternoon, I felt so homesick for California I wanted to cry. Each time I smelled the little sprigs of eucalyptus in the boughs of greenery decorating the counter, I thought about the old eucalyptus trees lining the streets around my mother's neighborhood, the old orange grove on the hill behind her house, full of nearly ripe oranges this time of year. The avocado, the grapefruit, and the lemon trees bearing fruit now and no one there to collect it, unless neighbor kids (or the trolls) climbed the wall. Beside the front gate, the magnolias would soon start budding. This was the green time of year in Southern California, and I imagined walking my usual route up Ridge at night, looking at all the Christmas lights on the houses and the lights of the San Bernardino valley below, Gorgonio and San Jacinto looming dark in the distance. I imagined walking again through Caroline Park, driving through San Mateo canyon with its horse farms and old orange groves, canyons and arroyos.

If I were still in my apartment in Echo Park, I'd be waking up every morning to sunshine and blue skies. This cool time of year, Kylie and I often started our workday with a hike in Griffith Park or a bike ride on the trails. I hadn't considered how confined I'd feel in a Nebraska winter, not being able to be outside like that, but now as I thought about winter, the cold, dark days stretched ahead of me. It would go on for months, Audra had told me, not knowing how much it upset me when she said the worst of winter was yet to come.

Maybe this is why I dialed my mother's phone number, which I'd long ago memorized. The phone rang a long time before she finally picked up with a wary hello.

"Hi, Mother."

"Oh, bug. I didn't recognize this number."

"I'm using a friend's phone. So how are you?"

"It's perfect here! We just got back from swimming at Magens Beach."

"That sounds wonderful."

"You should come visit! Mr. Gaston's villa has plenty of room, and I know he wouldn't mind having you here."

"I'll give it some thought." I paused then before changing the subject. "I've been thinking about the way we used to go to the Mission Inn this time of year. Remember?"

"Of course I do. That was fun. That dog with the sunglasses . . ." She laughed. She always loved hearing that hound.

I was smiling as I said, "Those were nice times."

"They were," she said, but I heard a little hesitation in her voice. "Are you feeling nostalgic, buggy?"

"Maybe. A little."

"You know, there's a reason why in ancient times nostalgia was considered a mental illness. You want to be careful with that. It can really hold you back."

I bit my bottom lip and waited for a couple beats. "Good to know." While I was saying this, I heard her cover her phone and mumble something. "Do you need to go, Mother?"

"Oh, our guests just arrived, but I have a few minutes yet to talk to my girl."

"I don't want to keep you. I just wanted to say hello."

"I'm so glad you did."

"And to wish you Merry Christmas, Mother."

She hesitated for a long time before saying, "Are you okay, Vivi? Are the meds still helping you?"

"They are. I'm doing great. Just a little bout of nostalgia. That's all." I hoped my laugh would reassure her.

"All right then, and do think about coming to visit. It'd be so fun to have you here."

In the days leading up to Christmas I'd been watching the neighbors decorate for the holiday. No surprise, the Clarks decorated on a big scale: white icicle lights along the peak of their house and colored lights in the bushes and trees out front. A massive Christmas tree decorated with thick off-white ribbons and large dusty pink and burgundy ornaments filled their big front window.

Mary Garlic and Tillie also put up a big tree. Their family tradition involved going to a tree farm outside of Lincoln and cutting down a live tree. Once home, they all worked together to hang their eccentric collection of ornaments, mostly things the kids had made over the years. This year the little kids added ornaments they'd made with Styrofoam balls and fabric scraps. Mary Garlic had found three strings of vintage colored lights at a local thrift shop.

Even Audra brought up from the basement a tall, slender artificial tree. She and Jim had bought it years before, and she decorated it in the same simple way they always had with white lights and silver ornaments.

I can't say I was entirely surprised when Ivan showed up at my door on the morning of the twenty-third holding a woebegone cedar tree. He must have looked hard to find a tree so lopsided and ugly. I laughed when I saw it, and I guessed he'd hoped for this response, his sneaky way of getting me to accept it. Who could say no to such a loser tree? He'd brought all the things to make construction paper chains, and cranberry-and-popcorn garlands—just like I remembered making in grade school one year—and a string of colored lights.

We worked together all morning to make our decorations, and by the time Ivan left, as the gloom of early afternoon was closing in, I had to admit that ugly little tree with its colored lights and homely decorations cheered me. Ivan had been almost giddy that day about leaving for Wilbur where he'd spend a little over a week with his family. His devotion to them was as foreign to me as any single thing about Nebraska.

Given the neighbors' fervor about decorating, I wondered later how I hadn't guessed they'd include me in their giving traditions. On Christmas Eve morning all of them brought me gifts of food.

Lake, Kettle, and Spur were so excited about the sugar cookies they'd decorated especially for me that they insisted I try one while they watched. They'd used red and green frosting to make what they told me (I wouldn't have guessed otherwise) were Santas and elves, reindeer and roosters (Spur's idea). Audra brought homemade fudge, a recipe passed down for generations in her family in Arkansas, and Bridget and Chuck delivered a box of elegant chocolates Bridget had made.

I suspected I was committing a huge social faux pas by not reciprocating, but I couldn't think of how to make up for my obtuseness about the holiday. My mother and I had never exchanged gifts with one another, let alone with the strangers who lived in all those neighborhoods while I was growing up.

Since the storm, Audra and I had continued to cook together most Tuesday and Thursday nights, maintaining the easy routine we'd established in October. We planned our menus for the coming week each Thursday evening. I brought ingredients for Tuesday meals and she for Thursday's. We cooked together those nights, making enough for each of us to have leftovers for another night's meal.

Like she had at Thanksgiving, Audra celebrated—if you could call eating off a tray in a nursing home celebrating—Christmas Day with Jim, but she invited me to share a roast chicken on Christmas Eve. After we'd eaten, she handed me a small, exquisitely wrapped box, waving away my embarrassment at not having bought her anything by telling me it had been an impulse buy. She'd seen it when she was shopping for her nieces. I rarely wear jewelry, but the silver necklace with its tiny silver bird was perfect, distinctive without drawing attention to itself.

It felt like a holiday for me that week and a half the kids were out of school not to have to get up early to help Mary Garlic. Between Christmas and New Year's the Wednesday night movie, *The Wizard of Oz*, was another of their holiday traditions. As usual, in Tillie and Mary Garlic's drafty house, the "big people" were wrapped in blankets and sitting on the couch and chairs of the common room, while the little kids snuggled inside sleeping bags on the floor, Mr. Shipley snoring between them. Even The Lord joined us most Wednesday nights, sleeping through the movie on Harmony's lap.

Aside from Bill, who I took a treat to each weekday morning after he'd been let out into the Clarks' backyard, I rarely saw anyone at the Clarks' house during the break. Now and then I glimpsed Bridget and the kids coming and going, but I never saw Chuck, who, when he wasn't traveling, left for work very early in the morning and didn't get home until well after dark. It appeared he didn't get much time off, even during the holidays. From previous conversations with Bridget, I knew she struggled with depression in the winter, and I guessed Chuck's work obligations didn't help.

I enjoyed my ridiculous little Christmas tree so much I didn't want to take it down after the holiday and kept it up well after the neighbors had taken theirs down, as quick to end the season as they'd been to embrace it.

After the new year, the cold deepened into a kind of pain. Nothing had prepared me for it. The wind lurked, throwing its weight into the cold, so the cold was almost unbearable. None of my winter gear kept me warm enough. The sun was a thin, white disc in a pale blue sky. It hurt to look at that sky. When I felt pent up in my cottage and had to get out, I drove into the countryside where beneath the sky, the land seemed defeated, the dry prairie grass flattened against the earth, the fields blank and exhausted. Birds huddled together or shivered alone on telephone wires. In the pastures, cattle stood, heads down, resigned. An ice storm near the end of the month made the roads treacherous. I wasn't used to driving in such conditions, and after a heart-thumping skid that nearly landed me in a ditch, I stopped driving out of the city.

I now understood what was meant by the phrase *dead of winter*. The cottage wasn't as cozy as it had been in the fall. The windows were drafty, and the cold came up through the crawl space under the wood floors. The furnace wheezed and chuffed with effort, not quite powerful enough to heat the drafty rooms on the coldest days. There were days—more than I'd like to admit—when after helping Mary Garlic with the kids and taking a treat to Bill, I crawled back into bed and didn't get up again except to make a peanut butter sandwich, before going to work at the Bean, and returning to bed again as soon as I got home, where I spent evenings huddled under the blankets with a book, except on Tuesdays and Thursdays when I basked in Audra's warm house and dreaded returning to mine, sometimes enticed to stay over with her those nights if I couldn't face my cottage.

After I finished rereading Cather's novels, I started going to the public library downtown for more books. Those cold days, I reread the novels I'd loved as a kid: *Pride and Prejudice, Portrait of a Lady, Anna Karenina, Madame Bovary, Wuthering Heights, Jane Eyre.* When I was younger, I'd read those novels compulsively, for escape and companionship, and that's how I read them again, in long gulps, without discrimination, with no purpose except to see what happened next, anything to escape from the reality of my cold cottage, my extreme boredom. And just as books had saved me as a child, they saved me now. At least for a while. But books can only do so much.

The last week of January was beastly. Brittle, windy, cold. If it hadn't been for my commitment to help Mary Garlic get the kids ready for school, I would have stayed in bed until I went to work at the Bean. As it was, I got up before the sun, threw on fleece pants and a fleece top and my down coat, and raced across the street. I was still committed to leaving Bill his treat each morning. I worried about him being outside in the cold, and on a few particularly awful days, when any sane person would agree it was wrong for any creature to be outside without shelter, I took him back to the cottage with me, returning him before Roger and Sophie got home from school. If Bridget hadn't been so sensitive about it, I would have suggested I be Bill's doggie daycare while they were away, but I knew enough not to bring it up with her.

I might have gotten away with this little deception if Bridget hadn't come home early one day. I panicked when I saw her car pull into the driveway and watched from the kitchen window as without hesitation, without any apparent doubt about where he might be, she walked across the street to my cottage after not finding him in the backyard.

I leashed Bill and met Bridget at my front gate. To my amazement, Bill wagged his tail when he saw her.

"I was worried about Bill being outside in . . ." I started to say before Bridget grabbed his leash from me. I couldn't tell if she was angry or just tired as she turned to leave with saying anything.

"I'm sorry, Bridget. I should have asked . . ."

She paused for a second. "Vivi, just stay away from my dog. Stop coming into our yard and taking our property."

Bill looked back at me then as if, like me, he was horrified by what she'd said. *Property*. She'd given herself away yet again. To her, Bill was the equivalent of a piece of lawn furniture, not a part of the family but a possession, while for me, he represented everything that was good in the world. The only living being I trusted.

Not long after this confrontation with Bridget, on another dreary day—clouds dragging their knuckles across the earth, the wind a pugilist pummeling from every direction—I crawled back into bed after helping Mary Garlic and lay in a stupor all day, not stirring from the bed, not reading or sleeping but simply staring up at the ceiling. It came to me in this weird state that there was no reason for me to continue this ordeal. My commitment to being away for a year wasn't a promise or an obligation. I was the only one who would be affected either way. It wasn't an assignment. I was free to leave that day if I wanted. I could pack up the car and leave Nebraska as easily as I'd left California. It would be far easier, in fact, to leave Nebraska. There was nothing at all keeping me here. On my return trip, I'd know how to read the atlas. I could make it back to sunshine and a civilized life in three days.

I obsessed all day about it, playing over and over again the details of my escape from the cold and the mindlessness of this unnecessary, awful choice I'd made. I feverishly rehearsed this plan as I lay beneath the blankets, occasionally glancing at the clock on the bedside stand, surprised to see how many hours had passed in this way when it had felt like only minutes.

It wasn't until the next morning, after a night of recurring dreams so boring I dreaded sleep, I finally understood I was sick. Later, when I heard a knock at the front door, and then a key in the lock, I knew it had to be Tillie or Mary Garlic. Outside the bedroom door, Tillie said with a little laugh, "Are you decent?"

"I think I'm sick."

She came into the bedroom. "Oh, yes, Gigi, I can see that. When you didn't show up this morning to help Mary Garlic, she figured something must be wrong." Tillie put her hand to my forehead, the most maternal thing I'd ever seen her do. "You're really hot, Gigi. What is it, do you think? What are your symptoms?"

She frowned as I told her how I was feeling. "I think you'd better come stay with us until you're feeling better."

"Tillie, I couldn't go to your place if I tried. I've never felt this rotten in my life. I can't even lift my head."

"Well then, we'll just have to take care of you here." She left the room and came back a few minutes later with a wet washcloth. I groaned when she laid it on my forehead, its clammy weight excruciating. She removed it immediately. "Okay. That doesn't seem to be helping. Listen, Gigi, I'm going to call our doctor to get her advice. I'm going to leave for a little, but I'll be back."

She smiled sadly at me, but I lacked the energy even to return her smile. Before she left, she insisted on helping me to the bathroom. I groaned with every painful step, every little bump an agony for my aching muscles and my throbbing head, and groaned again with the shock of the cold toilet seat on the backs of my legs.

I have no idea how long it was before Tillie came back. She hesitated in the bedroom doorway, watching me for a while before she held up a thermos. "I've brought some chicken noodle soup. It's supposed to be good for you when you're sick." As she helped me sit up in bed, she told me their family doctor had said there was a nasty strain of flu going around. The doctor's advice, according to Tillie was: fluids, sleep, and time. Tillie had brought ibuprofen to help with the pain. She'd been instructed that if anything changed with my condition, I needed to get to the hospital immediately.

I slept then. For days I slept, only vaguely aware of Audra helping me to the bathroom now and then, feeding me, straightening the room. I woke up a few times to find Ivan sitting on the edge of the bed reading aloud to me. He'd come by after I'd missed work, and Audra had enlisted him in my care.

After a week of this, I felt well enough to sit up for a few hours, even looking through one of the *People* magazines Harmony had brought for me. I was sure I was turning the corner until the next morning when I experienced a setback and was out for another three days. It was like being held under water, this weakness. No matter how hard I struggled to get above it, I couldn't. My body had let me down, and I had to submit to the humiliation of my dependence, so sick I couldn't even feel ashamed that, once again, the neighbors had come to my rescue.

Ivan told me later how he came most nights to sit with me for a couple hours. He'd been "so bored in my boring house" he'd finally brought over his old CD player and some discs, telling me they were mine to keep since he couldn't imagine how I managed to live without music. I remembered then how I'd woken up at some point, thinking I heard Nick Cave, before concluding I was hallucinating. But no, Ivan admitted he'd been listening to, of all things, Nick Cave's *Murder Ballads*. He'd been so bored, he'd also started reading aloud to me from *My Ántonia* and told me he'd almost forgotten the story about the Russian bachelor farmers throwing the bride and groom to the wolves.

"That's going into the musical!" he said. He'd convinced Moss to read *My Ántonia*, and together they'd decided the last musical of the Attic Theater would be *My Ántonia, the Musical.*

"Moss loves that scene with the wolves!" Ivan snapped his fingers then, interrupting himself. "Oh, I almost forgot. Bridget wanted me to tell you, she brought her dog—Bill?—over to see you. She thought he'd cheer you up, but you were so out of it you didn't even notice him."

"Bill was here?" I felt some big emotion bubble up in my chest. It came out in the form of a suppressed sob that I tried to hide with a cough, and which Ivan politely ignored. I wondered then what might have happened to me if I hadn't had all of them to watch out for me.

Ivan's thoughts seemed to have gone in a similar direction. "Man, if I didn't have family nearby, I don't know what I'd do if I got really sick. I have some good friends, but my neighbors? Forget it. They don't even know my name. They wouldn't notice anything until my dead body started stinking up the neighborhood."

Ordinarily I would have laughed along with his gruesome joke, but right then it felt a little too close to reality. It was clear to me that after this I couldn't just disappear and go back to California like I'd wanted. Not without saying goodbye to the neighbors. I felt I owed them too much to leave in the middle of winter, as if it would be selfish to abandon them to the dark and the cold while I was enjoying the warm sunshine.

I felt I needed to find a way to thank them for their help. I imagined how I'd bake a pie and invite all of them to share it with me. It would be the first pie I'd baked in over a year. It felt like progress that I could even think about baking a pie without wanting to cry. I imagined taking out of the closet the box with my grandma's baking things. I imagined mixing and rolling out the dough. I'd bake something simple and old-fashioned, something the gardener might have made for himself, a chess pie maybe. Or maybe a lemon meringue, something bright and cheerful to help us forget winter. No, that didn't seem right, lemon was too loud, too sharp a taste for winter. A peach pie maybe. While I watched gray clouds scud across the sky outside the bedroom window, I craved something sweet and rich. Pecan pie, or old-fashioned apple crumble. A chocolate pie. A rosemary pear pie. Suddenly, I was overwhelmed by all these choices, exhausted by so many possibilities.

Still, I turned to Ivan. "Would you like to help me bake a pie?"

He looked a little startled. After all, we'd just been discussing the reek of undiscovered dead bodies. "Sure." He sounded hesitant.

"When I'm feeling better, I want to bake a pie and share it with everyone to thank them for helping me."

"Okay." He still sounded hesitant. "You sure you're up for that?"

I knew what he meant, but that day I wanted to pretend everything was fine.

CHAPTER 24

There's Cold and Then There's Cold

I have no idea how it was possible, but winter only got worse after that. The short, dark days of mid-February were even more brutal than those at the end of January. Since recovering from the flu I'd felt wobbly. I was sluggish and dull, as if I couldn't quite wake up. Tillie and Mary Garlic noticed I wasn't myself; they kept reminding me the days were getting longer now, as if that would help. Oh, yay. Longer, miserable days.

Audra admitted it was an unusually harsh winter. "We usually have a lot more sunshine." We were sitting in front of a crackling fire having just finished eating the lamb stew she'd made for dinner. "The thing is, Vivi, you have to just get out into the cold. You have to embrace it." She sounded way too chipper. "Come on. Don't look at me with that sour face. Why not give it a try?"

She glanced out the window. "Part of the problem is there's no snow, so we can't go snowshoeing or cross-country skiing. We can't play outside." She said this as though everything would be fine if only we could do these winter activities. "I know what. Let's go winter hiking. Tomorrow. Let's go tomorrow." I must have looked dubious because she went on to diagnose me with a case of the winter blues. "It'll do both of us good to get out, Vivi. Trust me. You have plenty of good winter gear, and you'll be surprised at how quickly you'll warm up once we're moving."

The next morning I reluctantly walked to Audra's house where she looked over what I was wearing. "You need another pair of socks and a silk undershirt." She went to her bedroom and came back with both things. Motioning with her head that I should go into what she called "your bedroom" to put them on. When I came back out, she declared me ready to face the elements. We drove to Wilderness Park, where there were several other cars in the parking lot. The same park I'd hiked in the fall looked very different now in winter, its bare tree limbs like charcoal scribbles against the milky gray sky. The footprint of the park seemed smaller now that the leaves were down, and nothing muffled the sound of traffic on nearby Highway 77.

Audra took the lead on the narrow trail, and although she was over thirty years older than me, I had a hard time keeping up. She walked briskly, her back straight, rarely slowing even to step over or around exposed tree roots and rocks on the trail. I was so busy complaining to myself about the pace she'd set that I didn't notice for a while that I wasn't cold.

We walked for an hour, the only interruptions, brief pauses now and then as Audra wordlessly pointed out birds along the trail. She was a birder, and I knew she was taking note and would tell me later what we'd seen. The muscles in my shoulders and back started to relax. I felt the loosening of a constriction I hadn't been aware of in my chest, allowing me to breathe more deeply. My mind wandered as we walked. I didn't linger on any thought for long. Mostly, I observed: the beauty of a tree's bark, how the evergreens stood out against the pale sky, the way the yellowed grasses stirred in the slight breeze, the hush of the forest punctuated by an occasional birdcall or the rustle of rodents in the leaf litter. Despite the cars we'd seen earlier in the parking lot, we didn't encounter a single other hiker on the trails.

By the time we got back to the car, we were both pink cheeked and a little breathless. It was only as I waited for Audra to unlock the car that I felt the bite of the cold again. We were both shivering as she turned up the car's heater. The cold had made us giddy, and we laughed together as she pulled out of the parking lot.

"Let's stop on the way home for a cup of coffee at the Mill in the Haymarket," Audra suggested.

They were such normal, little things—getting into a car, driving somewhere, walking, getting coffee—but they felt miraculous to me that day, like going from a world in black-and-white to a world in color. Audra had told me I couldn't just talk myself out of feeling gloomy, I had to make choices. I couldn't be passive. I had to act to get myself out of my winter funk. Did other people just naturally know these things?

Over coffee, we talked in the digressive way we always did. At one point Audra was going on about trees, saying that if it weren't for the trees, Wilderness Park would just be an extra wide shoulder along Highway 77. "The trees create the perception of a space that exceeds its actual size. The forest is *more* than the trees." She went on to compare it to the way flour and water became something exponentially greater when yeast is added. "There's a kind of magic in a lot of natural processes, making them far greater than the sum of their parts, or ingredients." She smiled then, one of her startling smiles, a kind of magic itself, I thought. "Like love," she was saying. "Love works that way too." I knew Audra thought Ivan and I were dating, and I assumed she was going to say something about my relationship with him. I hoped she wouldn't. I didn't want things to get weird with her the way they often did with my mother, whose only interest in my life seemed to be in trying to understand what was wrong with me for not being obsessed with men the way she was.

But Audra wasn't going there at all. "I'm not a religious person, as you know," she said, "but I suppose this fundamental magic in the world, the way something like *bacteria*, lowly bacteria, or fungi for Pete's sake, are at the root of so much that's essential to our lives, that sort of elementary mystery about life, is as close to holiness, to the sublime, as I can imagine."

The idea of bacteria being sublime, holy even, made me laugh. She smiled. "You laugh all you want, Vivi Marx, but it's true."

After the success of our morning hike, we agreed to meet and walk together two mornings a week. "We'll go more often if you'd like," Audra said, "until the days get longer and the weather starts to get warm again." She hadn't said it, but I knew she was worried about me, that she suspected what was going on with me went deeper than the winter blues. I hadn't told her about how homesick I'd been or how before I got sick I'd been ready to pack up and leave, but I guessed she knew me better than I thought she did.

And if Audra knew me, well, I knew her too. I knew she was suffering in ways I couldn't fathom because of Jim's illness. In spite of that, or maybe because of it, I trusted she knew what made life worthwhile. She gave me a little key to happiness.

As we turned onto Fieldcrest Drive, she invited me up for lunch, saying she had a nice beef barley stew and plenty to share. I didn't have to work at the Bean that day and agreed to stay. Inside, her house was filled with the smell of the stew she'd left simmering in the slow cooker. I set the table while she cut a loaf of bread. It was like I'd never tasted stew before. After our vigorous walk, I felt I'd earned that bowl of stew.

It reminded me of Archbishop Latour's gratitude for the soup his friend Father Joseph made for him. She knew what I was talking about; she'd been inspired to read Cather after I'd talked so much about her. "Yes," she said and got up and returned with the novel, thumbing through the pages until she found what she was looking for. She glanced up quickly. "How funny. I'd underlined that section. Here it is: 'When one thinks of it, a soup like this is not the work of one man. It is the result of a constantly refined tradition. There are nearly a thousand years of history in this soup.'"

She smiled then. "Add soup to my list of magical things."

CHAPTER 25

Bliss = Bill

I hadn't seen Bridget for weeks when she invited me over the third Saturday in February. Bill was so happy to see me he broke one of her cardinal rules and jumped up on me. She scolded and smacked him across the nose but otherwise seemed to be in a good mood. In fact, she was beside herself with excitement about their annual trip to Cancun. She'd told me before how their winter trip was a time when she and Chuck got away together without the kids. Her winter tan made it clear she'd been going to a tanning bed in preparation for the beach.

"I have a big favor to ask you," she finally said. "Would you be willing to stay at the house while we're away to keep an eye on the kids. They'll be no trouble, but we don't want to leave them alone either. They're teenagers after all, and, well, you never know." Bridget and Chuck seemed to be the only ones who didn't know their kids were trustworthy. I knew the kids wouldn't need me, but Bill . . . ten whole days to spend with Bill. I couldn't say no to that.

After a couple glasses of wine, Bridget grew talkative. She admitted this winter had gotten her down more than usual, repeating what Audra had said about it being an exceptionally harsh winter. "I don't dare talk about things like this around Chuck. He's all about being up. If I say anything the tiniest bit negative, he makes this gesture with his fist, 'up, up, up,'" she said, mimicking the gesture. "Whenever he does that, I always say to myself, 'up yours.' Isn't that terrible?"

She laughed at herself. "The kids mock him when he does that too. Behind his back, of course. I know I shouldn't encourage them, but it always cracks me up."

She told me then how Chuck had grown up in Nigeria. His parents were missionaries, something I would never have guessed. Bridget thought that's what had made him stand out to her. He had seemed so much cooler, so much more mature, than the other guys she'd met that first year of college. "I envy his experiences, his travels." Apparently, though, Chuck didn't see it that way.

"Chuck thought the whole missionary thing, especially for a kid, was pretty awful. I mean, his parents put him on a train by himself when he was only five years old and sent him clear across Africa to a boarding school in Zimbabwe. He never saw them except for summers when the whole family came back to the States to raise funds, going from church to church 'begging,' as Chuck says, for money so they could go back to Nigeria for another year."

"Chuck hated every minute of it. And boarding school, well . . . boarding school is where he learned the hard way about real life, from the older kids. And . . ." she looked at me significantly before adding cryptically, "from one kid in particular. He was adamant that he'd never allow our kids to go to a boarding school, as if that was ever a possibility." She laughed at the apparent absurdity of sending kids to boarding school.

She gestured silently to ask if I wanted another glass of wine. I nodded, and while she filled our glasses, I glanced toward the mudroom where Bill was watching us. I caught his eye and his tail thumped loudly on the tile floor. "I'll never forget my dad's face when I told him Chuck and I were getting married," Bridget said. "I mean, they didn't even know Chuck, and it wasn't what they'd wanted for me, to have to grow up so quick like that." Bridget had a way of being in constant motion, even when she was sitting. She threw out her arms extravagantly now, moved forward and then back in the chair abruptly, before going on. "Chuck had to tell his parents we were getting married in a letter. I wish sometimes I'd kept the letter his mother wrote back, a *long* letter, like a sermon, full of quotes from the Bible. Chuck said it was typical of her, but when I got to know her better, I knew it was typical of her only when she was really pissed off. She's a bit of an oddball, like you'd expect, but she's a good egg."

She rolled her eyes. "Chuck's dad's another story. They've only ever visited us a couple of times. When they were here his dad was always quiet and polite, but inside I could tell he was seething the whole time. I keep waiting for him to blow up. There's something really tamped down inside him. Plus, he always looks dusty to me. Every time I see him I want to dust him off. The poor old guy has no sense of humor at all. I honestly think it drove him nuts to visit us. We're all so loud, including Chuck. Well, actually, Chuck is the loudest of all. You get a couple beers in Chuck, and he won't stop. He's like one of those machines you can't turn off. You just have to wait for him to run out of steam. He's the life of the party, though. I promise you. He tells the funniest stories you'll ever hear."

By this time, she'd opened another bottle of wine, and we'd moved into the den off the back of the house where there was another gas fireplace. It was cozy there, just the two of us. The kids were at an out-of-town basketball game, and as usual, Chuck was traveling for work. After she adjusted the fireplace, she sat down in one of the leather chairs facing the fire and tucked her long legs under her. "I think Chuck wasn't allowed to be a very sincere person growing up. Just watching him with his parents you see the woodenness. They're so formal. It's like they're always performing. The opposite of my family. Chuck was shocked the first time he met my family. The five of us kids all tease each other something terrible, and we tease our parents too. We like to insult each other and play practical jokes. I guess that's how we show affection. We get into terrible fights, and then we get over it, and laugh and hug each other. Chuck can't understand how we can laugh things off like we do. Even after eighteen years, he doesn't get my family. I suppose we're a classic mismatch, Chuck and me."

We both looked out the window into her backyard. In the fading light, she silently pointed out a colony of cardinals pecking around under one of her yew bushes. There were several males in the group. I was sure these were the same birds Audra and I had been watching in her backyard all winter. I told Bridget what Audra had told me, that our neighborhood must be especially good for food since male cardinals are usually very territorial. I also mentioned how Audra was trying, not very successfully, to teach me to paint those birds.

"It's so nice of you to spend time with Audra like you do," Bridget said as though I was doing Audra a favor, as though it wasn't possible we could be friends, before she changed the subject. "I always wanted to be creative, but I don't have a creative bone in my body. Some of my friends say I'm a good decorator, but that's not being creative. I just steal ideas from home design sites. Same with making quilts or knitting. You just follow a pattern. Any moron can do that. When I was little, my mother put me in a ballet class." She laughed at this memory. "I don't know what she was thinking. I towered above all the other little girls, like a big giraffe. We had to watch ourselves in the mirrors, so I had to see the whole time how ridiculous I looked. It was a pitiful sight. That didn't last long, thank goodness."

"I have no ear for music either. The Johnsons are definitely not a musical family. And neither was Chuck's family. We can't figure out where Roger and Sophie get their musical talent. I mean, Chuck and I can't even carry a tune, but the kids are talented, don't you think?" She asked this in such a naïve way it took me off guard. How could she not know how talented her children were?

"They're very talented, Bridget."

She smiled. "They are, aren't they?"

We were quiet again as we continued to watch the cardinals, only shadows on the ground now in the waning light. It felt good to sit in silence with Bridget. I'd reached this place with all the women in the neighborhood where we could sit comfortably in silence together.

After a while, Bridget broke the silence to say, "I wish I could paint a picture of those birds."

CHAPTER 26

Too Fine a Cut

The morning Bridget and Chuck left for Cancun in early March was the start of what would be the coldest week of an already colder than usual winter. The actual temperatures were well below zero, add the wind chill (a new concept for me), and the temperatures felt like double-digits below zero. Now I understood why Dante's *Inferno*, which I remembered only vaguely from high school English, depicted the deepest parts of hell not as a kingdom of fire but a kingdom of ice. That week the weather was indeed hell.

I took advantage of the comforts of the Clarks' house: their gas fireplaces and luxurious cashmere throws, no drafty window, no cold floors, no wheezy, old furnace. In fact, the thermostat was on a timer, as was the coffeepot, so I woke up every morning to the smell of coffee in a warm house. Bridget had stocked the cupboards and refrigerator with food. Everything was so comfortable, I came to agree with Bridget that I lived in a hovel.

Roger and Sophie were away at school all day, and most evenings they were busy with extracurricular activities. Sophie had a major role in the school's spring play and was at rehearsal most school nights, while Roger was either practicing or performing with the concert band or the pep band. When they were home, they were usually at Tillie's house working on the summer musical.

If the weather was hell, having that time with Bill was pure bliss for me. The day I arrived, he pounced on the stuffed duck I brought him and carried it with him everywhere, even keeping it beside him while he slept. I'd never seen any other dog toys at their house and guessed this might be the first toy he'd ever had. Except for helping Mary Garlic each morning and working two afternoons at the Bean, the only times I left the house during those ten days were the short walks I took with Bill twice a day. I'd never seen anyone walk him, and I was determined to get him out every day.

Bill was cowed the first time I clipped on the leash I'd bought for him at the same time I'd bought his stuffed duck, but once we were out of the yard, he went berserk, pulling and straining against his collar, barking at squirrels and later at cars on the streets beyond Fieldcrest Drive. He was such a sweet creature, though, only wanting to please, it didn't take him long to figure it out and to start to behave on our walks. We never went very far because of the cold, but I discovered a new side of the surrounding neighborhoods from Bill's perspective, as he stopped and sniffed under every bush and around every tree.

Bridget sent daily emails to Roger and Sophie, always instructing them to tell me hello. A few times when they showed me the pictures she'd attached, I'd see her slightly sniping message about how she couldn't copy me because of my "weird internet thing." In the photos she sent, she and Chuck looked happy and relaxed: on the beach, in front of their condo, at the bar, on a sailboat, and getting ready to go diving. As we looked at the photos, the kids and I invariably complained about how they were having so much fun while we were stuck slogging through the cold in Nebraska.

For the first couple days I rigidly adhered to Bridget's rules for Bill and made sure he stayed in the mudroom at all times. But really her rules were a little ridiculous. The kitchen was tiled after all, and there wasn't anything he could hurt there. And the basement family room also had a tile floor. What could it hurt to let him into that room if I was watching him? All he did was sleep for hours on the floor beside the lounge chair I'd colonized.

At night, the temperatures dipped even further, and once I discovered the mudroom didn't warm up like the rest of the house, it felt cruel to make Bill sleep in the coldest part of the house, especially during such unusually cold weather. The first night I let him into the bedroom I was using, he didn't wait for an invitation before jumping onto the bed with me. I started to tell him to get down, but he looked so happy, I couldn't do it. From then on, I waited until the kids were both home and in bed before I let him into my room, and mornings I was careful to get up before they did so Bill would be back in the mudroom by the time they came downstairs.

I suppose it was inevitable that we'd get caught. It happened one morning near the end of my stay when I'd forgotten both kids were leaving early for school that day, and I opened my bedroom door just as Roger and Sophie were in the hallway. They both glanced into my room just as Bill was jumping off the bed.

Until I saw the shock in their eyes, I hadn't allowed myself to think about what I was doing. Neither of them said anything for a few seconds before they doubled over in laughter. They encouraged Bill to get back on the bed again, and Sophie snapped a photo before I could stop her. Afterward, they teased Bill about being a "lady's man." Co-conspirators, they promised not to tell Bridget.

After that, I abided by Bridget's rules. Bill was the one who suffered for my previous lapse in judgment. The first few times I insisted he stay in the mudroom, he ignored me and came into the kitchen, tail wagging, obviously confused and hurt when I scolded him. One night I woke up and heard him in the hall outside my door whining to get in. I'd created a monster, and I was afraid of the consequences for him once Bridget got back. That night I roughly dragged him by the collar down the stairs and into the mudroom, where he stood with his head hanging and his tail tucked between his legs, breaking my heart as I told him sternly to stay.

The night Bridget and Chuck came home it was very late. They were exhausted after their trip, so I didn't see Bridget again for a couple days. By then, the cold front had moved through, and the temperatures had warmed enough for me to head out for a morning walk. Bridget was getting into her car to go to work when she saw me. She walked down the driveway and met me on the street in front of their house.

I could see she wasn't happy and knew immediately she'd heard about my transgression with Bill. I felt a sharp little sting of hurt that the kids had betrayed me, until Bridget said, "Did you really think I wouldn't find out? Every night Bill tries to follow me upstairs. I finally confronted the kids, thinking it was them who'd broken the rules, but it was *you*, Vivi." She seemed genuinely bewildered as she asked me why I had been so cavalier about respecting the rules of her house. More than that, she was bitterly disappointed, she told me, that she'd entrusted me with all the things most precious to her: her children, her house, everything she owned, and I'd let her down. "What would make you betray my trust like that? What did I do to make you dislike me so much?" she finally asked. "Help me understand, Vivi."

I didn't have an answer for this, didn't understand myself why my obsession with Bill had led me to believe it was only right he should be my dog, not theirs, to think I knew what was best for him.

"You act like you've fallen in love with my dog, Vivi, and I really don't get it. I don't understand you at all." If she'd said this with disgust, if she'd been snide or sarcastic, I might have been able to defend myself, but instead she'd said it with concern, almost with compassion, as though I was a child, and posed that way, I had no defense.

In that instant, I understood I'd lost more than the thread of my life. This situation wasn't just a regression. It was revelatory, revealing to me, and to everyone else, a serious character affliction, a flaw at my core, the horrible realization that maybe I'd never had a core to begin with, that I was in fact an empty person.

I was far more shaken by Bridget's disappointment than I would have been if she'd been angry with me. In spite of all our run-ins about Bill over the past few months, she'd always recovered quickly, willing to forgive and to look past my lapses in judgment, still seeing me as a capable adult. But no longer.

I wanted to apologize, to admit I'd acted rashly, to acknowledge I'd behaved in ways I wasn't proud of and didn't understand myself, but as she waited for my response, I felt a shame so acute, I couldn't even look at her, let alone speak. I couldn't explain the way Bill seemed to fill a desperate need I had. The devotion of that dog was the closest I'd ever come to unconditional love. He made me feel safe and whole in the world.

Here's the thing about being broken. There's nowhere to go. Nothing left to cling to. My misery must have been obvious, because her expression softened then, and she pulled me under one of her long arms into a rough side hug. "It's okay, Vivi. I forgive you, of course. I do. It isn't a question of forgiveness. I'm just trying to understand. As neighbors, I hope we can get past this."

Oddly, just then her forgiveness was too much, her understanding too fine and fatal a cut. It felt like the worst thing—her mercy. It was devastating, and distraught, I stepped out of her embrace, and gestured that I couldn't talk.

Maybe there's something about the rock bottom of your soul. Maybe all energy at that point becomes generative instead of destructive, because I felt a strange stirring of emotion, something akin to annoyance, a tiny resistance pushing against Bridget's generosity, warding off her mercy.

And later that evening when Bridget knocked at my door to drop off an exquisite little Christmas ornament she and Chuck had found for me in Cancun, it was too much. The timing was off. If she'd let things settle for a few more days; if she'd waited just a little longer, I might have been able to handle it, but somehow, her generosity so soon after my offense felt like heaping on, an excessive, even aggressive gesture. I felt a confusion of emotions—gratitude, of course, humbling gratitude, but also a keen little shard of anger at being forced to go along with her version of things, to accept her sense of reality as the only version of the truth. What at that moment looked like magnanimity, also appeared to me as enormous self-regard, forcing me to accept her forgiveness, to go along with her largesse, without having to take responsibility for the way I'd wronged her. I wished then I could summon one of my mother's irrational outbursts, one of her righteous bouts of bad temper in which she could so clearly articulate her displeasure, the way she could confront the lie and then move on, even if in the wake of her tantrum others were confused and battered. But I couldn't do it. I'd honed my emotions so carefully over the years, kept myself in reserve, become so expert at not being like my mother, second-guessing and keeping my feelings carefully in check lest someone else suffer needlessly for my excess, that I couldn't respond at all, not even to properly thank her for the gift.

I'd blatantly, deliberately wronged Bridget, and a part of me was still unrepentant about it. Given the opportunity I might well have done it again, and accepting her forgiveness made it all too neat, a cheap shortcut to resolving our conflict. I didn't question her ability to forgive; after all, I'd experienced her forgiveness many times already. But I didn't believe she forgot offenses, and her big gestures of forgiveness felt pro forma. It didn't bring relief but indebtedness.

CHAPTER 27

Spring Clean Up, Spring Screw-Up

Every morning the first week of April I woke to a ground fog so thick it obscured everything around me. The songbirds were raucous those mornings, so loud they woke me at 4:30. Half asleep, I stared out the window into the gloom, straining to see but not seeing. I got up early and while I drank my morning coffee kept an eye on the clock until 7:00 when I walked to Tillie's house.

The fog so obscured our little street I felt like the last person alive after the apocalypse. Once past my front gate, I couldn't see any of the houses on the street, including my own. The fog pressed against me. I followed the street until I felt the brick walk beneath my feet, trusting it to lead me in the direction of their back door, still surprised when I came upon it, invisible to the last moment.

One of those mornings, it wasn't the songbirds that woke me but the sound of crows squabbling in the tops of the tall cottonwoods around the creek. The morning of the crows, Mary Garlic was running late. She hadn't dressed yet for work when I arrived, and she was circling the kitchen table trying to get the little kids fed.

"Am I ever glad to see you. I don't know what's going on with all of us today, but we can't seem to get ourselves in gear."

I gestured for her to get herself ready while I took over the breakfast chores. Harmony, sleep-tousled, came into the kitchen, nodded silently at me, and poured herself a cup of coffee. This was a rare sighting of her in the morning, and I gathered she hadn't needed to go to school early that day. She sat down at the table and idly ate a piece of sliced banana off Kettle's plate.

"I can't get Moss to budge," Mary Garlic said when she returned a few minutes later, dressed for work now in jeans and a button-down uniform shirt.

"I'll get him up later," Harmony said. "He has a light schedule today."

"He should be taking advantage of that light schedule this year to take the college courses they offer over there. Those are free credits," Mary Garlic grumbled.

Harmony shrugged. I knew the question of college was a fraught one in their house. Tillie felt it was up to Moss or Harmony if they wanted to go to college, while Mary Garlic was adamant they both get degrees. I'd overheard more than one argument between them about it. During one of these arguments, I remembered seeing Tillie look at Mary Garlic with a sort of wonder, "Even after all this time," her expression seemed to say, "you still don't get it," but Mary Garlic, who never missed much, did get it.

"Tillie, this isn't only about money. Not everything is about money." Before Tillie could protest, Mary Garlic continued, "There are things in the world, in the *real* world, like work, that can be meaningful. Work can make your life better, and the thing is, I don't want the kids to have to work the way I've had to. I want them to have choices I didn't have."

"But Mary Garlic," Tillie said, "you don't have to keep working at the rail yard. How many times have I told you that?"

At this, I'd noticed Mary Garlic's back stiffen a little. After many hours in their house, I knew how this part of the argument went too. I knew the kids didn't have the choices Tillie thought they did because once in a rare, confiding mood Mary Garlic admitted to me there wasn't all that much money in Tillie's trust fund. The truth was, they needed the income from Mary Garlic's job, and they needed her job for their health insurance. Everyone—including the little kids—knew this except Tillie, and all of them conspired to go along with her delusion.

Without her ever saying it, I suspected even if there had been enough money to support them, Mary Garlic would have still wanted to work because she didn't like to be dependent on anyone, not even her beloved Tillie. She referred to herself as a "working stiff," and she worked hard, the only female mechanic in the local Burlington Northern shop. She wanted something more for the kids, but she was proud of her work, and she valued her independence.

I thought that morning as I washed little hands and faces around their kitchen table that it might have been good for Tillie to have experienced a little more of the real world. Mary Garlic had once described Tillie as feral, a fair enough description of someone who'd never had to live with a schedule, or to conform to anything or anyone, someone whose biggest challenge and struggle in life had been to raise five children with the help of a good and grounded partner. Tillie wasn't spoiled. It wasn't that. Instead, she seemed arrested, and like the members of her family, I loved her *for*—not in spite of—her childlikeness.

Mary Garlic was always in a hurry those busy mornings, so I noticed it when she paused a second longer than usual at the back door. She seemed to have something on her mind. Harmony had gone back upstairs to get ready for school, and the little kids had left the kitchen to gather their things, so it was just the two of us.

"You okay?"

She frowned slightly. "Have you noticed anything off about Moss lately?"

"No." The truth was I hadn't seen much of Moss. He'd missed the last two Wednesday movie nights and had slept through several Sunday morning brunches. I knew Mary Garlic tended to see the worst of any situation, and given her preoccupation about the kids doing well in school, it was no surprise that she and Moss clashed about school. He often played hooky, reliably driving Mary Garlic bonkers.

"I'm just not sure Tillie and I know how to raise a boy to be a man, that's all," she said, musing in a way that struck me as out of character.

"I'm not sure I understand what you're saying, Mary Garlic." I stopped swiping the dishcloth over the mess the little kids had left on the table. "Moss is a wonderful boy."

"*Young man*. He's nineteen," she corrected me, sounding a little peeved. "I'm not really questioning Moss's value . . ." She started to say more before she waved it away. "Tell the kids I'll be in the car waiting for them, will you?" She paused again. "And thank you, Vivi, for helping out like you do every day."

Maybe it was the fog, or the weird conversation with Mary Garlic, but that morning after they'd left, instead of going back to my cottage like usual, I poured myself a cup of coffee and sat down. Mr. Shipley was snoozing under the table, in the middle of some doggy dream that made him twitch and yelp periodically. I liked Mr. Shipley, but for reasons still mysterious to me, I didn't love him the way I loved Bill.

Since the meltdown with Bridget, I'd avoided the Clarks' house, not even taking treats to Bill every day. I hadn't allowed myself to think about it much, but that morning I thought about my strange, possibly perverse, feelings for Bill. I was thinking if I ever loved a man the way I loved Bill I'd be in big trouble, when Tillie appeared in the kitchen. She rarely woke before eleven, so I was surprised to see her up. She was so intent on retying the trailing sash of her robe and complaining to herself about "those damned crows" that she didn't at first see me at the table.

When she did, she smiled sleepily. "Oh, it's you. Good morning, Gigi. Where did all the *nice* birds go? Did those horrible beasts chase them away do you think?"

"They'll be back tomorrow. How about a cup of coffee, Tillie?"

"Oh, thank you, Gigi." She sat down and placed both hands flat on the tabletop as if steadying herself for the day ahead. When I set a mug of coffee in front of her, she cupped her hands around it and bent her head to breathe in the steam. Knowing as I did that she was slow to wake up, I didn't initiate a conversation. We sat together in silence until Moss joined us. He slumped in a chair without greeting us and studied his phone intently. His long hair was tangled and he wore only boxers and a T-shirt, as he often did around the house, despite the drafty windows.

"Morning, Moss," I finally said.

He mumbled something without looking up from his phone, and I saw what Mary Garlic said was true. In the past few weeks, since I'd last seen him, he seemed different somehow. He was still thin, but he'd added bulk in his chest and upper arms like he'd been working out. Inexplicably he still seemed to have his summer tan, and I wondered briefly how he'd managed to keep it through the winter.

He continued to ignore us, even after Tillie got up and silently poured him a cup of coffee. "He used to tell me everything," she said, hoping, I knew, to chasten him for his rude behavior. "He doesn't tell me a thing nowadays, though." She smiled, but I saw she was a little confused when her effort failed to get his attention.

"You going to school today, Moss?" she finally said.

"Mmmm."

"Is that a yes?"

"Yeah, Til."

"What's that you're so intent on there?"

"Just texting a friend."

"I can never understand what people find to text about all the time," Tillie said to no one before finally saying to Moss, "well, if you're going, you should probably get a move on."

"I know what time it is, Til." I had never heard Tillie encourage timeliness, nor had I heard Moss raise his voice to her.

Equable as always, Tillie apologized for pushing him. In the past, I felt sure, her apology would have elicited some joke from Moss acknowledging that he'd overstepped, but this morning he was so distracted he seemed not to have heard her at all, his thumbs flying over his phone keyboard, his brow furrowed as he stopped now and then to read a reply.

I recognized something in Moss then I didn't think either Tillie or Mary Garlic had seen, that he was suffering, and I suddenly knew there was a girl, and that he was being tormented in some way by her. I'd had a lot of unrequited crushes in my life, so I knew something about that kind of suffering. I wanted to reassure Moss, to tell him I understood, but of course I couldn't acknowledge something he hadn't shared with me.

The next day the wind blew without stopping, and in its wake two days of rain. The entire city seemed to have been waiting for the sun to come out. When it did, the neighborhood came to life, the city was transformed. Every day something was in bloom. Maybe you need winter to really appreciate green and growing things, because I couldn't get enough of it.

Between Audra and Harmony, I learned the names for all of the early bloomers and the names of the budding trees: redbuds came first, even before the rain had passed, their rows of tiny purple buds seeming to glow in the gloom; crabapples, their gnarly branches heavy with pink buds, spirea, lilacs, sand cherry, plums and pears, forsythia. Tulips and daffodils, hyacinth and snowdrops bloomed overnight.

For a week the sun shone in a soft blue sky. Fat white clouds drifted into one another like drunken bumblebees. I sat outside on my front stoop in a sweater as if drunk myself, breathing deeply the still slightly chilly air, and watched the sky. I watched the neighbors, too, as spring loosened winter's stranglehold and all of us emerged from our winter cocoons, peeling away layers of clothes, opening doors and windows, reentering the communal life of the street that had gone dormant during the winter months. I was part of the neighborhood now, no longer a stranger. Between the October storm and the extreme cold of the winter, I felt we'd all survived something together. Things still weren't right with Bridget, but we carried on respectfully at arm's length. Fortunately, I hadn't expressed any of my irrational rancor, and despite my earlier doubts about her ability to forget my bad behavior, she showed no sign of holding a grudge. We'd established a friendly truce, something resembling our former neighborliness.

While I watched the neighbors, I found they weren't as pleased as I was. Until now they hadn't known the extent of the damage done to trees and bushes during the October storm, and I overheard them telling one another about what had been lost or seriously damaged in the storm. They listed their losses in mournful tones as if they'd lost old friends.

Tillie and Mary Garlic were worried about a red maple they loved, struggling for life after having lost two major branches in the storm, and a hedge of lilac bushes on the north side of the house was so damaged it wouldn't recover.

Bridget, along with the rest of the neighbors, grieved the loss of what all of them called "the old lady," the large, old weeping willow that had shaded part of the Clarks' patio. Beyond that loss, she seemed most upset about the cost of replacing three small ornamental trees in the berm in their front yard.

It was Audra, though, who mourned the deepest for a spindly dogwood tree she'd brought as a sapling from Arkansas and had nurtured for years. She'd worked late into the fall to try to repair the most serious damage, a major split in its trunk, but it was obvious now her efforts hadn't worked. There were other losses, too, and she enumerated them but always returned to her sadness over the little dogwood. The lost dogwood seemed to embody the other major loss in her life, Jim. She'd lived in this house longer than she'd lived anywhere since marrying him, and she told me once she expected she'd live there the rest of her life. She hadn't added the word *alone* but it was implied. I understood she couldn't bear to lose anything else in her life just then.

In October, two of the big cottonwoods along the creek had come down in the meadow behind my cottage. When they'd first fallen I'd thought of them as giants asleep on the meadow, their huge leafy heads lying on the ground under the snow. Now, though, seeing their dead branches, I couldn't think of them in such a whimsical way. Instead, each time I glimpsed them out the back windows, I felt a little pang of sadness, a tiny glimpse of how the neighbors felt.

Later that week, I heard Mary Garlic rototilling Harmony's vegetable garden plot. Through the open attic windows, I sometimes heard Tillie busily sewing costumes for the musical. Chuck had taken off a few days to work alongside the yard crew they'd hired to get their yard in shape. Inside the house, we'd all been told Bridget was doing her annual spring-cleaning. I could almost feel a hum of energy coming from their house. She'd once told me how each spring she moved every piece of furniture and washed the walls. She removed everything from all the closets and drawers and cleaned them too. The few times I glimpsed her that week, she was in a frenzy. Each day Roger and Sophie scattered out the back door as soon as they could escape whatever chores she'd assigned them.

Harmony came over to "wake up my garden," by which she meant thinning perennials and clearing debris from the flowerbeds. I offered to help, but perhaps sensing I'd only be in the way she'd told me not to worry about it.

Instead, I wandered over to admire Audra's orange tulips. She was happy to have my help clearing the winter muck from the beds of blue star juniper and the tall fescue that grew along her bluestone steps. She showed me how to cut back the dead grass to make room for new shoots. As we worked we couldn't help but notice all the activity at the Clarks where Bridget was now talking animatedly to the pool guys.

"Bridget's part porpoise," Audra said. "She'll be in that pool while the rest of us are still wearing sweaters." I'm not sure why we found this so comical, but we both laughed to the point of tears at Bridget's expense.

For that week the neighbors seemed a little crazed to me. I'd thought at first their mania was caused by the extra work of clearing the remnants of the storm's damage, but I later learned it was an annual condition. In fact, Mary Garlic and Bridget had both mentioned their annual spring cleanup, a communal workday they set aside each year.

Watching them reminded me of how the gardener must have worked long days this time of year when Fieldcrest Manor was still a grand estate. I sometimes felt he was there alongside me watching all the activity in the neighborhood with approval.

I knew Bridget had finished her spring cleaning when she called me over to look at the pool, ready for summer now that they'd pulled away the cover. Rain had moved in again that morning, and we stood together on her patio as the wind whipped the rain around us. Bridget didn't seem to notice or care about the weather, fixated instead on the minute she could jump into the water, practically vibrating with pent-up energy after the long winter.

She rubbed her hands briskly together. "First warm day in May, I'm in that water," she said glancing from the pool to Tillie and Mary Garlic's house before grabbing my arm with excitement. "I just bought three new swimsuits!" She told me she'd gained a few extra pounds over the winter, but she was working extra hard to get them off. I knew, come May, she'd once again be the goddess of the neighborhood.

Even before I got inside the Bean, I could see Ivan was excited about something. "You aren't going to believe what I've got," he said once I'd closed the door. "Sufjan Stevens at the Orpheum this Saturday." He held up two tickets.

"I'm totally jealous."

"I know. My buddy Mark got them for me. I want you to have the second ticket. You could meet my friends." For a split second I was tempted by the offer, but when he mentioned meeting his friends, I balked. He talked a lot about his friends from high school, what he called his posse. Without my saying anything, he saw I'd lost interest,

"You'd like them, Vivi. And I know they'd like you. It doesn't have to be a big deal."

He made it sound so reasonable. It was spring, and I felt liberated after the long winter. It sounded great to go to a show again, and I said yes before hearing all the details. Those details were concerning. The show was on a Friday night. We'd drive up after our shift at the Bean, meet up with the others at the show, stay overnight with his buddy Mark who had plenty of room, and then hang out with them on Saturday before heading back to Lincoln. Seeing my reaction to these plans, Ivan rushed to reassure me. "It'll be cool," he kept saying.

I knew I'd made a mistake giving in as soon as we got in Ivan's car on Friday to drive to Omaha. He was excited to see his friends, and to go to the show. He played Sufjan Steven's music in the car as we drove. I couldn't get as excited as he was. Is there anything worse, really, than being a drag and trying, for the sake of other people, not to be?

The Orpheum was a beautiful old theater. The show was great, the crowd cool, but I was emotionally wobbly all evening. It was exhausting to be polite meeting Ivan's friends, all these people I'd never see again in my life. They were all nice guys, just what I'd expected from Ivan's friends, but it required more than I wanted to give right then. Fortunately, I didn't have to talk once the show started, and it was late by the time we got to Mark and his Linda's house. They'd made up the bed in the guest room for me, and Ivan took the couch.

From the start, though, on Saturday when we all met up for breakfast at La Buvette in the Old Market, everything hit me wrong. It didn't matter that Omaha was pretty that spring day—the hills along the river a vivid green, the blue, scrubbed-clean sky. Everything about Omaha felt manageable. I saw the appeal in that. On the way to the Old Market, Ivan had detoured to show me a few up-and-coming neighborhoods downtown and in Midtown—where his friend Jack and his girlfriend had just bought a townhouse that cost a fraction of what it would have in downtown LA.

His friends were all relaxed, natural, happy, unguarded, but I was jangly. My awkwardness only made it worse. I felt so uncomfortable about being there, I started making weird little verbal jabs at Ivan, teasing him with an edge of cruelty. When Ivan's friend Leo made some crack about the freeways in LA being nothing but a gigantic car lot—something I'd said myself in the past—it hit me wrong. Maybe I was looking to be indignant. Whatever it was, my mood soured even further.

At least I had the good sense to shut up. Still, I couldn't seem to stop making silent comparisons. Omaha seemed like a toy city, everything about it small and insignificant compared to LA. Yeah, there were a few cool neighborhoods. So what? There were some interesting things going on with music and art. Okay. But it was trivial compared to what was happening in LA. Their pride in the city struck me not only as naïve but stupid. I decided they were all boring. My stubborn unresponsiveness to every effort they made to introduce me to Omaha only made clearer my disdain. Not only was I unimpressed, I was incapable of being impressed. In fact, the harder they tried, the more I withdrew. While I didn't actually say anything derogative, it was obvious I was judging not only the city but them too.

I knew I was messing up, but everything they did annoyed me: their inside jokes, their horsing around. They seemed like frat boys as they teased one other. And the more miserable I grew, the more I blamed Ivan for having pushed me into this outing.

By then I'd made assumptions about Ivan's friends. They were so laid back, so unpretentious, I took it as evidence they were slackers. I thought they were small-town kids who'd moved to the city and that was all they had going for them. I felt a barely concealed contempt for them, so I was embarrassed later to learn they were all accomplished guys. If anything, Ivan was the slacker among them. They'd been having fun that day, that's all. Hanging out, being themselves with their oldest friends. I didn't have a group of old friends like that. I didn't know how to goof around with people. I'd never been relaxed the way they were with each other. Not even with Kylie.

A familiar tape started to play in my head, a tape I played when anything went wrong in my life, whenever I thought someone might be judging me. The truth was, I envied Ivan that day. I envied him horribly.

For a while my standoffishness put a serious damper on their fun. I finally went too far and made a sarcastic remark about Saddle Creek Records to Brian—who I later learned was an oncology resident at the University Med Center—that made everyone wince. Ivan, loyal to everyone, scrambled to do damage control, begging me with his eyes to tone it down, while trying to laugh it off, trying to pass it off as an awkward attempt at humor rather than evidence of my scorn.

I seemed to snap out of my bad mood after that, and somehow got my act together enough to salvage a little bit of our time together. Even so, by the end of the day when Jack and Brenda invited me to their annual Fourth of July barbecue I knew it wasn't a sign they liked me so much as a sign of their love for Ivan. I saw they were worried about Ivan, hoping he was telling the truth when he'd told them we were only friends.

Ivan was quiet for a long time as we drove home on Saturday night, and I knew he was thinking about what had happened. He wasn't one to ignore things. He'd seen a side of me—some need for one-upmanship, some kind of social competitiveness—he hadn't seen before. He finally asked what it was I'd been competing for? He was gentle as he posed this question.

"Were you trying to prove LA has more going on than Omaha?" He didn't wait for an answer before adding, "Isn't that sort of like comparing apples to apple trees? You've never acted that way around me before."

"I shouldn't have accepted your invitation, Ivan. I'm not ready yet for this sort of social thing. I'm awkward in the best of circumstances; it was too much, and I should have known it about myself, but . . ." I looked at his profile, lit by the green light of the dashboard, and he glanced at me quickly before turning back to the road. "You have to believe me when I tell you I've never been rude before the way I was with your friends today. I'm really sorry for that. I feel awful about how I acted."

I had no excuse for it. He knew it, and I knew it. I had no explanation for my behavior except that I'd been a jerk. It was as simple as that. He didn't say anything, but without taking his eyes off the road, he held out his hand to me. I took it, thinking it was a gesture to shake hands, as if agreeing it wouldn't happen again. Instead, he closed his hand around mine and held it for a long time, only letting go when he had to make a turn. We drove in silence until we got to Fieldcrest Drive.

It was a little past midnight, but even in the dark we could see the neighbors had been hard at work. Leaf bags lined the street as did neat piles of the uncollected limbs and branches that had come down after the October storm. The street looked more vivid and alert. Something about this broke the silence between us. We exchanged a glance and smiled. Just as Bridget's fervor earlier in the month had struck Audra and me funny, thinking about all the neighbors working away like little ants all day seemed funny too.

The next morning, I went over to Tillie's to help Mary Garlic and Harmony make Sunday brunch for the clan. Like always, I walked in the house without knocking. As soon as she heard the door Harmony yelled, "We're in the kitchen, Vivi. Coffee's made."

I walked through the house, stepping over toys, and discarded backpacks, and roller skates, and skateboards, and bicycles to get to the kitchen I loved—where Harmony's smile greeted me and lit me up from the inside. She couldn't have known how much I appreciated her kindness just then after the disastrous trip to Omaha, but my happy little high came crashing down as soon as I saw Mary Garlic's scowling face.

"Well, if it isn't the lady of leisure herself."

I wasn't sure what to make of her unexpected hostility. I smiled and tried to ignore her, thinking she was in a bad mood.

"Don't just stand there smiling like an idiot," Mary Garlic said, mimicking a fake smile. "You've got a nerve."

I'd started to sit down at the table but caught myself as she said this and remained standing. "What's going on?"

Mary Garlic looked at Harmony with mock amazement, causing Harmony to blush and look away. "All innocent to boot," Mary Garlic said. "You know, when people are depending on you, it matters. That's the test of who you really are. That's the kind of thing that tells people if you're someone who can be counted on when things need doing, or not."

Here's the deal. I miss things. A lot goes completely over my head. In fact, I miss really big things, including, apparently, the fact that there was an expectation that *everyone* on Fieldcrest Drive help with the spring cleanup. True, they'd never had a renter before, and they hadn't thought to communicate their expectations to me, but that was beside the point. As Mary Garlic put it, I'd let them down, and I'd done so without explanation. In fact, I'd been so lazy I'd left town to avoid helping, behavior so shocking and egregious she didn't even know how to classify it.

I started to explain, but she cut me off, "Miss La Di Da. Miss California. Miss We *Pay* People to Do That Sort of Work. That may be how things are done where you come from, missy, but around here we *all* pitch in and help. We all do our share. Even the little kids. Even *Tillie*." She said this with the same amazement I felt upon hearing it.

"But I had no idea . . ."

"I don't want to hear your excuses. You were told."

"But I'm a *renter*, Mary Garlic. I misunderstood."

I must have whined a little when I said this because Mary Garlic answered with a tone I'd only heard her use when scolding the little kids, "I don't want to hear any of your damned whining. You're in the doghouse around here." She waved her hands in a sweeping gesture of utter frustration, dismissing both my bad behavior and me. "I don't want to talk to you anymore about it. I can't even look at you right now."

Once she'd left the kitchen I turned to Harmony. My face must have reflected how stricken I felt because she crossed the room to give me a hug. "I know you didn't mean anything by it, Vivi. You just didn't know."

"I *didn't* know," I repeated.

She nodded. "Some things are just assumed. If I'd thought about it, I would have let you know, but . . ." She shrugged and shook her head as if she was as bewildered by Mary Garlic's reaction as I was.

"It's not your fault, Harmony, but this place is a mystery sometimes." She sighed but said nothing.

"I'd better get out of here before Mary Garlic comes back."

"Oh, no." Harmony reached out to stop me. "Don't do that. It will only make it worse. You know how she is. She blows up and then she gets over it. It might take a while, but don't run away. And don't keep apologizing either. It'll just make you look guiltier to her."

Who *was* this girl? She smiled and gave me another hug. "I'll pour you a cup of coffee." While reaching for a mug she seamlessly changed the subject. "I want to try this new recipe I found for rosemary, gruyere, radish omelets."

"That sounds excellent," I said gratefully.

"Doesn't it!"

Through all of this, The Lord had been licking and preening himself on his cat bed in the corner by the stove, but he stopped his grooming now and looked at me with contempt, admonishing me with silent loathing to get my act together.

CHAPTER 28

A Kolache Action

Ivan seemed eager to move past what had happened in Omaha. Too eager actually. When I next saw him the Monday after our trip, he blamed himself for having pushed me, telling me he should have known I wasn't ready.

"Stop making excuses for me, Ivan," I finally said. "Just face it, I can be an obnoxious brat." He smiled, but after that he made it clear he didn't want to talk about it anymore.

It left me feeling something was unresolved. I kept waiting for an irruption, which is why in the middle of May as we were closing the Bean when Ivan said, "Vivi," with a certain cautious tone, I was on alert. "I want to talk to you about something, but I don't want to upset you."

Here it was, what I'd been waiting for all along. He hadn't forgotten, and now he was going to tell me he'd been kidding himself. Anyone who could be so rude to his friends wasn't someone he could spend time with. I had to wait for him to finish moving two chairs back into place before he said, "I've been thinking about it, and I want to organize something like . . . something inspired by the pie-actions."

I hadn't seen this coming. He rushed to clarify. "Not a pie-action exactly, but something else, to get attention for that bill, the one we've been working on since the fall, to help kids with autism. The legislature agreed to hear it, and it's coming up on the floor at the end of May."

I kept sweeping for a few seconds. When I finally glanced up, Ivan was watching me closely. I stood up straight, the broom handle in front of me. "Congratulations, Ivan. I know how hard you've worked on this. But you know I can't help you stage an action here. It makes me really uncomfortable to even think about doing something that might get the attention of the trolls."

"I get that, Vivi, but what I was thinking was that maybe my mom and her friends could make kolaches and bring them for the state senators. A kolache-action, a Nebraska version of a pie-action."

I pictured his mother and her friends, sweet, small-town Nebraska women carrying trays of kolaches into the state house. I could imagine it getting media attention. Almost in spite of myself, I said, "Ivan, that's . . . that's actually a pretty good idea."

He smiled tentatively. "You think so?"

"I sort of love the idea. Would your mom do it?"

"I know she would."

I moved the broom to one hand. "You promise you wouldn't do anything to connect it to PIE?"

"Scout's honor." He raised his hand as if taking an oath. "Can't you just see it, though?" he said, dropping his hand.

"I can. Grab a piece of paper and a pen." I put away the broom and dust pan while he went behind the counter. We sat together and sketched out the details for the kolache-action, laughing now and then as we pictured the ladies from Wilbur in their role as activists.

As fun as it had been to talk to Ivan about the kolache-action, after a week went by and he hadn't mentioned it again, I was a little relieved, thinking it had been a fun exercise and nothing more. But when I came in for my shift on the twenty-first of May, he was beaming. His mother had recruited sixteen other women, and they were coming to Lincoln in four days for an action they were calling Kolaches for Kids.

"I took the day off work, so I can go. Want to tag along?" He smiled hopefully.

"I don't want to get on any videos."

"Of course. I promise, we'll stay in the background."

It was a perfect May morning when we met in front of the state capitol an hour before the action was to begin. The cloudless sky was so saturated in blue it felt as though you could almost see the curve of the earth. The air was still, the only sound the cooing of a mourning dove.

As we climbed the steps to the big front doors, I told Ivan I'd never been inside. Another weird omission in all my earlier sightseeing.

"I bring my Life Skills students here every year for a field trip," he said as he played tour guide, showing me all the art deco details and going out of his way to point out all the pagan symbolism. We were standing on the mezzanine level, admiring the mosaic tile floor of the rotunda when Ivan's mother texted that they'd arrived and were heading into the building. I followed Ivan downstairs, both of us hanging back to watch. We couldn't see the women at all from where we stood because of the crowd of journalists surrounding them.

"Stay here," Ivan said. "I'm going to get a little closer, but I'll be back soon." I watched him lope away.

Once they were all inside, Ivan rejoined me. We followed at a distance and climbed the stairs to the viewing gallery where we watched the debate start on the floor below.

Ivan had done a good job of enlisting print and online media. Every few minutes he checked his phone and gave me a thumbs-up to indicate people were posting about the action on social media.

Not quite understanding the nature of what was happening, several of the state senators, sensing a ripple of excitement as the crowd thickened in the galleries above them, and noticing the larger than usual media presence, responded by debating even more vehemently against the bill. The legislators were mostly white men and a few white women, with one significant exception.

"That's Ernie Chambers from Omaha," Ivan whispered to me. "He's famous."

Chambers stood out not only because he was Black but because he was dressed casually in jeans and a gray T-shirt where most of the other men wore suits and ties and the women skirt suits with hose and heels. "That's his uniform," Ivan whispered again. Chambers was one of only a handful of senators in favor of the bill. The women from Wilbur had come to support them. As Chambers spoke, he quoted from what he called "the bibble," by which, I finally figured out, he meant the Bible, to make his points about doing the right thing. The other senators ignored him.

When there was a break in the debate, the women from Wilbur went into action, each of them going to the offices of the senators she'd been assigned, giving their aides a dozen kolaches, and delivering, along with the treat, a request that the senator reconsider his (or her) vote. For those few senators in favor of the bill, they delivered two dozen kolaches and thanked them for their support for the state's children, who, they reminded them, "are the future of Nebraska."

Afterward, Ivan told me Ernie Chambers, who had a longstanding rule against accepting gifts of any kind, politely refused the kolaches, but made everyone laugh by composing on the spot one of his limericks:

There once were some ladies from Wilbur
Who came to the state legislature
They brought something sweet
To make people Tweet
And all for the sake of the future.

News of the Kolaches for Kids action spread, and that evening every radio and television station in Lincoln and two of the Omaha stations aired it. The event drew condescending chuckles from some news anchors and a bit of head scratching from print journalists, but except for a few state senators who expressed outrage and consternation, there was no overt criticism. No one in mainstream media quite knew what to make of it, but social media loved it. Although the bill didn't pass for days afterward, social media across the state buzzed about it.

CHAPTER 29

Chuck's Not-So-Funny Tales
of Sexual Humiliation

As soon as school was out, the teenagers on Fieldcrest started working double-time to finish the script and the score for *My Ántonia, the Musical.* I stopped by Tillie's house late one windy Friday night to help her cut fabric for the costumes she'd designed, some of them repurposed from the previous year's homesteader outfits. Once we'd finished, Tillie asked me to stay for iced tea. We were sitting in the living room listening to the kids working upstairs. She'd just told me how much she liked to hear all them working together when we were interrupted by a sharp knock at the front door.

"Uh oh," Tillie said. I followed her eyes to the clock on the mantel: 10:15. "That'll be Bridget. The kids missed their 10:00 curfew." She chuckled as she got up to answer the door and tossed over her shoulder in a loud whisper, "If it weren't for the musical, she wouldn't be caught dead coming here." For some reason I was surprised she knew about Bridget's disapproval of her family, mistaking her customary spaciness for obliviousness.

Before Tillie reached the door, I watched through the windows as Mr. Shipley jumped on Bridget and rested his front paws on her shoulders. He was a large dog, and on his back legs he was almost Bridget's height. "Tillie! Mary Garlic!" Bridget shouted. "Come get this creature off me."

Tillie collared Mr. Shipley, and I heard her say, "You know, Mr. Shipley wouldn't hurt you, Bridget. He just can't resist a beautiful woman."

Bridget wasn't amused. "Where are my kids?"

Tillie gestured upstairs where we heard Harmony sing a few bars. We couldn't make out the words, but whatever they were made all of them erupt in laughter. By then I'd come out to the hallway to greet Bridget, but when I saw her unsmiling face, I stayed quiet. "They were supposed to have been home fifteen minutes ago."

"Yep. We all lost track of time. I'll get them for you." Tillie opened the door wider to let her in. "Come inside and wait."

"No thank you, Tillie. Just send them home immediately."

We watched Bridget leave before Tillie went to the bottom of the stairs and called up that it was after 10:00. We heard a frantic shuffling before Roger and Sophie clattered down the stairs and out the door. Moss and Harmony followed them downstairs, and all of us watched them sprint toward home.

"She must make life hell for those kids," Tillie said, almost under her breath.

Moss looked at her sharply. "It's not *her*."

Later that night, as I was getting into bed, I heard the wind come up. It howled in the trees, and a branch on the big maple tapped urgently on the roof. A few minutes later, I heard a metallic rapping against the front of the house and guessed the wind had knocked a gutter loose. I couldn't sleep with what sounded like a drum line on the cottage and thought instead about Moss's cryptic remark earlier that night.

Only a month earlier I'd been invited to one of the Clarks' patio parties for the first time. They'd been slow to invite me, and I suspected I was being punished a little for what had happened with Bill in March.

They were good hosts: festive lights around the pool, sultry jazz over the outdoor speakers, cocktails, hors d'oeuvres, good food from the grill, everything perfect really. I'd been cautious about showing too much affection toward Bill, but as soon as he saw me, he grabbed his stuffed duck and wagged his tail wildly, his rear end swinging from side to side. Seeing this, Bridget said, "He won't let anyone touch that stupid duck you gave him." And while she'd said it dismissively, I'd felt myself flush with happiness.

That was the first time I heard Chuck's legendary stories. Bridget had been right; they *were* the funniest stories I'd ever heard. In fact, I've never laughed so hard in my life. It was painful laughing like that. The other guests seemed to feel the same way. We kept saying things like, "Chuck, I'm dying, man. Give us a break." We begged him to stop. "You're killing us," we said. It was terrible; no one could resist it. The next morning my whole body ached because I'd laughed so hard.

Chuck had kept us enthralled, one story quickly following another. He was a kind of comic genius, a comedy machine, and it's impossible to reproduce the effect. As they say, it's all in the timing, and in the deadpan delivery. The first time I heard his stories I couldn't take my eyes off him. It was like falling down a rabbit hole, his voice leading me, controlling me, pulling me along while everything else disappeared.

While I'd been listening, I couldn't take seriously his tale about the troubled eleven-year-old boy, the little sadist, who had tormented and tortured Chuck for a year at his boarding school in Africa when Chuck was nine. Even as I heard the horrifying details of the abuse, registered how disturbing it was and how powerless Chuck had been to stop it, I couldn't think of it as anything other than Chuck's hilarious past.

Not until the next day when I recalled the details, no longer diverted by that insane laughter, did I grow uneasy. The morning after that first party, I'd felt nauseated as I thought about what had happened to Chuck. The feckless adults in his stories had been as manipulated by that sick boy as Chuck had been, enablers of a malevolent culture of abuse.

I couldn't hear the gutter hitting against the front of the house and guessed it had come down. I'd have to talk to Mary Garlic about getting it fixed. I wondered what my grandma, the sanest adult I'd ever known, would have advised Chuck when he was a boy? I remembered how she'd listened to me when I was a kid. She'd never condescended or dismissed me.

She was kind but firm. She didn't shirk from the truth or pretend everything was all right when it wasn't. A pragmatist, she'd spelled out the facts as they were. She believed in facing reality head on but didn't argue with my perception. She acknowledged my concerns at the same time she wouldn't indulge my self-pity. Every summer I asked if I could come live with her, and every summer she said the same thing, "You have to go home to your mother. She's your mother." I'd add another story of my mother's wrongdoing as evidence I should stay, but Grandma only shook her head. She'd say something like, "That was wrong—bad—rotten—unlucky"—whatever characterized my complaint. "But what are you going to do about it?" she'd ask, making me look at myself, take responsibility for my own behavior, my own decisions, my own choices. And then she'd asked me to think about who or what helped? "What do you need to do next?" she'd ask. Did I need to apologize? Speak up? Remove myself? Denounce something? Be unafraid? Confront? Or simply move on?

When I was a kid, her questions made me furious. I think now she'd be accused of blaming the victim, but I can hear her saying in response to that, "Phooey!" She believed in knowing your enemy, and knowing your own power (for good or ill), your own potential (for beauty or for dishonor), and your own ability to act (to correct action or to redirect it). "You can't change other people," she'd say. "You can only change yourself and try to make the world better."

She'd been trying to teach me how to think, how to grow up. Why hadn't I remembered any of her advice this past year? I hadn't occurred to me to employ any of her lessons when I'd been dealing with Kylie, let alone Bridget. Now, though, thinking about Chuck's ordeal, I questioned the limits of her tough love. I couldn't see what Chuck could have done in his situation, except to try to get help from the adults in charge. And what adult, even the best-intentioned adult, hearing his outlandish stories involving such elaborate, sick abuse, wouldn't maybe doubt him? Hadn't I, more than once, in the midst of laughing my ass off at his stories, thought to myself, "He has to be making this up?" Hadn't I, the next day sometimes questioned Chuck's mental health? Not seeing him necessarily as the victim but somehow the perpetrator in those revolting stories? Wasn't I complicit in some way by questioning the veracity of his outlandish accusations? I argued back and forth with myself as I lay awake that night. Didn't we have to question accusers, too, since not everyone who claims to be a victim is in fact a victim? I decided this had to be why Chuck told his stories the way he did. Humor was the only way he could get anyone to listen.

I felt sure Chuck had been abused exactly the way he claimed, but I wondered if maybe he hadn't learned a few things from his tormenter. At the most recent party I'd attended at their house only a few days before this, I resisted getting caught up in the hypnotic pull of Chuck's stories by focusing on Bridget instead. I saw she was immune to his stories. She didn't once smile, let alone laugh, during his routine. As soon as he started up, she busied herself cleaning up, but her movements were restrained. Even though she appeared to ignore him, she was keenly aware of Chuck, working hard not to betray any emotion, just as she had the night of the storm, because Chuck was watching her the whole time. No matter where she was his eyes were locked on her.

CHAPTER 30

A Lady Lost

The next morning I had to fight a hot wind to move the gutter that had fallen in the night. The sky was a dusty gray and the wind blew all day. Late afternoon, as I was leaving the grocery store, there was a brief lull before the wind shifted and grew cold; dark clouds churned overhead. I'd barely finished loading my bags into the back of the car when I heard a loud crack of thunder close by followed immediately by a long streak of lightning. In seconds rain fell, big, plopping drops. I made it into the car just as the storm broke. The wind seemed to come from all directions, and together with a heavy rain buffeted the car as I drove slowly toward home barely able to see the road. I could hardly see to make the left turn on Forty-Eighth Street. Water gushed against the curbs flooding the streets. I squinted to see bushes and trees thrashing. I glimpsed someone walking on the sidewalk, drenched and bent into the wind. I was feeling sorry for her until I recognized it was Audra. She must have gotten caught in the storm as she was coming home from visiting Jim.

I honked to get her attention and pulled over to the curb. Seconds later, she climbed into the passenger seat. Like everyone, she'd been unprepared, dressed for summer. She was shivering with the cold and could hardly speak. I cranked up the car's heater for her. She was still shivering when we reached her house and she invited me to come inside.

The cold outside had made her house chilly enough I asked if I could start a fire as Audra went to change into dry clothes. Later, as we sat together drinking hot tea, we reminisced about all the gloomy days we'd spent together in front of her fire that fall and winter. I'd spent a lot of warm June days with my grandma when I was a kid, so Audra hadn't needed to tell me this was a highly unusual situation.

Jim's condition had continued to deteriorate, and she told me again how horrible it was that he couldn't communicate with her. As long as he'd been able to acknowledge her, she'd felt like she was dealing with a living man, but now, his frozen face, his perpetual stare—she shuddered as she told me this—it felt like he was judging her "even more than usual." To hide her emotion, she looked down and pretended to be preoccupied with the inside of her tea mug, before she recovered herself and sat up straight. "I've had plenty of time to adjust to this. Jim would be very upset that I haven't done more to prepare for the inevitable. I just haven't known how to move ahead." She looked toward the windows overlooking her backyard. Because of the rain, the only thing we could see were the frenzied trees. I thought about her cactus garden, the way I'd dismissed it that first day, and how much I now appreciated it.

"Right now what's motivating me are growing things," she said. "I just want to be around living things. I crave it the way someone who's starving craves food." She was quiet for a long time. I gave her time to gather her thoughts. She wasn't glib or quick. Conversations with her sometimes required patience. "Today," she finally said, "when I was visiting Jim, I couldn't take it anymore." She looked down briefly. "When I left, I twisted his big toe. Hard. I don't know what got into me. I guess I just wanted some kind of response, but, Vivi, there was nothing." She said this with a look of horror. "Some days . . . I'm just so tired. I want to be done with it, but being mad at Jim isn't going to change anything. I've decided I have to start dealing with reality. First thing tomorrow I'm calling the crematorium and our attorney. I've put it off long enough."

I didn't like it when Audra talked about Jim. It made me uncomfortable to talk about things like funerals and death and cremation. My one glimpse of him in October had been enough for me, and I didn't like to think about him. Usually, when she talked about him, I just listened, but now I said, "That must have been a hard decision for you."

"Oddly, no. Putting it off has been exhausting. I feel relieved now."

It didn't take much for her to persuade me to stay for dinner. She'd made a puttanesca the day before and asked if I'd mind sharing the leftovers. I set the table and opened a bottle of wine while she reheated the pasta. We listened to the rain beat against the windows as we ate. At one point she said as if stating a fact, "You'll stay the night." That winter, I'd often spent the night at her house after one of our Tuesday or Thursday dinners. Until I got to know her, I hadn't appreciated how unusual it was for her to bring me into her life the way she had. She was a private person. Shy. She'd told me before how she didn't like the fancy dinners and cocktail parties she'd had to host when Jim was working. She was at her best one on one in this sort of spontaneous situation.

Audra wasn't much of a drinker, so she surprised me that night when after dinner she opened a bottle of Jim's bourbon. She seemed to want to commemorate her new resolve to face the future. The bourbon burned my throat as it went down. It clearly affected Audra, too, as she coughed a few times. Despite this, we each had a second glass. The summer storm seemed to have shaken us out of our routine. I say this, to explain that things felt different that night.

We weren't drunk, I don't think, but we were tipsy. We were definitely relaxed as we sat up later than usual talking. Her voice changed. She assumed a dialect I'd never heard her use before. She told me a story about how as a little girl she'd had a speech impediment, and the school had assigned her a speech therapist, Mrs. Parrish. "Imagine a little tiny girl like me from a great big family living out in the boondocks, getting that sort of special attention from a grown-up twice a week!" Audra said. "She was such a nice woman and she took a liking to me."

"Mrs. Parrish told me I could be anything I wanted, that I could go to college and become somebody." Audra looked at me wide-eyed when she said this, as if it still amazed her. "Even then I knew that wasn't true what Mrs. Parrish was saying. My family couldn't afford to send me to college. Even as a child I knew things weren't equal between people, but she'd put an idea into my head, and from then on I set my sights further. I worked hard in school, and of all things, I got a scholarship to the university."

She paused and smiled to herself, still pleased with the memory of her achievement. Almost immediately, though, her expression darkened. "Even with Jim nosing around and wanting to marry me when I was just a girl, just a kid without any wherewithal at all, in spite of that, I didn't lose sight of my goal to finish my degree, not for a while anyway."

Her voice brightened a little artificially as she went on to tell me how much she owed Mrs. Parrish, and I was struck by the falseness of her forced cheerfulness, especially after the terseness in her voice as she'd mentioned Jim's pursuit of her. In previous versions of that story, she hadn't described herself in quite the way she did that night, as the victim of a predatory man.

She went on to tell me about how after they left Fayetteville, they'd moved to where Jim was a dean at a small college. She was working as a bookkeeper at a hardware store down the street from where they lived. "Every morning on my walk to work and every evening on my walk back home, the old Italian man who lived on the second floor of one of the triple-deckers along our street tapped on his window as I walked by and blew me a kiss. Of course, I blew a kiss back to him. He did this with all the women who walked on that street and whose names he'd learned on the nice summer days when he could maneuver his wheelchair onto his front porch."

She smiled at the memory. "Such a simple gesture, but it guaranteed Tony would be blown kisses every day through the winter, and winters can be very long in Boston. So smart of him, don't you think?

So healthy. So life-affirming. He was grabbing life, finding a way to be engaged in spite of his confinement. I've thought about that many times since then. It makes me mad at myself for being so cowed always, so retiring and fearful all these years." I wasn't surprised when she blamed Jim for her caution and repeated what she'd told me before that "Jim always emphasized to me before one of our parties that these were his colleagues, not our friends, and that I should 'comport myself with care.' I was not to talk about personal things. No jokes. No sarcasm." As she said this, she flashed one of her beautiful smiles at me. "It's hard to believe now, but at some point, earlier in my life, I must have been capable of such things for him to have made such a show of cautioning me against them." She laughed, but I thought it sounded a little bitter.

She changed the subject then, and we talked about the theme for this summer's musical. We were both looking forward to it. She hadn't known until then that the inspiration for this year's show had grown out of Ivan's boredom while waiting for me to recover from the flu.

She smiled. "Do you know, when Moss and Harmony were toddlers they used to walk over to our door and leave little offerings for us: a frog in a box, a wilted flower, a few feathers, a caterpillar, treasures they'd found, you know. I never discouraged their visits, but it irritated Jim their bringing 'junk' onto our front steps. He thought it was wrong that they were allowed to trespass on our property. I've always wondered if maybe Mary Garlic . . . it wouldn't have been Tillie . . . didn't overhear Jim one day complaining about it—which he did loudly every time he found one of those offerings—and made them stop bothering us." She looked at me. "It's always made me sad to think that."

The room had gotten chilly, and she stood to turn up the fire, "That's better," she said, before sitting down again. "Roger and Sophie were a little older when the Clarks moved into the neighborhood. They were never allowed to roam the way Tillie's kids were. Bridget runs a tight ship over there." The sarcasm in her voice as she said this alerted me. Audra had her complaints about the neighbors, but she was never one for gossip. Now, though, she'd made no effort to hide the bite in her remark, and she went on to speculate. "I can't say if that's a happy family or a sad family. It's those kids that give me pause. They're so polite. Too polite if you ask me. But I'm sure you've noticed that." I didn't say anything, embarrassed all over again about what had happened with Bill that winter. "They don't seem to have any friends, apart from Moss and Harmony, which puzzles me since Bridget and Chuck are so social." She paused for a beat longer than expected before adding, "The only kid I see regularly at Bridget's is Moss." And again, I heard the edge beneath her words. The conversation had begun to feel dangerous.

I didn't have to wait long before she asked outright, "Have you noticed anything *funny* next door?" I was tempted for a second to quip, *I've heard Chuck's stories*, as a way to avoid an uncomfortable conversation, but something in Audra's tone cautioned me not to make light of it.

"That depends on what you mean by funny."

She fidgeted slightly before she abruptly stood up to clear our plates. "Oh, never mind."

After our long evening of confiding, it seemed odd that she'd stop now when she so clearly had something on her mind. "Audra, what's going on?" She was in the kitchen rinsing dishes and appeared not to have heard me, so I repeated it, "Audra, tell me what's going on."

She turned off the water but stayed at the sink for a few seconds before she finally stacked the dishes on the counter and came back to the living room where she poured both of us another glass of bourbon before she sat down. "I shouldn't be saying anything. I'm not clear about my motives here." She stared into the fire, as if to take her own measure, when for some reason, maybe still thinking about Chuck, I said, "If you've seen something . . . is someone being hurt?"

"No, it's nothing like that. I'm sure it's nothing. I'm just . . . I've probably misunderstood. I shouldn't speculate."

For several minutes we watched the fire in silence, before I surprised myself by asking, "Does Moss have anything to do with this?"

Her eyes opened wide. "How did you know?"

"I don't." I paused and shrugged. "It's a lot of things."

"What do you mean?"

"There's something that's bothered me since last summer. A weird vibe, that's all." I shrugged again. "It was just a feeling, one of those things you sense but you can't say for sure." And I went on to tell her about the bonfire after the Break-a-Leg party, how Bridget had been there. And Moss. The bottle of Jim Beam.

While she was listening, Audra had been leaning forward. She caught herself now and sat back against the couch cushions. She shook her head. "That's not all, though, is it? What else?"

"It was Bridget . . . The way she was acting. A little too familiar—with Moss. And Moss seemed . . . I don't know, disrespectful isn't the right word, but the way he was teasing . . . it felt off. It made me uncomfortable."

"Were Bridget's kids there?"

"No, but I remember thinking they'd be dying of embarrassment if they had been."

Audra shifted before saying with finality, "I don't want to start rumors."

"You're right. Bridget was just having a little fun, drinking around a campfire. Not a big deal."

When Audra stood up again, I joined her to help clean the kitchen. When we'd finished, she asked if I wanted something for dessert?

"No. I should probably get to bed."

"Are you sure you won't have a brownie? I made a pan last night, and I can heat it in the microwave."

"I don't want to trouble you, Audra."

She laughed. "Microwaving a brownie?" She paused. "How nice it is to spend this dreary, stormy night with you, Vivi. I'm sorry for talking so much, burdening you with my issues, but it felt good to get some things off my chest." And that's how she persuaded me (I make it sound like I had no agency in the matter) to stay up just a little while longer that night.

We sat at the kitchen island to eat our brownies. From the wide panorama of her front windows, we saw the lights on the Clarks' patio. Amazingly, even in this storm, they were entertaining guests. I could make out dark forms milling around in their kitchen, while outside, in the gloom, Chuck stood at the grill, holding a flashlight. He'd moved the sun umbrella on their patio over the grill to keep the rain off. I knew how inside the house Bridget would be laughing and talking, refilling glasses, flirting, making everyone feel comfortable. Did I envy her social skills? Did Audra and I both perhaps take consolation for the limitations of our own personalities by suspecting something unseemly about her?

I knew the neighbors had complaints with one another, but I'd wisely avoided gossiping with any of them. I hadn't told Audra about what happened with Bill in March, embarrassed by my own behavior, of course, but also knowing Audra wouldn't want to be involved in my spat with another neighbor. What I had to admit to myself that night, though, was the spiteful, irrational resentment I still felt toward Bridget. Maybe it was true what my mother always said, that "we can never forgive the people we've wronged the most."

Audra interrupted my thoughts then. "I didn't really *see* anything." She paused for a second, "But more than once last summer I *heard* them—Bridget and Moss—while her kids were away at camp and Chuck was traveling for work. You know yourself; it's impossible for me not to see Bridget's yard from my house. My windows," she gestured toward them, "look right onto her patio. Moss has been going over to swim with her for years now, so it's no big deal, but last summer, something changed. They were laughing and carrying on so much it attracted my attention, but then things would get quiet, and I'd see them going into the house together and not coming out again for a long time. Oh, I had a bad feeling about it, Vivi, a strong suspicion.

It went on like that for several weeks. I told myself to mind my own business, and I did. But now . . . well, now that she's back in the pool again . . . I saw Moss over there last week when Chuck and the kids were gone, and it happened again just like last year."

I knew as soon as she said this, that it was Bridget Moss had been texting in April. His winter tan wasn't a holdover from the previous summer. They'd been going to the tanning bed together. I saw it all as clear as day.

Audra seemed disgusted, whether with herself or with them I wasn't sure. "It's just circumstantial, but I'm not blind." And then she backpedaled. "I'm sure it's my overactive imagination. Besides, Moss isn't a kid anymore. You know yourself he and Harmony turned nineteen this spring."

I remembered Audra's earlier description of herself as "just a girl" and said now, "Still, Bridget shouldn't be taking advantage that way. It has to be confusing for a boy—a young man—like Moss."

Audra looked at me. "I've struggled with this. I've wondered if I should have confronted Bridget last summer? If maybe I should have warned Tillie, but I didn't want Mary Garlic to get riled up about it."

"Oh, Audra," I said, not sure myself what I meant by this exclamation.

"I don't want to accuse, but . . ."

"But it doesn't look good," I finished for her.

"No. It does not." She smiled sadly. "I'll bet you've never lived in a small town, have you, Vivi?"

I shook my head, not wanting to get into the story of my vagabond past, and wondering vaguely where she was going with this.

"Well, there's an interesting thing about small towns. Everyone knows everything about everyone. And that's no exaggeration. They know exactly how much money you have and how much you owe. They know everything you've ever done in your life, both the good things and the things you're ashamed of. Not only that, they know all about your family as far back as they can go. Small towns pass down stories about one another from generation to generation. They know if your great grandfather was suspected of robbing a house when he was young, and they know if your mother was engaged to another man before he broke it off with her, and the judgment about all of those things carries on for years."

She looked at me to emphasize this next point. "And no one, not a single person, will ever say anything about it. It's just understood. Always there. And everything you do in your life they understand through your past. You can't escape it. There's no privacy, and the only way it works is that everyone pretends none of it exists. It's a kind of open lie. A code of discretion that allows everyone to pretend they have privacy. It's deeply strange now as I think about it, but it's how a neighborhood like ours works too. The truth is, I'm mad at Bridget right now for being indiscrete, putting me in this terrible position of having to break the code and say out loud what should remain unspoken."

I thought about Tillie's attic workshop and its perfect view of Bridget's pool. While it was possible Tillie hadn't noticed anything, living in her head the way she did, I thought it was just as likely she did know and didn't care. She didn't share Audra's small-town version of discretion, but the world worked differently for Tillie. She'd blithely told me one day how she'd lost her virginity when she was fourteen on a beach in southern France with a boy she didn't know. It was the only time I ever saw Mary Garlic take serious offense at something Tillie said. "It's all been wonderful for you, hasn't it, Tillie?" she said, her voice dripping with sarcasm. "Well, life isn't quite as special for some of us, like how I lost my virginity when my fuckhead uncle Johnny raped me." I'd looked quickly at the little kids who were in the room with us that day. They hadn't seemed the least bit disturbed. I guessed they'd heard it all before.

Maybe it was because of this memory, I said, "Shouldn't we be thinking about Moss."

"I don't see why?" Audra said, and I heard impatience in her voice. "It's unseemly, but it isn't illegal. I don't think Moss is being abused. If anything, he's the instigator."

She clearly wanted to end the conversation, but since she'd poured each of us yet another glass of bourbon, we stayed where we were, both of us taking a sip, and another and yet another, until somehow over the course of finishing a fourth glass, we found ourselves on another side of the argument. Would our feelings be so ambiguous, we wondered, if it was Chuck who was possibly involved with Harmony? Both of us reacted viscerally to our hypothetical and later questioned ourselves.

Until then, I'd felt pleasantly intoxicated, but now, with the mention of Chuck I thought about all of his guns. Something cold clutched my heart, and I felt very sober, unable to get out of my mind a macabre image of Bridget and Moss floating in the pool, the water red with their blood, reminding me of the gruesome scene in *O Pioneers!* after Frank Shabata shoots Marie and Emil under the mulberry trees.

I whispered, "The guns," and Audra looked at me in alarm.

She swallowed hard and shook her head. "We can't say anything about this to anyone, Vivi. We absolutely cannot. We have to keep it to ourselves." After a pause, she added, "Please, Vivi. We have to be discrete. I made things worse talking about Jim the way I did earlier. You have to understand, please, I'm angry with him right now. It isn't rational what I'm feeling. And what I told you before isn't the whole story of our relationship; it's just how I'm feeling right now. I'm sad. I'm grieving."

I knew this was true, but yet, perversely, I felt myself dig in. Clearly, I was more drunk than I thought because for a few minutes that night, I believed the only way to prevent the violent scene I'd imagined was to tell Tillie and Mary Garlic what had been happening right under their noses. I watched Audra's face grow ashen as I said this. She kept trying to reason with me, afraid of her inability to control the situation, afraid most of all of me up on my high horse.

CHAPTER 31

My Mortal Enemies

The temperatures stayed lower than normal into June. The unseason-ably cool days a strange reversal from the stifling heat of the previous summer. We all laughed about having to wear sweaters to watch the fireworks Chuck and Roger set off on the Fourth. It wasn't long after the Fourth that I began to feel a different kind of chill. I began to feel subtly excluded. Conversations seemed to stop when I joined them. Audra was still friendly but a bit guarded. I caught Mary Garlic watching me intently before turning away when I noticed.

On the sixth, after a rehearsal of the Attic Theater, Harmony knocked on the door of the cottage. As soon as I saw her face I knew something was very wrong.

"Can I come in for a few minutes, Vivi?"

"Of course."

She turned down my offer of something to drink but joined me at the kitchen table. She took a deep breath. "I feel like I need to tell you something."

I had a terrible foreboding, a sudden salty, metallic taste in my mouth made me think I might vomit. "Go on."

"You know how boys are," she said. "Roger and Moss."

I shook my head, confused about where this was going. "What?"

She pulled her sweater closer. "Roger had this picture of you and Bill on the bed," I felt myself blush as she said this. "He sent it to

Moss. A few months ago. And they started creating memes." She pursed her lips slightly. "They have this whole paracosm about you and Bill being in love." I winced. "It's just silly stuff," she said and shook her head. "Nobody takes it seriously. You know those two. They think everything is funny. But then a couple weeks ago Moss sent one of the memes to Bridget, and since then, well, it's sort of gotten out of control."

"What do you mean?"

"Oh, Bridget started saying things about you being irresponsible when you were housesitting for them." I felt my stomach drop when she said this. "And then MG, well you know how MG is, she got started complaining about how you were rich." She blushed before going on, "But you still took money from her every week to help with the little kids."

"But, Harmony! I didn't want to take that money. I thought she'd be insulted if I didn't."

"And you're right. She would have been."

"But this makes no sense."

Harmony smiled a little ruefully. "MG is . . . she isn't always . . . she has her own ways of thinking about things."

I shifted in my chair, suddenly angry with this hypocrisy. Harmony made a pleading gesture. "It isn't fair," I said.

"I know, Vivi."

"And the others?"

"Audra loves you. You know that. She's worried that maybe you might be unhappy here."

This stung too, knowing Audra had been involved, talking behind my back this way, and telling a lie to cover for herself. I'd regretted immediately the way I'd behaved at her house in June, but I thought she knew that without my having to reassure her I wouldn't be a selfish, indiscrete shit. And here all this time she must have been terrified I'd spout off and destroy the finely calibrated peace on Fieldcrest Drive.

"And Ivan? Is Ivan involved in this too?"

Harmony's eyes pleaded with me again to try to understand. She looked down at her hands. "He's been defending you for a while now, asking Roger and Moss to tone it down."

"A while? He's known for a while?" I blinked away the tears I felt gather in my eyes. Ivan had known about this and hadn't told me? But why? And then I thought about the oafish way I'd behaved in Omaha and guessed he probably hadn't wanted to risk my overreaction.

"I don't know what to say, Vivi."

I interrupted her then. "Is Tillie involved too?"

She rolled her eyes a little. "Oh, you know Til. She couldn't care less."

"And you? What about you, Harmony?"

"It's been me and Ivan trying to get everybody else to settle down."

How bad must things have gotten that she felt she needed to come here to warn me? "So, why are you telling me this now? What's the worst that can happen, Harmony? I'm not a criminal."

"I know that, Vivi, but . . ."

I sighed and sat back against the kitchen chair.

Harmony reached across the table toward me. "Everything'll be okay, Vivi. It's just a misunderstanding, that's all." But as she said this I saw a sliver of doubt in her eyes, and it shook my confidence. "I think the problem is that we've accepted you, we all like you, but we don't really know you that well. And now there are questions."

I remembered Tillie's cryptic remark the day we'd stood together looking out the window of her attic about how "no life bears scrutiny."

I thought about Bridget and the boys texting back and forth, joking for weeks at my expense. The irony didn't escape me: while I'd been distracted by my suspicions about Bridget and Moss, they'd been using the same measure against me. I knew Harmony hadn't told me everything. I wondered how wildly they'd all speculated about why I'd really come to Nebraska. Once they'd started to doubt me, how easy it must have been to suspect me of all sorts of things. It wouldn't have taken long for them to fixate on my many oddities, especially my being de-gridded, to support an accumulation of possibilities, one more sordid than the next.

As if she'd read my mind, Harmony said, "I tried, Vivi. I kept telling everyone they should talk to you rather than making up things, but . . ."

"You're a true friend, Harmony. Thank you."

That evening, Ivan stopped by. He brought his customary six-pack of Pabst, and we sat together on the little back patio of the cottage. The evening was cool enough I'd brought out a blanket.

"Harmony told me she came to talk to you earlier today." I nodded. Knowing me the way he did, he guessed what I'd been planning. "I don't want you to leave, Vivi." He looked at me for a few seconds. "I want you to stay and work this out. If you go back before this gets resolved, it'll hang over you. Your neighbors here . . . there've been some hiccups in the past few weeks that have made them wonder about you. You can't blame them for that. I could only defend you so much. I didn't think you'd want me to tell them why you're here. That isn't my story to tell."

Ivan seemed confused when I didn't respond but I told this story instead: "There was this homeless guy that lived on a street near my condo in Echo Park. He was always angry; he'd hit himself really hard in the head all the time. The first time I saw it, I was so upset I told him to stop, but after a while I got used to seeing him beat himself up every day." I looked up to gauge Ivan's reaction to this. He was listening, waiting for me to go on. "Well, that's how I felt this afternoon after Harmony left. I felt like that homeless guy. I was so mad at myself I wanted to punch my own head." I looked at him again, and he met my glance. "I've fucked up so much this year, Ivan, on top of fucking up in California, it just felt like too much."

"Vivi, you didn't fuck up here or in California."

"I did, though. I really messed up. Not the trolls. They're another category and don't count here. But with Kylie and with the board. I royally screwed that up. It was stupid and immature, but I could find a way to excuse myself until here I am doing it over again, and I have to acknowledge a deep, repetitive compulsion. It's like something got short-circuited in my brain after the trolls, and I keep looking for ways to punish myself for it."

Ivan didn't say anything. Instead, we listened as a screech owl whinnied in one of the trees on the creek. Fireflies lifted into the air. A full moon cast the shadow of the cottage across us.

"Promise me at the very least you won't leave without saying goodbye to me, Vivi."

"I promise."

CHAPTER 32

Pies4Peace

For the next couple of days I avoided everyone on the private way, hearing all the while the voice of Myra Henshaw, Cather's most bitter character, saying, "It's all very well to tell us to forgive our enemies; our enemies can never hurt us very much. But oh, what about forgiving our friends? . . . that's where the rub comes!" Each time I thought about leaving, though, I remembered what Ivan had said. He was right. This wasn't how I wanted the year to end.

Still, how do you forgive friends who betray you? I understood the neighbors had complaints with me, but this? It felt over the top in some way. What had started as a teasing little game had somehow grown into outright suspicion. And I guessed now that once Mary Garlic got involved, things escalated quickly. I remembered how Tillie once described Mary Garlic as the German shepherd at the door of their house. She was right. What'd I'd interpreted as porous boundaries—the unlocked doors, their welcoming demeanor—distracted from the fact that they weren't a family that embraced just anyone. Mary Garlic didn't merely suspect the worst about people, she assumed it.

I hadn't appreciated the rarity of her trust, the ways I'd been allowed access to their family. Of all the neighbors, Mary Garlic would be the most disappointed in herself for letting down her guard. She'd always seemed a little clownish to me. Did I feel this way because she was so transparent about her worries for the family? Was it because she couldn't help but be exactly who she was? Because, out of all of us, Mary Garlic wasn't a liar, ever, and wasn't afraid to act on her beliefs, to be unashamedly, unapologetically on the side of love for Tillie and the kids. She was both feet in, heart fully on her sleeve.

Why had I been so secretive with the neighbors about what had happened in California? By now, it had shrunk in significance.

It took me longer than it should have to know what I needed to do, but once I decided, I didn't hesitate. I went to the closet where I'd stowed my grandma's pie tins and rolling pin in August. Cather had started out as my guide to understanding Nebraska, but I'd since made her a sort of coach for navigating life. I summoned her full-on embrace of life and her regard for order as I grappled with my unruly, troubled self that day. I channeled my grandma. I could hear her telling me I needed to wake up. I needed to believe—to *know*—I had choices. What did I want? My impulse I saw now, like my mother's, was to disrupt rather than to preserve. It was a deeply pleasurable habit to stand at a distance and observe, to criticize and not participate in the culture of a new school, or a new neighborhood, not to have to maintain friendships.

I'd bake three pies: Grandma's go-to pie, an old-fashioned lemon meringue, the same pie that in a roundabout way launched PIE all those years ago; a Mexican chocolate pie with a hint of red pepper and cinnamon inside a hazelnut crust; and I'd show off a little and make a peach pie with a lattice crust.

Only after I'd returned from the grocery store with all the ingredients I needed to start baking, did I think about how I'd bring all the women in the neighborhood together. I looked around my little cottage. There wasn't room at the table to seat all of them. And not enough chairs. I'd have to buy more plates and silverware.

Later, Audra couldn't hide her hesitation as she answered the door. She'd been avoiding me, too, and when I said, "I have something important I need to say to all of you," I saw the wariness in her eyes. "It's not about Bridget," I said. She still seemed hesitant, but she agreed to invite the neighbors for an afternoon get-together.

I baked all day on Saturday—the cottage filled with the comforting smell of buttery piecrust, fruit and sugar and chocolate—and with me I felt the presence of all my familiars: Grandma, of course, so close it seemed she was leaning over my shoulder noting along with me how the old Hotpoint oven had a tendency to bake a little unevenly; Willa, watching with approval from a chair at the kitchen table, believing as she did that food was among the most powerful of civilizing agents; and the gardener—my beloved, mysterious gardener—watching with a benign smile over everything, the way I'd imagined him all these months in his green tweed coat, dark pants, and a brown riding cap.

I'd enlisted Ivan to help me carry the pies up to Audra's house that Sunday afternoon, and as we started out the tall fescue dipped and swayed in the breeze seeming to usher us up the bluestone steps. Audra met us at the door.

"Did you make all of these, Gigi?" Tillie asked as Audra handed her the pie I was carrying.

"I did."

Audra had gone to a lot of trouble. She'd opened the dining room table and set it with her best dishes. She'd laid out a crisp white tablecloth and freshly ironed linen napkins. She'd made coffee and heated water for tea. In the past I would have dismissed it all as overly fussy, but now it all seemed so civilized, so intentional.

After Ivan left, as Audra was filling our cups, Mary Garlic asked, "So what's the occasion? Is it your birthday, or something, Vivi? Cause if it is it'd have been nice to . . ."

"No, it's not my birthday." I laughed. "I come in peace bearing pies." They laughed along, but they were clearly confused. But the pies did their work. They were impressed by them. Everyone wanted to try a small slice of each.

I knew if I waited too long, I'd lose my courage, so once Audra and I had served everyone, I said, "I owe all of you an apology."

Bridget looked up from her plate with a quizzical expression. "What are you talking about? These pies are amazing!"

I laughed. "Well, thank you. I'm glad you like them. But that isn't what I meant. I meant that I've sort of taken some things for granted this past year. I never really thanked all of you for the way you saved me not once but twice, during the storm and while I was sick." Audra shook her head dismissively, as if to say that's what good neighbors do, but I went on, "No, hear me out. I didn't reciprocate at Christmas when all of you gave me such beautiful gifts. I didn't get it that I was expected to help with the spring clean-up. I . . . well . . ." I glanced at Bridget but didn't elaborate. "I haven't always understood or respected the rules. I apologize for everything, for being thoughtless, careless, indiscrete, secretive." I'd started to ramble a bit, and the more I talked the quieter all of them became until I noticed they'd all stopped eating and were staring at me.

Finally, Mary Garlic broke the silence, "Geez, this is the weirdest thing I've ever been to," which made everyone laugh.

"Vivi, I don't understand what you're talking about," Bridget said.

"Maybe apology isn't the right word. What I really want to say is that I owe all of you an explanation about why I'm here." When I said this I felt a frisson of some unspoken emotion move around the table.

The story poured out, and as I talked I saw it the way Mary Garlic might: privileged white girl starts a successful business, things go wrong, and she loses her best friend; bad people hurt her, she has a breakdown and makes bad decisions.

When I finally finished talking, they were all quiet. They looked down at their plates as if thinking about what I'd said but not certain how to deliver a verdict. Once again, it was Mary Garlic who broke the ice. She held up her plate. "Well, whatever. Could I have another round of those peace pies, peaceful pies, whatever the hell they are?"

She continued to make silly, off-hand remarks while I served everyone seconds, getting the biggest laugh when she called the pie-actions, pie-infractions. We were all still laughing at this when Audra excused herself to answer the phone. We continued to laugh as we watched her write something on a notepad. We couldn't hear what she was saying, but we noticed when she stopped writing mid-motion. We looked at her, a silhouette in front of the big windows, standing very still behind her kitchen island. We stopped laughing then. We waited together until finally, as if in slow motion, she hung up the phone. She stood alone for a few seconds. She was very alone. And even when she rejoined us we saw she wasn't herself.

She seemed dazed. "That was the nursing home," she finally said. "I need to go sign some papers." She looked up at us, her expression so vulnerable and exposed it felt like a violation to witness it. "Jim just died."

Without hesitation, we all got up from the table and surrounded her. Audra seemed completely incapable of making decisions. It was Bridget who took charge.

"Audra, I have numbers for all your emergency contacts. Do you want me to start notifying people?" Still dazed, Audra looked at her gratefully and nodded. "Do you want me to contact the folks at Wyuka Cemetery too?" Audra nodded again. "Anyone else I should call?" Audra looked at her with a beseeching expression. "Audra, don't worry. You don't have to make decisions right now," Bridget said. "We'll get through this."

I'd never been this close to death before. I'd been devastated when Grandma died, but I'd been shielded from the gritty details. Audra nodded dumbly, childlike where she was usually so reserved, so serious, so adult. She folded in on herself like a little moth. Insubstantial and small, she seemed to have lost her animating spirit; she opened herself to our mercy.

"I'll drive you to the nursing home," Mary Garlic said. "I'll get the car and bring it up here to the door. Just come out when you're ready, Audra. We'll get you there."

Mary Garlic was halfway out the door when she shouted back to Bridget. "I'll have my phone. Let me know if you need anything after you make the calls."

"Will do." They left together, and I watched as Mary Garlic sprinted down the street toward her house and Bridget sprinted in the opposite direction toward hers.

Tillie glanced at me. "I'll stay and help Vivi clean up."

"Oh, yes," Audra said, as if only now seeing the remnants of our afternoon, the plates of half-eaten pie, the still full cups of coffee and tea. "Yes," she repeated.

With her customary smile, Tillie took Audra's arm. "Let's get your purse and whatever else you need to take with you." Still stoic, Audra couldn't seem to allow herself actual tears, but she released a shuddering sigh and slumped against Tillie before being led back to her bedroom.

Knowing Audra's kitchen as well as I knew my own, I began to clean up, stopping only when Audra and Tillie emerged from the bedroom. Audra seemed a little calmer now, but when I hugged her, she wept.

Mary Garlic was already waiting behind the wheel of the car. Seeing how well Tillie was able to comfort Audra, I said, "I'll be fine to clean up here alone. Why don't you go along to the nursing home, Tillie."

Tillie nodded, but once she'd gotten Audra settled in the car, she came back inside. "Audra's worried about notifying people at Wesleyan. She doesn't want them to hear secondhand, but she doesn't have the president's phone number, and . . ." She glanced at me in an appraising way. "Do you think you can use her laptop to find the number?"

Something shifted inside me, a shadow lifted and lit a part of my mind that had been in darkness. I watched Mary Garlic slowly back the car down Audra's narrow driveway before I began to clean up the mess: I hand-washed and put away the silver and Audra's best dishes, wiped down the counters, swept the floors, removed the leaf from the dining room table and put it back where it belonged in the basement, straightened the area rug in front of the fireplace, and moved the living room chairs back into place. That's when I saw the copy of *Lucy Gayheart* I'd loaned to Audra from the gardener's collection sitting on the coffee table.

Blue sticky notes indicated two places she'd wanted to share with me. I picked up the book and read the first passage she'd marked: "In little towns, lives roll along so close to one another; loves and hates beat about, their wings almost touching. On the sidewalks along which everybody comes and goes, you must, if you walk abroad at all, at some time pass within a few inches of the man who cheated and betrayed you, or the woman you desire more than anything else in the world. Her skirt brushes against you. You say good-morning, and go on. It is a close shave. Out in the world the escapes are not so narrow."

I understood immediately why she'd noted this passage. I could almost hear Audra say that people who lived anonymous lives simply didn't understand how much personal differences had to be set aside to live a meaningful and dignified life in close proximity.

The second passage she'd marked was more direct and personal, and as I read I heard Audra's voice advising me, "Nothing really matters but living. Get all you can out of it. I'm an old woman, and I know. Accomplishments are the ornaments of life, they come second. Sometimes people disappoint us, and sometimes we disappoint ourselves; but the thing is, to go right on living. You've hardly begun yet. Don't let a backward spring discourage you. There's a long summer before you, and everything rights itself in time."

Oh, Audra. How she broke my heart.

Already, our conversation that afternoon seemed like the distant past. I almost couldn't remember now what all the fuss had been about. My own secrecy seemed pointless, like a non-problem. The neighbors had made clear they'd moved on. "Enough of this," Tillie had said at one point. Yes, enough of this.

Finally, I went to the den and without a flinch turned on the computer. The screen flickered to life, and the whole time I felt . . . nothing. No buzzing. No panic. No breathlessness, no jolt to the heart. I was on familiar territory and quickly found the information I needed. I used

Audra's landline to call the president's office at Nebraska Wesleyan and left a voicemail message.

After the call, I sat in the chair I liked best and stared into the dormant fireplace. I thought about all the time I'd spent in this house throughout the past year. I looked at all of her things the way you do when you're really looking at things for the last time. Outside, the evergreens bordering Audra's backyard were full of birds. I watched them flit between the branches. I looked down at the street below where everything seemed to be caught in the amber light of late afternoon. The sounds beyond the neighborhood traveled farther and took on a peculiar resonance. The air, like the light, suspended life in some way for a short time.

I'd wait here until Audra got home. I'd stay as long as she needed me. I'd help her with whatever paperwork needed to be done. I'd make phone calls to insurance companies. Whatever she needed, I'd help her through it. My lease would be up soon, but I'd talk to Mary Garlic. She'd be fine with a month-to-month lease so I could stay a while longer.

Such practical thoughts about staying made me think about leaving. Already we knew Fieldcrest would be different next year as the three older kids left in August after the musical: Roger for college at St. Olaf in Minnesota; Harmony for Chicago and the Culinary Institute; and Moss for New York. He had friends in Brooklyn who'd told him he could stay with them. He wanted to see if he could make his way there. It was a long shot, he admitted, but all of us on Fieldcrest believed in him. I tried but couldn't imagine not being there still when they came home to visit.

I'd never thought about the possibility of never seeing some of these people again. I couldn't imagine not having Audra nearby. And what about Bill? I couldn't face the thought of leaving Bill. Not yet. And Ivan? As I thought about not seeing Ivan I saw the ways I hadn't let myself see that he cared about me.

I thought about all the ways the neighbors had allowed me into their lives, how they'd been friends to me through this entire lonely year. On Fieldcrest Drive, I'd sometimes felt too closely scrutinized by other people, but I'd been a part of something too. What I hadn't seen until now was how lonely I'd been *before* I arrived on Fieldcrest. For years, I'd mistaken my engrossment with PIE for engagement with life. What had felt normal now seemed insular and confining. I'd been so preoccupied about losing the thread of my life I hadn't stopped to question what kind of life it had been. I hadn't chosen it. Not really. It had chosen me. And I hadn't considered the possibility I could choose differently.

The quiet house lulled me into a stupor. I daydreamed a little. What would happen if I stayed here in Nebraska? Maybe Audra would help me make the cottage more comfortable. I could offer to pay for improvements like new windows, and a new furnace, insulation in the crawl space so it'd be more cozy next winter. I imagined Ivan, and I might confess how we'd both felt that tiny jolt of electricity that passed between us the first time he said my real name—Vivienne. And Bill? Wasn't it possible I could get a dog of my own one day.

And while I was daydreaming, I imagined how after all these months I might call Kylie. A sobering prospect. She'd be pissed with me. And who could blame her? She'd say something like, "Jesus, Vivi. What's wrong with you, disappearing like that? Would it have been too much for you to have at least let me know you were alive, for chrissakes? I thought you were dead. Did you think about that? Did you think about how much I might have been worried about you? So, when are you coming back?"

"That's just it," I might say. "I'm not coming back to California. I don't know yet what I want to do, but I think I want to make a big change in my life. I just don't know what it is yet."

She'd be silent for so long I'd finally have to ask if she was still there. "I'm here, but have you completely lost what's left of your mind?"

I would laugh and say, "Not completely. Well, maybe a tiny bit. I don't know. Listen, I won't leave you high and dry again. I'll meet you somewhere like Chicago, and we can work out the details of my exit plan."

"I don't get it. Why are you doing this?"

"It's hard to explain. I feel at home here. That's all."

"All right," she'd say, making it sound like it was anything but all right.

"I found something here that makes me happy."

"Are you in love, or something?"

"That might be some of it. I'm not sure yet, but if so, that's good, right? We're friends, he and I, and as Willa says, 'It's best when friends marry.'"

"Willa who? Married? Are you getting married? Jesus Christ, you're scaring me, Vivi."

"Never mind," I'd reassure her. "That isn't the point. It's just a place. And during the worst year of my life, it's become *my* place."

"What the hell are you talking about? You're really worrying me, Vivi."

And my mother. I didn't even want to imagine the scorn I'd have to withstand from her. She'd likely at some point repeat her mantra about needing to avoid entanglements, but her advice to me all these years had been wrong, and her actions had always belied it. You can't avoid entanglements. It's part of the involuntary contract we all sign at birth. You can't avoid getting hurt, and you can't avoid hurting other people. But there's love too. There's love. I'd learned the hard way how much I relied on other people, and now I wanted the people I cared about to know they could rely on me.

By the time I stopped daydreaming, it was almost dusk. It had been fun to dream for a few minutes. I was reluctant to return to reality, finally laughing a little bitterly to myself that the future I'd imagined was about as likely to happen as the country electing *that man* as our next president.

I stood up and turned on the lamps around the house. Before I starting to make dinner for Audra, I put the leftover pie in her refrigerator. I washed Grandma's pie tins and set them on the counter by the door so I'd remember to take them when I left. If Audra wanted, I'd make more pies for the visitors I knew would be coming.

Baking a pie wouldn't solve anything. It had never solved anything. It was a gesture, that's all. The oldest kind of gesture, and like all such gestures, it was merely a small expression of kindness, a show of goodwill. "It's the thought that counts." I decided now that cliché wasn't as vacuous as I'd always believed. Thoughts did matter. Another puzzle that couldn't be solved—how small things counted, even thoughts, accumulating for good or ill, contributing to or taking away from our little lives, helping or hurting as each of us made our way through this short, perilous passage on earth.

Acknowledgments

I am grateful to the support of the early readers whose keen insights have made this a better book: Janet Silver, Bronwyn Milliken, Sherrie Flick, Jordan Milliken, Joanne Rossman, Beryl Aschenberg, and Joyce Kaufman.

Others listened, encouraged, advised, and offered emotional support at crucial times over the years it took me to complete this book: Alex Johnson, Mimi Schwartz, Margot Livesey, Roisin O'Gorman, Suzanne Berne, Ellen Duffer, Heidi Pitlor, Eibhear Walshe, Annie Weatherwax, Barb Straus, Theresa Blomstrom, Gretchen Henderson, Pamela Painter, John Skoyles, Heather Lundine, Janet Sternburg, Michael Lowenthal, Phillip Graham, Michele Morano.

Thank you to Courtney Ochsner who believed in and championed this novel at the University of Nebraska Press. And thank you to Clark Whitehorn whose generosity toward my work spans many years and astonishes me still. Thank you to all the dedicated professionals at the University of Nebraska Press whose integrity, hard work, dedication, professional knowledge, and talent made this book possible, especially Abigail Goodwin, Joeth Zucco, and Rosemary Sekora. I'm deeply honored to be included among their authors.

Finally, thank you, always, to my dear family.

To order or obtain more information on these or other University of Nebraska Press titles, visit nebraskapress.unl.edu.